Also by David Rowan

My Beautiful Memory, 2018, ISBN 978-1-78535-764-0

THE
VIRAL
A PANTOMIME
PRESIDENT

DAVID ROWAN

ARCHWAY
PUBLISHING

Archway Publishing books may be ordered through booksellers or by contacting:

Archway Publishing
1663 Liberty Drive
Bloomington, IN 47403
www.archwaypublishing.com
844-669-3957

ISBN: 978-1-4808-9879-0 (sc)
ISBN: 978-1-4808-9878-3 (hc)
ISBN: 978-1-4808-9880-6 (e)

Library of Congress Control Number: 2020921461

Print information available on the last page.

Archway Publishing rev. date: 11/30/2020

CONTENTS

PREFACE

You Really Cannot Make This Stuff Up!

Of course, we all are aware of the incredible events that 2020 brought us—pandemics, riots, and the rest—but this year has simply been the culmination of an epic period in our history, an era when people can get their news from multiple and disparate sources. This world of social media, cable news, Facebook, and Twitter has made many realize that there truly is such a thing as fake news and that stories are often skewed to fit a narrative. The media has much to answer for, and this novel is more an indictment of it than any one person or political party. Many scholars will no doubt win Pulitzers for their astute insights into the Trump presidency, but I thought it would be much more interesting to explore it through the context of a satirical novel based on all the recent unbelievable but true events.

This manuscript was finished in June 2020, and it's been fun comparing actual events with the book's storyline. For those who read this book and—due to their political affiliation one way or the other—pick holes in its details, please remember that it's just a story, albeit one with both feet in reality!

For Alex

ELECTION NIGHT

"So, what do you want to do about the victory party?"

"Goddamn it. I don't give a fuck about those fuckers at the party! They were supposed to bring me the win! Can the whole fucking thing!"

"You need to think about your concession speech, Madam Governor."

Stacey swallowed hard, choking down a lump in her throat. What had happened? She had the votes, she had the debate questions, she had the media, and she had the backing—why didn't she have the presidency? The lump in her throat traveled down to become a knot in her stomach.

"Give me some time. I need to, er, gather my thoughts."

"Okay, but you can't wait too long. I'll arrange the media for one hour from now." Her campaign manager hung up, leaving Stacey alone with her thoughts. How had that bastard beaten her? He was a fucking joke, zero political skills, mocked or hated by all her friends and associates, a no-chance loser who only got campaign coverage because the media loved to make fun of him. And yet, despite her promising exit polls last night, it was now obvious that he'd kicked her ass big-time.

Fucking electoral college, she thought. *What happened to democracy?* She forced back the bile to calm herself and compose the goddamn concession speech.

"And you're on in three, two, one."

"My fellow Americans, at this early hour of the morning, I'm addressing my campaign staff, my followers, and most importantly, those of you who voted for me. It's with a heavy heart I have to advise you that I have called Mr. Suit to congratulate him on his victory and to wish him future success in his presidency. Now, I know that you all worked hard and did your best, and I'm deeply grateful for the faith and trust you placed in me, but we fell short at the finish line. A last-minute groundswell of undecided and, in my opinion, uninformed, voters opted to support Mr. Suit's populist agenda instead of our caring, compassionate vision for America. I fear that our nation is now set on a new and dangerous course, but I must accept the electoral college count—even though I won more votes than my opponent. I plan to return to my home state to continue our fight for equality and women's rights. I'm particularly saddened that our country has been denied its first female president, and I know that you all are too. I feel so badly that, at least for now, our children will not be able to see how a young girl can grow up to become a president. Please try to be upbeat, continue pushing our agenda, and don't ever lose hope! Thank you and goodbye."

As the television lights dimmed, Stacey pushed back from the desk and stood to face the crowd. Sad faces stared back at her with tears in their eyes. The sounds of weeping and sobbing could be heard throughout the room. She began to move through the crowd, desperate to get out of the mob so she could grieve on her own. However, the short journey to the exit proved to be a long one, many hands of commiseration were laid on her shoulders, vacuous words of solace uttered, even the occasional encouragement given—"We'll get them next time!"—and Stacey's weary body began to droop even more under the weight of her well-meaning supporters.

A familiar face appeared through the throng in front of her; it was Bill, her campaign manager. "Come on, Madam Governor. Let's get you out of here," he said over the noise.

"Where the fuck have you been?" Stacey hissed into his ear. "Get me away from these idiots."

The two of them, linked closely arm in arm and with Bill's outstretched other arm forging a path, pushed their way out of the media room and into the hallway.

"Just get me to my room, Bill," she said. "I need a drink."

They entered her suite, and Stacey made a beeline for the minibar. She pulled out two small bottles of bourbon and dumped them into a tumbler. Its contents were gone in one long swig.

"Goddamn it. There's no more bourbon," she said. "Go get me your supply from your room."

"Madam Governor." Bill disappeared through the interconnecting door to his own suite, returning shortly with more booze.

By then, Stacey had flopped down onto the off-white overstuffed couch. She looked totally drained, a limp middle-aged woman who'd not slept for a long time. She had bags under her eyes and saddles around her waist, which bulged out from the expensive two-piece suit that was now creased and a little soiled. She seemed older than her sixty-two years and tired, so tired.

Bill poured another double shot into a glass and handed it to her, and then he sat down on an armchair across from the couch. "What now?" he asked after she'd gulped down the second double.

"I don't know, Bill," Stacey replied, suddenly too tired to even be angry or resentful.

"Any ideas?" He gently pressed her.

"Sure, Bill. I'd like to kill that motherfucker." She spat back, her venom making a sudden reappearance. But then, after a pause that was just a little too long, she said, "No, I think it's time to take a break, go up to the summer house, recharge, depressurize, and all that BS. Then maybe I can figure out what to do next."

"Sure thing, Madam Governor. I'll start demobilizing the team and wrapping up loose ends for you. Should I keep some key team members on board to plan the next campaign strategy?" Bill asked softly.

"Goddamn it, Bill. It's too goddamn soon to even think about that shit. I need to step back and take a deep breath before making any big decisions."

Inside, Stacey knew that it—she—was over, but she just couldn't give voice to that nagging knowledge. A life of public service had taken its toll. Politics is a tough business with lots of casualties (boy, didn't she know it!). It just grinds you down—all the lies, all the deceit, all the toadying to assholes who are important to your career. The backroom deals, the knives in the back. Sure, a life in politics brings big-time monetary rewards, but was it now time to count the winnings and get up from the table? Her head was telling her yes, but her ego kept a doubt alive. *Maybe one more run at it?* The most powerful job on the planet? Wasn't that her birthright, her destiny, her entitlement?

"Arrange the car, Bill. I want to go to the lodge today. No interviews or press for at least a week. Let them all go after Suit. I'm sure the news folk are just as pissed as I am and will want to question the hell out of him. He won't know what's gonna hit him when our media machine cranks up."

"I don't know, ma'am. He's pretty savvy … made his name on television," Bill quietly replied. "I'll organize the car." He rose and left the suite.

Stacey's angry eyes pierced holes into his back. *Pretty savvy? He's a moron!* She suddenly remembered that this moron had just beaten her in a presidential election.

❧

Just outside Chestertown, the Lincolns' summer retreat sat in iron-gated solitude. Although she was the governor of New Jersey, and had been for some years, Stacey found that Chestertown's proximity to DC was perfect, and the family had spent many weekends and summer months there. Washington is the heartbeat of America and its seat of power. Who wouldn't want to spend as much time there as possible, soaking up its buzz, particularly someone destined for the presidency?

They had bought the estate a long time ago. It was priced way over their heads, but friends in the right places had stepped up to help. Tom, Stacey, and their two young children began to commute whenever possible between Trenton and the Lodge. *Who wouldn't, given a choice between Trenton and a beautiful waterfront secluded haven?* Throughout Tom's two terms as governor, they regularly relaxed at the lodge as a family or entertained the people who mattered in DC and around the nation and world. It was not just a retreat; it was a nerve center for strategizing, planning, and now, regrouping. Back when Tom was about to be term limited out of governor's office, it was here that they began their plans for restructuring his political life. Tom had been a popular governor, known for his quick wit and down-home, working-class approach to running the state. Stacey had ridden up on this goodwill and enjoyed statewide popularity too, although not to the same extent as Tom.

Of course, that was where Stacey had made the momentous decision that set her on course for the presidency. It was at the lodge that Stacey began her true political career following Tom's terrible accident. The same friends who had guided her through those trying times also stepped up when, commencing her own second term as governor, Stacey had set eyes on the top job: president of the United States of America. Influential friends had guided her, opened doors, built up war chests, and wrangled the media in their efforts to get her elected. Now, like a house of cards, it had all collapsed.

Stacey sat on the veranda and looked out glumly over the water. Her plans in pieces—what should she do now? It was time for sage advice from those same friends who'd oh, so nearly gotten her to the top. She took out the secure phone and scrolled down through her contacts. One name sprang out from the screen. *He will know what should happen next,* she thought.

MR. BIG

There really are billionaires' clubs. In fact, there are several. Many people know about the billionaires who have signed a pact to give away X percent of their fortunes before their death. Such acts of charity and selflessness get good publicity, but a little analysis of these types of agreements might give pause. Vowing to donate large sums of money to good causes is, of course, laudable, but someone giving away fifty million dollars who has a net worth of, say, twenty billion is a bit like you or me dropping ten bucks into the red bucket at Christmas (except that we don't get press coverage and plaudits from newspapers and other media that are as likely as not owned by those same billionaires).

In addition to the acceptable face of billionaires' clubs however, there are other less-known, covert, and shadowy groups. These are cartels of like-minded influential individuals who see it as their duty to steer the nation to a future in line with their own ideals. Such idealism always includes an element of control over the masses, because everyday folks simply cannot be trusted to have their own opinions or make their own decisions. They need to be quietly steered toward a way of life that allows the club's members to abide and thrive.

As you might expect, these individuals do not seek the spotlight.

They prefer to operate behind the scenes. The most shadowy club of all calls itself simply "the Group." You could make educated guesses about some of its members. Does the billionaire have significant control over some aspect of communications, say a newspaper or a social media platform? Is the billionaire active in financial markets to the extent that he can actually influence them? Does the billionaire own a portfolio of companies that offers products or services that are needed by a large chunk of the population? Identify these individuals, and you'll probably ID the members of the Group. Such people might share common political viewpoints, often Democrat, because of that doctrine's basic tenet of centralized governmental control. However, in reality, it's not about ideological goals, whether liberal or conservative. It is more a desire to control and manipulate the masses. Thus, they shape views, guide opinions, and mold the great unwashed public to suit their ends. All this makes them more money, massages their massive egos, and strengthens their need to control. Thus, their "virtuous" cycle perpetuates.

Milos Kunis is one of leading lights of the secret society of "controllers and shapers" and is the de facto leader of the Group. Once in a blue moon, his name may come up in alt-media pieces, or when a particularly huge deal is being closed, but mostly Milos is content to quietly toil away behind the scenes, under the radar, shaping the world to his ends. His origins are unclear, the son of an Eastern European family whose place of birth is not known for sure. Ukraine? Russia? His country of residence likewise is questionable. Being a billionaire, Kunis enjoys a string of houses scattered across the globe. He may be seen wrapped in overcoat and scarf taking the air in Central Park, Hyde Park, or Gorky Park. He could be spotted lounging from the deck of his yacht in Monte Carlo Harbor, Sydney Harbor, or Guanabara Bay.

Milos is a true global man, a globalist who wants the world to bend to his will. His wealth came initially from the ruthless world of hedge funds. Using other people's money, he parlayed their seed capital into a highly profitable fund via a series of high-risk investments. The greatest and most well-publicized play he made was a foreign exchange trade deal where he managed to perfectly time a contrarian position in an East European country's currency. This was perceived at the time by most experts as a crazy move, but it paid off massively. His giant windfall drove that nation's economy into recession, but Milos was indifferent to the travails of its people. It was not his fault that he had outsmarted them. What luck he had had with that deal—or was it? Subsequent investigative journalism found that several members of his fund were coincidentally members of the government in question, their ownership obscured by shell corporations and offshore entities. Although their poor population all took a severe hit following the massive sell-off in their currency, these few countrymen came out smelling like roses. Such is the ruthless world of big business.

Following this amazing transaction, Milos became a hot item in the world of finance. Success begat success, and his wealth grew. The richer he became, the more elusive he was, discreetly spreading his empire via corporate acquisitions, buying and selling companies. As with his currency play, there was never any regard for the welfare of employees; he always focused on the return on capital employed. Such a callous approach to business brought him immense wealth. As his fortune grew, Kunis began to discreetly support and fund political and social causes that took his interest and furthered his goals. Such support was always via third, fourth, or fifth parties; he did not want the spotlight, and he did not want the world to see the details of his sly attempts to bend the populace to his will.

One obvious area of his focus was politics. Any governmental system that strives to exert centralized control was of interest; he could buy off just a few politicians and get massive leverage. Smaller government made things more difficult; bigger government was the way to go. New Jersey is an industrial state, and some of Kunis's acquisition targets were industrial complexes there. Having a senior politician in New Jersey could be beneficial, allowing access to inside information—or giving him the ability to shape regulation in a manner that could make his assets more profitable. This is why the Lincolns and Kunis met. Back then, Tom Lincoln was a young congressman with ambitions. New Jersey has a two-term cap on governors, and then-Governor Graham could not run again. Tom saw that, given the right team, party backing, and a dab of luck, he could conceivably become the state's next governor. He'd begun his exploratory campaign two years before the election, and, of course, Stacey was all in for this potential step up the political ladder. More connections and more influence—what wasn't to like about becoming the state's next First Lady?

It was at a Democratic fundraiser that wheels were set in motion between Kunis and Lincoln.

"I'm told that you have your eyes on the governor's seat," Kunis commented as he sat next to Tom during dinner (the seating arrangements were by no means coincidental).

"As I'm sure you know Mr. Kunis, I've been thinking of it," replied Tom. "Our state needs some fresh blood, someone with new ideas. Don't get me wrong … we've had eight solid years under Governor Graham, but I feel like our traditionally Democratic voters are looking for a shake-up. I believe that I'm the guy to lead that change, and if my exploratory team concurs, we'll be making our announcement in the not-too-distant future."

"Well, I wish you good luck," said Milos. "It's always good to see new ideas in our party."

"Hell, I may even be knocking on your door soon, looking for more than just moral support!" Tom chuckled.

"I'd be happy to talk. Tell me, what are your thoughts on the current state labor laws? They've always struck me as a little constrictive."

Tom was nothing if not quick-witted. He realized that Milos's question was not idle chitchat.

"Well for sure, a new look at outdated laws is part of my agenda. Our state needs more employment, and I've often thought that some of our existing laws restrict growth. Perhaps a new broom will be able to sweep out a few dusty old rules and free up our potential for creating more jobs."

At the big round banquet table for ten, Stacey chatted with other diners, but all the while, she was bending her ears toward Tom's discussion with Kunis—and she was pleased by what she heard. Maybe a connection to him was the start of the road to the top?

Tom's campaign kicked off, and Milos kept a watchful eye over his progress. It became apparent that he was well-liked by the party, but more importantly, by the public. His GOP rival was an established older politician, and New Jersey seemed to want young blood. Tom was light on his feet, quick with an ad-lib, and looked good on the screen. His wife too was an asset, supportive yet independent, a partner to him and not a kowtower. She was a strong, independent woman who complemented him perfectly. Milos began to discreetly support the campaign, both financially and via his network of influencers around the state and country.

The election results were decisive. The Lincolns moved into the governor's mansion and basked in the limelight, enjoying the victory that New Jersey-ites had given them. Kunis did not visit them there, but on his frequent visits to New York, dinner arrangements would be made, and Tom (sometimes with Stacey, sometimes without) became a close ally of Milos. As their friendship blossomed, New Jersey enacted several new labor and environmental regulations, all to the benefit of Milos's companies.

"Look, Tom, I'm a staunch union supporter: We need unions to keep bad employers honest. But when union leaders get too much power, they can stifle the workers. Mandatory union membership has always struck me as draconian. Shouldn't an individual at least have the right to choose?" Minos opined one night over a late supper. "And some of the regulations over industrial health and safety surely need a revision? They too make the workers' lives so much more difficult. Just a slight relaxation of a few rules could unchoke the state's economy and send your citizens on the road to prosperity."

Tom had known that this, or something like it, was coming. He'd already weighed the options. Changing labor laws and/or health and safety rules could be perceived as antidemocratic, but he also agreed that such changes would almost certainly increase employment. The workers would end up having fewer rights and protections, but on a day-to-day basis, so what? More jobs equals more state revenue, and surely that would be good for the state? Welfare programs could be increased, and the overall population would eventually benefit. Tom needed to be sure that he could make these changes without detriment to his reputation or chances of reelection.

On the trip back to the mansion, he concluded that if he was to make controversial decisions, now was the time—while he was still the state's favorite governor.

Stacey agreed and did all she could to publicly support his actions. She found such a rush in being involved with public life; it was as if she'd been made for the cut-and-thrust of politics. What a team they were making! There was resistance and dissent to his new initiatives, but thankfully, the media protests were muted and buried. The message was spun as "more jobs, good."

❧

"Milos, so good to hear your voice. I'm glad that you picked up." Stacey was sitting on the veranda of the Lodge, looking out across the water.

"Where are you, my dear?" Milos replied. "It is a terrible thing that happened. I simply cannot believe that that boor could become the leader of the free world. My team is running a postmortem on the campaign, and I'll let you know what they find. We should have won comfortably."

"I'm at the Lodge. I think of you every time I come here. I needed some alone time to consider my next move, and I so value your advice. You've always made the right recommendations." Stacey was still reeling and resentful about the loss. Her mood pendulumed between anger and resignation to her fate. She desperately needed guidance.

"Now is not the time for rash actions. You must let the dust settle. I suggest you go off the grid for at least a few weeks. Relax, take a hike in the woods around the Lodge, and empty your mind. Meanwhile, my team will determine what happened. Once we know that, we'll know what our next steps should be. You must remember that I've always had your best interests at heart, poor Tom's too. We made such a good team when both he and you held the governorship, and I'm certain that we can come back from this."

Stacey let his words sink in. He was correct of course: depressurize, clean out her negative thoughts, and get refreshed for whatever comes next. "As always, Milos, you give good advice. It's so reassuring to know that you still value our friendship and history. Now, I think I can hear a Blanton's calling my name …"

"You are welcome, Stacey. Don't overdo the bourbon, but if it helps you relax, there's no harm in winding down like that. I'll be in touch on the secure phone. Take care, my dear."

Milos hung up. Of, course he could have gotten angry about the election results: so many years quietly shaping the election to his will, so many favors called in, and so much political and financial capital expended. But the way is forward—and the kingmaker and chief puppet master had plenty more tricks up his sleeve.

Meanwhile, Stacey gulped hard on her bourbon. "president-fucking-elect Suit," she bitterly said to herself. "What a fucking joke."

The rest of the drink slid down her throat, and she stood to refill her tumbler.

UNSUITABLE

"Hello audience! What a beautiful day in America. Now, let's find out if tonight's news suits you!"

These had been the opening words of *Unsuitable* (Weekday nights after the news—don't miss it!) for more than a decade. Ronald George Thomas Suit had hosted his talk show since its inception. When media company executives threatened to replace him because of his outspoken views, RGT—Ron—had simply beaten them to the punch by migrating his show to cable TV, where it morphed into *Not Suitable for Watching*—or "NSFW" as its massive fan base liked to call it.

The format was a mix of politics, guests, and silliness. Each night, Ron kicked off the program with a completely ad-libbed monologue covering the day's news. Here, his surprisingly conservative opinions were expressed but always in a snarky-witty way and always balanced by potshots at Republicans too. Guests on the show might be Hollywood types, but they just as easily could be politicians, journalists, or pundits. It was *The Tonight Show* meets *Face the Nation*. Most nights, there'd be a recurring set piece such as "Birthday Suit," whereby Ron would interview a guest in just his underwear, with the guest usually stripping down too (or sitting uneasily fully clothed). Or he might go full-on serious with a guest in a quick-fire set of questions that would test the victim's professed knowledge or expertise in a given area. The show endured because it catered to all demographics: short clips to keep millennials' attention, gossip to attract the *People* readers, and politics to keep the more mature viewers engaged. Of course, the main reason it endured was Ron, who juggled perfectly that fine balance of entertainment and information.

None of this had come easily; the show was no overnight sensation. Ron Suit was a Houstonian who grew up with a Texan's innate sense of conservatism and independence. His family had its roots in oil and gas, but they were also tightly connected to the Bush dynasty. Growing up, Ron was at ease interacting with executives, politicians, or social titans. As he aged however, he had no desire to enter the family business. Instead, he capitalized on his keen interest in current affairs and intense curiosity about people. He took a degree in journalism at TCU's Bob Schieffer College of Communication. Following graduation, Ron found that certain media had a hunger for his kind of commentary. Using the family's network as a calling card, he made many freelance connections, initially getting gigs on PBS TV and radio, where he was allowed to express his right-leaning views. Being naturally on the conservative side, such appearances were not too frequent, but his quick wit tended to soften the liberal media's dim view of him. This attitude softened further when he married Megan Scott. She was a Hollywood darling, attractive, smart, and the star of several TV series. They'd first met at a get-together in the Bushes' house. Despite there being an ideological divide in their politics, they were both smitten with each other. Against all odds and expectations, the marriage had survived, with Megan and Ron maturing into a close couple with feet in both Hollywood's cesspit of hypocrisy and the media's news cycle. This disparity of views often served as fodder for his skewering of the left. Megan gave as good as she got too, and such back-and-forth endeared them to the public throughout their years of marriage.

Ron became known for more than just his show. He appeared in a recurring role on several other series such as *Shark Tank* and *CSI*. He guest-hosted other TV and radio shows. He even had smaller roles in movies. Ron matured into somewhat of an institution, his podcasts had a huge following, and he commanded respect among his peers and disdain among his enemies.

The defining moment of Ron's life came as he was at the peak of his popularity and power.

✐◈✐

"Ron, you have to back off on knocking the president," the executive producer said during the daily morning planning meeting. "You can't keep taking shots at the guy just because you don't agree with his policies."

"C'mon, that's exactly why I have to knock him. The man is killing our country. Surely, even you can see that?"

Since the election of Peter Ludwig, Ron had felt an uneasy sensation of traveling backward, heading for a life that might be something like living in *1984* (the novel, not the era). He'd initially kept his mouth shut about these concerns and continued to bash both left and right on his show, acting in his usual equal-opportunity insulter persona. But now, eighteen months into Ludwig's second term, he could no longer maintain a dispassionate stance.

"We've got the highest welfare roll in history, we've got a recession, and we've got the frigging government getting more and more into our lives. Jeez, I should be giving him more crap than I do!"

"Look, Ron, the board needs you to tone it down. They're getting grief from the main shareholder, a big Ludwig supporter. I know we're cable and can, hell, *need* to be edgy, but please soften the rhetoric a little. Please."

Ron did tone down his sniping over the next few shows, and his producers let out a breath of relief. But his mind was ever-churning over new thoughts and ideas. Being told what to do did not sit well with Ron.

"Hello, audience! What a beautiful day in America. Now, let's find out if tonight's news suits you!"

Ron opened with his usual nightly welcome and moved over to the couch where he typically gave his monologue. As usual, this was an unscripted talk with his audience.

"Some of my more astute viewers may have noticed that I've been going easy lately on our commander-in-chief. Well, the powers that be decreed that I'm too rough on President Ludwig. Who knows, perhaps they're right? So, in the interests of fair play, I'd like to make a little announcement. Don't worry, I'm not quitting or having a sex change or anything. Entertainers like me can bash the president more or less with impunity 'cause he can't really come back at us, can he? That would be beneath the dignity of his office. Well, I'm going to give Ludwig the chance to bash me all he wants because tonight I'm hereby announcing my run for the presidency! Let's kick the bum and his crooked lackies out of Washington so he can spend his retirement criticizing President Suit. That has a nice ring to it, doesn't it?"

The audience cheered, and the producers groaned. Was this another one of his jokes—or a real declaration of intentions?

It didn't take long for the world to realize that Ron Suit was serious about entering the race. His social media posts soon made that clear. Public reaction was mixed. Some laughed it off as a publicity-grabbing stunt, and some were disgusted that he was demeaning the office of the presidency. A surprising number thought that he was just what Washington needed: fresh blood to shake up the disgusting career politicians who never do anything for the nation except line their own pockets. Popular media piled in on his decision to run. It was easy pickings for good ratings: a TV host runs for office!

As may have been expected, in the months that followed, Ron's cable show was canceled under the direction of its main shareholder. Fortunately, Fox had been quietly courting Ron for some time, and a deal was quickly done. The migration was a success, just like the move from broadcast to cable, and the show soon enjoyed the highest ratings of any late-night format on television. Of course, the move freed up Ron to more openly express his conservative views—and push his presidential run.

The campaign began in earnest, and Ron was helped by a small core of friends, family, and associates. While other Republican primary hopefuls struggled and squabbled for airtime, Ron remained a media draw, an endless source of fascination. Left-wing shows loved to feature pieces on him, citing his campaign as a sure sign of the GOP's hopeless lack of good candidates. He was an amusing diversion, a contrast to the serious firepower of the Democrat field, all of who were experienced politicians covering every demographic of the identity politics spectrum. Besides, all the mainstream talking heads knew that he'd be a short-lived phenomenon; once the primary debates kicked off, he'd surely be decimated by the experienced politicians who were his rivals. Unfortunately, these pundits were all failing to account for one key issue. After all his years of TV, Ron was very comfortable on the screen and had vast experience of ad-libbing and questioning. He knew how to work the camera. None of his competition came close. Oh sure, they had stood in front of teleprompters and given trite sound bites like all politicians, but thinking on their feet was not a skill most had mastered.

Meanwhile, over on the Democrat side, the potential CNCs were fighting their own wars.

"Isn't it time we had a woman president?"

"Isn't it time we had an LBGT president?"

"Isn't it time we had a president who is truly of color?"

"Isn't it time we had a Muslim president?"

Slicing and dicing their electorate in such a fashion was not doing the candidates any favors. As each of the runners made their pitch to their selected group, they were failing miserably to convince the rest of the populace.

The long election season ground on, and a majority of the nation quickly grew bored with the incessant coverage and daily news alerts or twenty-four-hour scandals. Ron Suit, however, could usually be guaranteed to deliver something entertaining or off the wall, and the viewing public warmed more and more to him. Conservatives liked his stance on important issues; independents were drawn to the concept of electing someone from outside of the political world; and even moderate Democrats could see that he plainly was trying to represent ordinary people and not just small minority sectors of the populace.

Throughout it all, the Group was quietly steering the mood of the nation to its own ends. Openly liberal media got behind their favorite Democrat candidates, playing the odds by focusing on the most-electable few. The "independent" media recommended Republican candidates who they knew would be the weakest opponent of the preferred Democrat contenders. Conservative media tried hard to discount Ron Suit as a credible candidate and went for the most-experienced politicians. Even Fox couldn't bring itself to truly get behind Ron, despite it being his employer (or maybe because of it?)

And so, the interminable, never-ending political coverage dragged on, grinding slowly toward the primary debates where, thank God, two candidates would finally be defined. This milestone would tell the public that, at last, the election was coming, would soon be over, and we could all get back to normalcy.

But who would come out of the sausage grinder as the respective Democratic and Republican candidates?

MADAME GOVERNOR

L ife as the First Lady of the state of New Jersey suited Stacey. The first four years slid quickly past, and Tom was easily reelected to his second term. Throughout their time in office, the Lincolns and Kunis kept close (but discreet) contact. Milos even helped them with their purchase of the Lodge in Chestertown, and this became their place for meeting and strategizing, out of the public eye. An idea matured that, after stepping down from the governor's office, Ron might get a role in the federal government, and in the longer term, he could even be groomed for the presidency itself. All options can be on the table when you have someone as powerful as Kunis in your corner.

During his second term, Tom's popularity remained high, but Stacey began to notice that perhaps it was a little too high amongst a certain demographic: women. The job kept Tom away from home a lot. He had long and erratic working hours, and Stacey could never be sure about when he'd be able to spend time with her or the kids. But, hey, these things come with the territory, and as long as they were a successful team, the disruption and stress were worth it.

"You look tired, Stacey," Kunis observed one weekend at the Lodge. He had come down to meet with Tom, but the governor was running late back at the Mansion, and so it was just the two of them, the kids tucked away upstairs in bed.

Stacey took a sip of her drink and sat silently for some moments. "Milos, I'm not sure I should be talking about this, but if we're to keep on climbing Tom up his career ladder, I think you need to know that Tom is screwing someone else, another woman."

"I know, Stacey. I know," Milos softly replied. "He has had a problem keeping it in his trousers for a while now. I'm just so sad that he is getting sloppy enough about it that you've obviously found out."

"Christ, you knew?" Stacey couldn't believe her ears. She rose and began pacing around the room like a caged tiger. "I gave up so much for that man. I could be anything I want, but no, I play the part of loyal wife sitting at the right hand of the great Governor Lincoln, and I was loyal. This is how the bastard repays me?" Her voice was now a shout, and the pacing became more intense. "And you, Milos, you knew? Fuck, who the hell can I trust anymore?" Stacey downed the bourbon in one gulp and headed for another.

"Stacey, in my business, I have to be discreet. What good would it have done for me to tell you?" Milos was now at her shoulder. He placed his arm around her, consoling her.

Stacey was trembling, not with sadness, but with rage. She turned to face Kunis. "I should have known. You should have told me."

"We need to keep this quiet, my dear. I will talk with Tom, but if the public gets to find out that he is not the perfect man they think he is, it will surely affect his path forward. Now, it's not too long before you'll be moving out of the mansion. We should keep up the façade of harmony at least until the next governor is elected. By then, I'll have him back on the straight and narrow, and we can carry on with our plans."

Milos returned to his seat, but Stacey continued to pace. "That fucker, double-crossing me, who does he think I am? I've given up so much for him. I could have been anything! Hell, I'd make a better goddam governor than him. I'd make a better anything than him!"

"You are probably, right Stacey. You have a tenacity that I've rarely seen. You are bright, attractive and, because of our long friendship, you have good connections in all the right places. But the right thing to do now is act as if you don't know about Tom's dalliances and leave the governor's mansion as a successful and happy family."

"You're right, Milos," Stacey said softly, forcing herself to calm down, "I'm making a mountain out of a molehill. Now, I need another Blanton's." But inside, she still seethed.

The call about Breitbart came late one evening. Milos's network had identified that the right-leaning media site was about to publish a piece about Tom's waywardness. They'd gotten interviews with some of the women involved—plus eyewitness statements from some of Tom's staff who had seen him "in action." It would be a damning piece that would surely impact his chances of future office.

Milos called Stacey on the secure line. "You need to know that there is about to be some heavy weather concerning Tom and his girlfriends. Breitbart is about to drop a hit piece on him."

"Goddam it, Milos," replied Stacey. "This could end his career and my reputation. What the hell are we going to do?"

"Well, it wouldn't be the end of the world if people find out that the god has feet of clay, but this is definitely a bump in the road. Perhaps we should play a wait-and-see game. Let the article be published, and I'll talk with my friends to keep the media reaction as muted as possible. No guarantees though."

"No, Milos. Think of the harm to me and my children when the story gets out." Stacey launched on another tirade, yelling into the phone as she paced back and forth, "I should have run for governor instead of him. At least I'd have the sense to keep on the straight and narrow. Now the son of a bitch will stigmatize us all for the rest of our lives."

"It is unfortunate, Stacey," Milos said. "There is something I could do, but it is radical. I hesitate to even suggest it."

Stacey pressed him for details of the potential lifesaver. They talked through Milos's plan, brainstorming options, examining potential downsides, and evaluating all the variables in outcomes.

"So, it's settled then?" Milos asked with a deadly serious voice. "I must know that you are 110 percent in on this. For me, it is an unhappy option, but I've been in such situations before, and these actions have worked out successfully. You, Stacey, must be on board before we go any further. I truly need you to tell me to begin this."

"Yes," replied Stacey. "Let's do it."

They hung up, and Stacey flopped onto a couch, a sense of dread mixed with exhilaration washing over her.

As usual, Stacey and the children traveled down to the Lodge for the weekend, leaving Tom to deal with matters of state (and other things) back in Trenton. The Breitbart piece had just come out and was getting lots of coverage. Oh, goodie, one of the Democrat's darlings was in trouble. Right-wing media had a field day lecturing the world on society's failing morals, while the popular press reveled in all the salacious and sleazy details. Tom's halo had slipped, and to say the least, he was not happy. His relationship with Stacey over the past days had been strained, although he almost had a sense that this was not news to her: Whenever he looked at her, she had a steely glaze in her eyes, a distant stare. The kids didn't know what was going on, but they clearly sensed the rift, seeing malevolent glares from Stacey's eyes being met by sheepish looks from Tom. He knew that he'd screwed up, but he'd gotten away with it for so long that the risk of being found had out ceased to be a deterrent. This was possibly the end of his future run for the presidency and probably the end of his marriage. Why did he always have to cave in to his sexual appetites? Oh, how are the mighty fallen! From hero to zero just because of a few meaningless bonks.

Tom sat at his desk, struggling to concentrate on his work while his brain kept tugging him away into despair. The private line rang.

"Hello? Oh, it's you. Yeah, it would be good to talk. I've messed things up, Milos. I know that. Maybe you can help me work through my options for salvaging something. Yes, I still go running most nights. I could meet up with you in the park later at the usual spot. No, no problem that it will be so late. I'm not sleeping much anyway."

Tom hung up. If there was anyone who could resolve this mess, or at least some of it, it would be Kunis. For sure, he'd know what to do.

Tom changed into his sweats and left the mansion at the appointed time in the wee small hours. He had taken late-night jogs on a regular basis pretty much since taking office. Sometimes the jogs were actual runs, and sometimes another form of exercise was involved. Regardless, security was used to seeing him with his AirPods hanging from his ears as he trotted off toward Marquand Park in the gloomy darkness, returning an hour or two later, sweating and panting from either type of exercise.

The meeting spot looked like the opening scene from *The Exorcist*: deserted, misty, and damp, with only a street light slicing down through the gloom. Tom stood not far from the entrance gates, jogging on the spot to keep his blood circulating while waiting for Milos to arrive.

In the distance, a pair of headlights pierced the mist. *Finally*, thought Tom as he stopped running on the spot and stepped off the curb to flag down the approaching vehicle.

The driver spotted Tom through the mist, but instead of slowing to a halt beside him, the engine's note increased as the car sped up. Tom's body arced almost gracefully about twenty feet into the air as two tons of metal smashed into him. The impact was such that he was literally knocked out of his Nikes and his sweatpants shot down to his ankles, unable to keep up with his acceleration from the impact. The car drove off into the dark, one headlight now nonfunctional. Silence returned to the avenue as the car's exhaust receded into the distance. Tom lay in a crumpled heap, legs akimbo, blood pooling under his lifeless corpse.

Nestled between Trenton's industrial mega-complexes stands the Lombardi Recycling Center. Family owned for many years, it specializes in metal recycling. That night, chain-link fence gates swung open to allow a single vehicle to enter. It was a late-model sedan, definitely not the typical delivery to Lombardi's, who usually dealt with old clunkers. But this car had noticeable damage to its front grille and driver's side fender. Only one headlight was working.

The driver stopped next to a crawler crane and exited the vehicle. The crane swiftly picked it up with a massive claw that slammed down and pierced through the vehicle's roof. The crane slewed round to drop the damaged automobile into a pit. A high-pitched whine pierced the quiet night as a hydraulic power unit was switched on. Pistons slid huge plates forward in the pit, crushing the car as it slowly turned into a rectangular block of metal about the size of a large coffee table. With the crushing done, the hydraulics shoved the block out through a chute in the side of the pit. Once again, the crane used its claw to hoist the block skyward and dump it onto a huge stack of similar crushed metal lumps.

Work finished, the driver of the car and crane operator stood together quietly for some time, remaining silent until another car approached. The driver got in, and the car disappeared into the night.

Mr. Lombardi shut down the equipment, locked the chain-link gates, and set off for home. He smiled to himself. *Big money for easy work—what's not to like?*

The Trentonian, The Times, The Star Ledger, and *the Jersey Journal* all screamed the same headline: "Governor Dead in Tragic Hit and Run!" The lieutenant governor assumed leadership and gave endless press conferences, vowing to track down the culprit. He promised to maintain the governor's policies and reassured the state's population that things would work out. All the while, he quietly thought that, in a way, this was an accident that would be good for him. With the governor's job up for grabs shortly, it would do him no harm at all to be in front of TV cameras constantly and in social media again and again. Surely his chances of being elected the next governor of the state of New Jersey had just skyrocketed?

I actually look pretty damn good in black, Stacey thought as she readied herself for the service. Of course, her persona was that of the tragic widow, adrift in grief after the sudden loss of the love of her life. The children were naturally upset while being young enough that their bemusement cushioned the pain a little. Stacey had convinced herself that they'd manage the loss and come out the other end just fine. *Yes, they'll hurt but they've got me,* she thought. *He didn't spend that much time with them anyway, always working—or fucking. And what kind of a role model would he have been once the kids were old enough to know all the details of his affairs?* No, this was a storm that the Lincoln family could surely weather.

The state service passed without incident, and local and national luminaries attended to give Stacey their condolences and offers of help in the future.

Milos did not attend. He thought discretion was the best policy, and besides, he was overseas in China closing an acquisition. He did call, however, to check in on how she was coping. "Are you managing, Stacey?" he asked, his voice full of concern.

"Everyone has been so nice," she replied, "even our asshole enemies. The lieutenant governor seems pretty pleased with himself; he can't wait to settle into the job on a full-time basis."

"Time will tell about that, Stacey. Time will tell. I will be gone for a few weeks, but meanwhile, my team is working on your strategy and speech. I'll have someone contact you with a draft once it's ready. The timing will be critical: too soon and you'll be seen as a callous woman, too late and we'll lose the sympathy of the voters. Just continue to play the heartbroken widow, use the children as much as possible, and accept every request for an interview. I'll see you soon."

❦

"Thanks, Lester. You know it's coming up to one month since Tom … since he … since the accident, and I've been so touched by the huge outpouring of love from everyone around me."

Stacey was being questioned by NBC. The interview had been arranged on a "tease" that Mrs. Lincoln would have an important announcement to make. Following questions about how she was coping, how were the children doing, the progress on finding the culprit, and so on, Stacey began her key sound bite, the entire reason she was doing the interview.

"Most of all, it's been the love of the New Jersey people that's kept me going through this nightmare. Our state truly is the best, most compassionate in the nation, and I'll never forget that. It's this love that has brought me to an inevitable conclusion: I simply cannot abandon the people. My husband worked tirelessly to defend and honor New Jersey-ites, and I was with him all the way. I am convinced that he greatly improved our state's fortunes during his tenure, and I'm sure that he would have continued to do so for his remaining term, even while dealing with the scandalous dirt that some hateful news sites had begun spreading just before his death. I have been totally involved with his governance, and I've worked closely with Tom on each piece of signature legislation we passed. So, it's no surprise that I feel a need—no, an obligation—to continue his work. For that reason, tonight—and, Lester, you're the first to hear this—I am declaring my intention to run for Democratic governor of the great state of New Jersey. I want to thank the people for their past and future support, and I want to assure everyone that I am ready for this. The pain of the past month has strengthened me and given me resolve. I hope to prevail, and with the people's help, I will!"

More questions followed, but Stacey was already switching off, her mind now concentrating on the campaign.

"Well, you heard it here first," said Lester as he wrapped up the piece. "I want to offer Mrs. Lincoln my sincere condolences—and wish her luck with future endeavors."

They went off the air.

Stacey had a flutter of butterflies in her stomach. *Now it begins,* she thought.

At home, the lieutenant governor's heart sank. *I'm fucked,* he thought. And he was. With a strong campaign team and heavy advertising courtesy of Milos Kunis, plus a massive outpouring of sympathy from the state's electorate, Stacey became New Jersey's second female governor.

WE NEED A WOMAN

Stacey quickly became the DNC's darling. A woman and a widow, if only she'd been black or gay, she could have had the trifecta, but two out of three was good enough. As her first four-year term unfolded, she enacted sufficiently liberal policies that cemented her place in the hearts of the party's leadership.

Throughout it all, Milos quietly steered her, offering counsel and help whenever necessary. He was playing, as always, a long game, and when not helping Stacey, he was talking with the president or key party representatives about her future. President Ludwig had begun his second term and was well on the way to fulfilling much of his progressive agenda. Kunis usually had the president's ear when required, although he sensed that sometimes Ludwig was marching to the beat of a different drummer; decisions were occasionally made that went against Milos's plans. Trying to understand him better, he had dug deep into Ludwig's background, but it all seemed clean—if not a little too clean. Politicians always had skeletons in their closets, something that could be used to "persuade" them when necessary. Ludwig's closet was neat and tidy, although sparsely filled, and with several empty shelves. No matter, as usual, Kunis was like a willow; he could bend with the breeze when necessary and adapt to changing circumstances. His business empire was successful and expanding, as was his influence.

The seeds that Milos planted took root, and it was inevitable that Stacey's name would eventually come up as a possible successor to Ludwig.

"We need a woman, George," the president opined one morning in the Oval Office.

The VP, George Burton, nodded in agreement. Burton was a lifelong career politician. He had made a run at the presidency once back in the seventies, but he had come up short. In the next election cycle, he'd be well into his seventies; he was tired and not as sharp as he used to be. Some time ago, he'd said, "Mr. President, I have no interest in participating in the next election. My life has been devoted to public service, and I've been fortunate enough to make some money along the way. It's time for me to ride off into the sunset, Peter." Burton's intentions had thus prompted the debate over who should carry the liberal torch for the next four or eight years.

"It's time for a female president," the president continued. "Let's get the team to put together a folder of potential candidates so we can run some due diligence on them. This will be an important election. For our policies to endure, we are going to need a Democrat president, a Democrat House, and a Democrat Senate. It's a tough ask, but we can do it with the right people and the right help."

The election committee began their search. They assembled a dozen candidates, some black, some gay, some Muslim, all women. A thinning-out process reduced this number to the final three. Each potential candidate was evaluated by a scoring system based on their track record, policies, race, religion, gender identification, financial backing, media footprint, reputation, and tele-visuality.

Of course, Milos was familiar with the party's methods. He had spent years shaping aspects of Stacey's life to best suit her potential as president. In the USA, anyone can run for president with very few barriers to entry, but it is always the party that steers things in their preferred direction. Sure, primaries are held, debates are organized, and party votes are taken, but it is the elite few who ultimately decide who their candidate should be. Kunis had been one of those elites for some years. If you kept on his good side, there was a strong chance you would be the chosen one. It was therefore no surprise that Stacey Lincoln's name was in the short list of three.

"Who've we got? Lincoln, Abrams, Warren. You know, any one of them could work, although Warren is so strident, and Abrams is so angry. Let's focus-group them to see who'd fit best."

Meanwhile in the wider branches of the party, away from its elite core, other hopefuls began declaring their intentions to run. The race was on. As in all presidential elections, the initial field was large, populated by a mix of experienced politicians, idealists, radicals, billionaires; every possible permutation of humankind presented itself as a presidential hopeful.

Stacey had seen all this coming and was very prepared, having been coached at length by Milos and his team. She entered the race with gusto, assisted by the Kunis money machine. Following mandatory rounds of television appearances and interviews on NPR, she began preparations for the caucuses.

"Who do you think will be the opposition, Milos?" she asked one night in the hotel after a heavy day of shaking rubes' hands and pretending to be interested in rural life. *God, the misery of flyover America! How can they put up with life in the sticks?* Stacey looked forward to getting back to civilization, although the façade had to be maintained while campaigning on the road.

"I think you are strongest of our field, my dear," replied Milos.

"No, I don't mean on our side. Hell, I know I'm the best candidate for our party. I meant for the Republicans; they have some strong players."

"I'm not so sure Stacey. Of course, there's Romney and Bush, but I think the public has seen a little too much of those two. Who else is there? They're all old white men—not a good fit against our candidate."

"You didn't mention Ron Suit," she commented. "What are your thoughts about him?"

"The media is enamored with him right now, but he is a sideshow attraction, an amusing diversion from serious news. They'll tire of him soon enough, and his fifteen minutes of fame will be over. Now, we need to get to bed. It's an early start in the morning."

⚭

As the media followed both Democrat and GOP candidates, one journalist in particular was especially interested in the Lincoln campaign. Breitbart's Joe Trubek had been the man who, some years before, had broken the news about Tom Lincoln's affairs. Although still young, Joe was an old-school journalist who required multiple sources before publishing any of his articles. He didn't resort to the "unnamed sources" trick that had become so common in nearly all journalism these days. If you want to write a hit piece, simply make up whatever lies you wish and then give them credence by citing unnamed sources. *Actually,* he thought, *the unnamed sources trick really only applies to pieces when covering Republican politicians.* For the past several years, the press had seemed to be in a coma when it came to the shenanigans of the president's party. It was always down to outfits such as Breitbart to report the truth rather than the watered-down fluff articles about Ludwig's administration. There had been so many instances of this willful ignorance, the latest being Ludwig's inexplicable shipping of literally billions of dollars in cash to the mullahs in Iran. Outrageous, yet most of the American press had ignored his actions or reported on it in passing as if it didn't really matter. Or how about the release of all those terrorists from Guantanamo for no reason—or the "One Voice" effort to sabotage the Israeli election? There were literally dozens of examples that a compliant media had downplayed or outright ignored. What had happened to investigative journalism where you followed the story wherever it led you, without regard for political affiliation or bias?

Trubek's continued interest in the Lincolns arose from the events that happened following publication of his piece on Tom's mistresses. It struck him as odd that immediately after the piece came out, Tom died—and even odder that his widow had seemed so well-prepared to run for governor's office. His reporter's nose was smelling something rotten; something just didn't sit well with him. He was taking a break with a colleague in their regular coffeehouse down in the Meatpacking District. It was a "shabby-chic" hipster joint: beadboard and exposed brick inside with holed linoleum flooring, and mismatched tables and chairs. The décor included rows of shelving with old coffee makers and obsolete coffee cans, some legible, some so rusted out as to be unreadable. It fit the vibe of the area perfectly.

"Everything happened just so neatly, didn't it? Lincoln gets caught with his pants down, and bam, he's dead. Then, suddenly, the glamourous widow rises from the ashes to grab the governorship. And what about the hit-and-run driver? Jeez, there must have been a ton of evidence available, paint chips, tire marks. Weird that the only surveillance camera that might have caught the driver making his escape was 'undergoing maintenance' at the time, isn't it? Then, poof, everyone loses interest in the whole thing, including the police. I'm telling you, Maury, there's a story in there."

His friend nodded in agreement.

Joe was like a pit bull. Once he bit on a story, he couldn't let go—not even if he wanted to. Sure, he'd dug around enough to unearth the whole Tom Lincoln bonkathon story; maybe there was a story in Tom's death too?

"Back to the grindstone, Joe," said Maury as he drained his latte. "Keep at it, man. Ciao."

"Sure thing, dude. I smell Pulitzer!" Joe yelled at Maury's back as he disappeared around the corner of the cobbled Lower Manhattan street.

Joe climbed the stairs up to his apartment and sat down in front of his laptop. *How to begin? Let's search for auto body shops in and around Trenton, junkyards, and maybe drivers with hit-and-run convictions,* he thought as the investigation began.

PRIMARIES

Every four years, the United States goes through a tedious process that is an essential part of its political theater. While the rest of the world typically elects its politicians after a campaign that might last a few weeks or months at most, America feels the need to beat itself over its collective head for years with an interminable round of talking heads, all of them speculating on who might be the next presidential candidate. This ritual usually commences within months of an inauguration. Such self-flagellation culminates in primary season. We all know the drill: the caucuses, New Hampshire, Super Tuesday etc., etc., ad nauseum. The public gets to see candidates looking awkward at county fairs, eating things they normally wouldn't dream of touching, or answering questions from hicks who normally wouldn't get within a hundred yards of them. But, if you want to become president, you must go through this ritual and endure the bullshit that goes along with all campaigns. And all the while, candidates have to pretend that they are enjoying it and that they actually like to connect with the flyover people. "Just vote for me. I'll promise you anything—and then forget you all as soon as I'm in power."

This primary season was no different to any other. Six Democratic hopefuls and the same number of Republicans worked the crowds, hopping from Iowa to Vermont to South Carolina, all trying to bribe the populace into getting their vote in exchange for empty promises. In corner cafes and town halls across the heartland, the same tired speeches were made, and a dozen egocentric politicians vied against each other, competing for attention from the masses and the media. Of course, the media plays along with the game, building up a different candidate each week, only to knock him or her back down the next. Every speech given, every word uttered is parsed and dissected by "experts." Depending upon which channels you watch, or if you tune into an AM or FM station, you'll be told that the weakest Democrat candidate is still a hundred times better than those lying GOP bastards, or vice versa. What a system!

Stacey Lincoln had an edge on the Democrat side due to her Kunis-provided team of experts. Pollsters, campaign managers, field workers—nothing was too much for the Elect Stacey machine. There were no guarantees. Some of her opponents were as well funded and managed as she was, and others ran shoestring operations as if they were not actually serious about being president and were in it for some kind of ego trip.

To the small section of the public who were actually interested in all this nonsense, Stacey was an appealing possibility. She had governorship experience and was therefore likely to be a capable leader of America. She seemed sincere in her stated wish to improve the lives of the people. She had a compelling backstory as a widowed mother who'd lost her husband in a tragic accident. Most importantly, she was a telegenic woman, and wasn't all of media insisting that the nation was way overdue for a female president? In our world of identity politics, gender trumps capability, so having a woman who also seemed capable was perfect. Voters could feel better about themselves for voting not only on gender but on capability too.

Over in the GOP camp, the same political dance went on, but one particular candidate was proving to have a big advantage. The public already knew Ron Suit; he'd been in their living rooms five nights a week for years. He was their friend, someone with whom they shared opinions, enjoyed skits together, and swapped stories. Ron was well aware of this and molded his campaign to match. While his rivals did all the usual primary stuff such as town hall meetings and hand-shaking, baby-kissing public appearances, Ron took a different approach. He livestreamed or broadcast blogs in towns throughout the heartland. The public loved this approach; it gave them the feeling that they were on his TV or radio show. Ron, of course, was highly skilled at ad-libbing in an amusing manner with anyone, and the broadcasts were always entertaining. He was also plain speaking about any subject, speaking his mind openly instead of parsing his thoughts through a politically correct filter. This endeared him even more to a significant bloc of voters, who were all looking for a sea change in Washington. Many of the people felt that the government was broken, full of self-serving weasels who got into politics not to change things for the better, but to line their pockets. The past eight years had seen a nation in decline; things needed shaking up!

Candidates on both sides were burning through advertising money at an alarming rate, at least all except one. Ron was good viewing, and the media on both sides simply loved covering him. He had no need to spend tons of cash on ads because he was enjoying hours of airtime for free. Even the left-wing coverage was still airtime, and when the talking heads of, say, CNN ran a piece that mocked his approach to the campaign, it only reinforced and built his base; viewers could see his sincerity contrasted against the snide, superior news host. Without realizing it, the opposition coverage was making him more popular.

Ron's added benefit was his wife, Megan. As a media draw in her own right, she contributed greatly to Ron's popularity—even though her political stance was opposed to his. Megan enjoyed a massive Instagram following, among other things. Her media posts generally ran along the lines of "I know he's a conservative, and I know I'm against a lot of his positions, but ..." She even posted sometimes about how some of Ron's campaign issues made sense. Thus, moderate lefties, especially young moderate lefties, became somewhat interested in Ron and his views. Drip, drip, drip. The democrats were leaking out into Ron's bucket.

"Hello, audience! What a beautiful day in America. Now, let's find out if tonight's news suits you!"

Courtesy of Fox, Ron had kept his NSFW high in the ratings. He was currently using it as an integral part of his campaign, and here he was, airing his show from Iowa in front of a big local crowd.

"Tonight, we're here in Ames, Iowa. Of course, it's pure coincidence that Iowa is one of the early primary states. I could have broadcast from Des Moines, but you know what? Ames is actually a very pretty university town, so it has loads of bars full of drunk students—and that's my kind of town."

The crowd cheered.

"Sitting with me tonight are four stalwart citizens of Ames who I picked at random—after they gave me envelopes full of money. I thought I'd start with a little quiz for you all. The winner will receive this new piece of merch that I reckon is an absolute collector's item already." Ron leaned down to pick something up from under his chair and held it up to the camera. It was a baseball hat, or gimme cap as he'd grown up calling it. Bright blue with white capital letters across the front that said "Ron Suits" and under that in crimson "You!"

Once again, the crowd dutifully cheered.

"Now," began Ron, looking at the four competitors, "you may not know this, but your hometown often features in crossword puzzles. I am a Zen master of the crossword, but I want to find out about your puzzle-solving skills. So, I'm going to give you a clue, and the answer will always be an anagram of Ames. Ring your bell to answer. Most correct answers get the cap. Are you ready?"

The four locals nodded their heads, each looking uncomfortable to varying degrees.

"Here we go. The clue is *alike*."

A blue-haired lady wearing eyeglasses with thin chains hanging from their arms, looping around her neck quickly hit her bell. "Is it *same*?" she asked.

"Yes, darling. It is indeed. You were quick off the mark there, weren't you, Betty? Okay, next clue is *flat top*."

The same lady rang once more. "Mesa," she said firmly, gaining new confidence in front of the cameras.

"Ladies and gentlemen, I think Betty must run the local Mensa chapter." Ron giggled, raising one eyebrow as if he was Dr. Evil. "You win again!"

The other competitors shuffled in their seats, abashed that this old lady was beating them.

"Right, last question. Car show."

This time, there was no immediate bell. After a few seconds, a ruddy-skinned, overweight man in bib overalls chimed in. "That has to be SEMA," he said gruffly.

"Yeah, you broke Betty's run. Sadly though, she gets the cap. Now, Betty, come on over to the couch so we can get to know each other."

Ron took Betty by the elbow, and they walked the few feet across the stage to a couch. He sat her down and positioned himself just a little too close to her.

Betty blushed.

Moving his head in close to Betty's, Ron purred, "Tell me, Betty, you are obviously a font of knowledge. What do you do for a living?"

"I'm a librarian at the university, Ron."

"What!" Ron leaped back on the couch. "If you're a librarian, I'll put money that you're a Democrat. What in hell are you doing up here with me?"

Betty blushed again. "Actually, Ron, I am a Democrat and have been for decades, but I've been listening to some of what you've been saying, and it seems to make sense. I thought I'd come and hear for myself."

"Well, thank you so much, Betty. You are *so* right." Ron became serious. "This country needs open minds. We're far too closed and polarized right now, and we have been for some years. In my view, it's because of someone you probably voted for. Peter Ludwig's eight years has resulted in us becoming a nation of opposites. You are either hard left or hard right—on my team or a sworn enemy. My view is that it doesn't matter. What do we need to do, audience?"

The crowd began to chant, "Kick the bums out. Kick the bums out. Kick the bums out!"

As the segment went into break, the camera zoomed in on Betty. She was wearing her newly won hat, grinning, and her lips were softly mouthing the words, "Kick the bums out. Kick the bums out!"

⚬⊶⊷⚬

Meanwhile, over in Stacey's camp, she began her stump speech in the same way she always did. "Isn't it time we had a woman in the White House?" she asked the crowd, and before they could respond she continued, "Of course it is. For too long, we have been suppressed. Even today, women earn significantly less than men for doing the same job. In my own state of New Jersey, I enacted legislation that requires equal pay for equal work, and my administration will enact similar laws, backed by a task force that will investigate every claim of inequality. If you, as a woman, can document that you are being paid less for doing the same job as a man, we will prosecute your employer to the fullest extent of the law."

The crowd—mostly women—clapped and cheered.

The rest of Stacey's speech unfolded in a similar manner: a series of statements that showed what was wrong with the country followed by what laws or restrictions she would introduce to fix them. At no point did she or the crowd reflect on the irony that her own Democratic Party had just spent the past eight years in power. Why weren't these problems already fixed?

Following the conclusion of her speech, Stacey walked down into the crowd and spent more than an hour with them, posing for selfies, giving sound bites, and generally acting like a consummate politician. There was no question that she was good at it. Eventually she was bundled into a car and taken to her hotel.

Bill, her campaign manager, was already in her room, holding out a tumbler full of bourbon.

Stacey grabbed it, flopped down in a chair, and took a deep swig. "Goddam it, Bill," she hissed. "How long does this shit go on? If I have to pose in front of another iPhone, I'll go crazy!"

"Don't worry, Madame Governor," Bill replied. "The deeper into the primaries we get, the less face-to-face you'll need to do. Following the debates, you'll be concentrating on arena venues and will be able to distance yourself from one-to-ones. But you always must keep your public face on: the fair-minded widow from New Jersey who will listen."

"Yeah, yeah, yeah. I'm going to bed. See you in the morning." Stacey rose to see Bill out of the room. *Fuck, it's a long road, but it will be worth it.* She flopped down into the bed.

As primary season dragged on, some attrition was bound to occur, and a few candidates on both sides dropped out. They got no support in the caucuses, or hardly any votes, and they bowed to the inevitable. In a final flourish of self-aggrandizement, some of these losers even had the temerity to make closing speeches where they endorsed others who were still running. What a joke. Quite obviously, no one cared about these candidates enough to pick them—so why should they care who they'd recommend? Of course, cynical observers might surmise that such endorsements are actually coded messages to the favorites: "Promise me a position in government after your election, and I will endorse you."

Heading into the party conferences, it was becoming clear that Stacey Lincoln was pulling ahead and solidifying her base. She'd been picked by all the pundits and media experts as the Democratic choice for president. On the GOP side, however, things were not so cut-and-dry. The party stood firmly behind Romney, a longtime senator with immaculate credentials and voting record; he was a hands-down favorite. Unfortunately, the electorate was not in agreement with the party; more and more, they favored Ron Suit. The primary debates had shown him to be light on his feet, quick with a riposte, and simple in his vision of what America should become. His popularity was cemented in one debate where he demolished all the other candidates. When asked by the moderator why he would be the best choice for president, Ron answered, "Well, look along this line of hopefuls. We've got the party favorite, the guy who everyone says will be president, except that they've said that twice before! He lost then, and he'll lose now! Then we have the egomaniac billionaire who seems to think that carpet-bombing us with lousy advertising will get him elected. He couldn't even be bothered to run in some of the primaries! Then there's a couple of career pols who are sleeping through the whole campaign—and, I might add, look asleep right now! Finally, there is your humble candidate who is not a politician, who is not a billionaire, who is listening to the pulse of the people. From where I stand, it looks like I'm the only candidate who makes sense. We have far too much government in our lives, and I promise you that when I'm in office, I'll be taking a big broom and sweeping all the corrupt politicians, useless regulations, and lousy lobbyists right out of Washington!"

Some in the audience began chanting, "Kick the bums out," but they were quickly shut down by the moderators.

All three primary debates unfolded in the same fashion; the other candidates spoke eloquently about their vision for America, while Ron maintained his same position. "These bums have been in Washington for decades and have achieved precisely nothing.

Yet they keep promising us that things will improve if only they get elected."

In the final debate, he said, "Well, here we go again, folks. More empty promises and glib sound bites. All I'm saying is this—and you can take it to the bank—you all better uncork the real bubble up and get the rainbow stew on the stove because this president will do what he says he'll do when he walks through that White House door!"

"Kick the bums out. Kick the bums out!"

The crowd loved it, while the other candidates at their daises looked at each other with puzzled faces. "What the fuck did he just say?"

MEET THE CANDIDATES

As the nation's public went cross-eyed under the nonstop bombardment of advertising, punditry, and point-counterpoint debate, time ground on inevitably toward the Democratic and GOP conventions.

Over on the left, candidates and delegates gathered together to begin the convoluted voting process that leads to selection of a Democratic presidential candidate. Almost five thousand delegates partied, wore outrageous clothing, and generally acted the fool in what should be a somber occasion. There were district delegates, state delegates, PLEO delegates, and superdelegates, all following their own quirky regulations for pledging.

A particularly odd aspect of the DNC primary process is the superdelegate; this mysterious and elite group tipped the scales in Stacey's favor from the outset by immediately casting their unfettered votes for her. Thus, 15 percent of the available count was pledged as a bloc before any other delegates participated, sending a strong signal that the governor of New Jersey was the DNC's favored nominee. Per the rules, other delegates must vote in compliance with the results of their caucuses or primary votes, but as usual, there was a chunk of unpledged votes up for grabs from the districts and states that had allocated pledges to candidates who'd subsequently dropped out of the race. This freed up the delegates to pledge for whomever they wished. The superdelegates bloc vote sent a powerful message to delegates that perhaps those unhindered votes should also go to Lincoln. This superdelegate tactic had of course been arranged by an elite few: Ludwig, the DNC chair, and select others, including Milos, had lobbied quietly but firmly to ensure that their choice, Lincoln, got a head start.

"A simple majority is all we need," said Bill. "Let's see if you can pull it off on the first round."

They did, receiving comfortably more than two thousand pledges. Stacey was the presumptive Democratic presidential candidate.

❧

"I'm told that this primary had the biggest voter turnout in the history of the party," Ron said as he accepted the party's nomination on the stage of the GOP convention. His wife stood by his side, looking sensational and glamorous. Ron continued, "I look out on the sea of faces before me, and I know that you're looking for change. I'm sure that the reason for the historic turnout is because people are sick and tired of our crappy status quo. We have a government that pretends to listen to us once every four years and then goes back to its self-serving business as usual. The high turnout also demonstrates the power of popular culture in our world today. You know, Peter Ludwig, our soon-to-be-ex president, tapped into an emerging social media structure back when he first won, and that contributed significantly to his election. Well, we noted that experience and used it as a key element of our campaign. We've shown that smart use of today's media platforms makes all the difference. With no apologies to my rivals in the race, a large part of why I got the nomination is because of my media footprint—plus, of course, the footprint of my beautiful wife, Megan." Ron turned toward her with a "ta-da" gesture. He paused to drink in the moment. Oh sure, he'd been a celebrity for a long time and was clearly used to adoring crowds and admirers, but this occasion was different, and he began to realize why. Not all of the crowd was friendly; he would have to work to convince people that he was the right choice. Continuing with his ad-libbed remarks to the convention floor, he began speaking once more. "You know, I totally get that a lot of you here tonight might not be 100 percent happy with the outcome of this primary. I totally get that some of you RINOs out there are pissed with me for snatching away your rightful candidate's coronation. I totally get that I could be perceived as a lightweight, an outsider who doesn't belong here, but I can totally assure y'all that my ideals dovetail perfectly with those of the Republican Party. I can totally assure y'all that I will follow through on all my campaign promises, and isn't that exactly what politicians are supposed to do? So, watch out, Washington, because this Suit is bringing a big broom—and he'll be sweeping out all the crap and corruption from the dark and dusty corners of our capital. America deserves an honest, minimalist government that frees up its populace so they can thrive and excel. That is the fundamental principle of Republicanism, and that's exactly what you're going to get from my administration when we win the presidency!"

Chants of "kick the bums out" began reverberating around the convention center.

Ron and Megan basked in the warmth that was beginning to emanate from the floor.

The GOP delegates had pledged per their districts' wishes, and those wishes were for Ron Suit. While the popular heart of the party had gotten behind Ron, the old-school core of leadership was clearly not yet onboard. His promises to shake up Washington would have obvious negative consequences for them. He was going to upset the applecart and jeopardize their power, money, and influence. That was not good.

❧

Finally, after years of talk, thousands of promises, and dozens of candidates, the parties' preferences were decided. Two tribes could now begin putting on their warpaint in anticipation of the final battle in a long war. Lawn signs and bumper stickers began cropping up across the country. "Stick with Stacey," "Let's make all fifty states the Land of Lincoln," and of course "Isn't it time for a woman president?" could be seen in Democrat strongholds, while "Ron Suits Me," "Suit up for America," and obviously "Kick the bums out!" sprouted in GOP enclaves.

No mercy was to be shown by the opposing and polarized sides, and their weapons of war were newspapers, TV, radio waves, and the internet. It was no surprise that left-wing organizations lined up behind the Lincoln campaign, and the *New York Times, Washington Post*, CNN, MSNBC, and all three main broadcast channels threw their weight into a nonstop vitriolic diatribe against Ron. However, they still had a morbid fascination with the man. He made for good press, and it had not been lost on them that circulation, viewership, and hits all went up whenever Ron Suit was in the piece. So, even though he was now getting negative coverage from this side of the media, he was nonetheless getting coverage.

On the other side, Fox, AM radio, the *Examiner*, the *New York Post*, and other outlets lined up behind Ron. Their coverage was tempered; he was the Republican party candidate for president, yet such an unconventional one! The mantra seemed to be this: "We're behind him, but guardedly, how will he cope if he wins?"

As the weeks passed, both sides asked, "What if he wins?" If an alien had landed in America during that period, unaware of the massive media bias inherent in news coverage, it would be certain in the received knowledge that this woman Lincoln was going to win the election. After all, overwhelming coverage showed her to be the "steady hand" and an "experienced politician." This man Suit was a "novelty," a "long shot," and an "inconceivable choice."

Interestingly, even Suit's supporters were often muted in their support. The guy was so out there that displaying a preference for him was often seen as a sign that you didn't take politics seriously—that you were a joke just like him. Better to remain silent and be thought a fool than to speak and remove all doubt.

Per the usual process, televised candidate debates were arranged, three to be held one per week on "independent" TV channels, moderated by "unbiased" hard news reporters. The first was scheduled for CNN, led by Anderson Cooper.

"So, when he asks about your view on LGBT rights, our focus group research shows that this is a differentiator between you and Suit. You have to capitalize on this and press home your openness to persons of all genders." Stacey was being prepared for the debate. Her team was running a mock debate, complete with one member posing as Ron Suit and providing the responses expected from him. They had spent days running through these rehearsals, posing every question, and coaching her on the correct way to respond.

"Okay, okay, we've been through these goddam questions a hundred times. I know the answers, but what happens when I'm asked about something I've not been prepped for? I need training up on good ad-libbing versus taboo topics. I've got to be prepared for all eventualities." The frustration in Stacey's voice was audible.

"Stacey!" Milos had been quietly watching the rehearsals, coming and going constantly, taking calls, but never offering advice or criticism. "You do not need to worry about unknown questions. I can assure you that we are going through every question that you will be asked."

Stacey looked puzzled. "Milos, how in hell can you say that? Do you have a time machine or something? I need to be ready for the gotchas, the surprise questions."

"I guarantee that these are the questions you will face, my dear. You should focus on these and these only. Now, relax and let us start over."

Once more, the Kunis web of influence had been at work.

Even though he was confident that Suit had no chance of election, he nevertheless had opted to tip the scales by ensuring that he got the all the debate questions ahead of time. In war, all tactics are acceptable—and the ends justify the means. Once more, the Group had exerted its widespread influence to control the layout, format, and outcome of the debates.

"Hello, welcome to the first presidential debate. I'm Anderson Cooper, and joining me as moderators tonight are Wolf Blitzer and Erin Burnett. We're going to run through tonight's rules of debate, but I must first ask our audience to refrain from outbursts or applause throughout the evening."

So began the debate. Stacey felt supremely prepared. Even though she couldn't be 100 percent sure that somehow it had been rigged in her favor, Milo's assurance that she would know every question was comforting. She could handle this talk show host.

Ron had been preparing for the event too. For this final leg of his campaign, he'd assembled a group of social, financial, and economic experts plus other specialists, all drawn from his wide circle of contacts, all of whom were keen to break Washington's status quo and give the Capital back to the people. Of course, like Milos's team, they too expected something from this work, perhaps a cabinet position or a "tsar" appointment?

The first question was designed to shake up the night by starting out a little controversially. "This question is for you, Madame Governor: How will your administration address LGBTQ issues in the USA? You have three minutes."

Stacey launched into her well-rehearsed reply. "Well, Anderson, I believe that for too long our country has repressed minorities, whether on the basis of skin color, religion, or gender orientation. My opponent's party has been particularly egregious in this area. When I am elected, we intend to form a Department of Gender Equality that will ensure equal opportunity for people regardless of how they identify. It will ensure that every piece of government paperwork will list all gender denominations. We'll also investigate offering a financial supplement where minorities such as transsexuals can qualify for additional Social Security subsidies to compensate them for the hardships they must endure. Our society must be a caring one, and my administration will work to ensure that the population follows the rules laid down by us. It's the government's job to care of minorities, and enactment of caring laws is the best way to achieve this."

"Mr. Suit, you have two minutes for rebuttal."

Ron was raring to go, getting the bit in his mouth. "Well, America, here we go again. You're going to hear tonight, and in every other debate, that Stacey's answer to everything is more government and more money thrown at the problem. We already have appropriate laws in place that cover this topic; in fact, we have too many. Less than 1 percent of Americans identify as transgender, so why are we even asking this question? Let's debate more important issues! Now I know, Anderson, that you and your network will label me as transphobic or gay-hating, but I assure you I'm not. My position on this topic is the same as Peter Pumpkinhead: any kind of love is all right! And speaking of minority groups, I'm pretty sure I just sealed the XTC fan-bloc vote with that reference! My administration will not operate on a 'divide-and-conquer' platform where we chop the nation up into little groups of 'oppressed minorities.' As far as I'm concerned, we're all Americans—and we're all God's children. God doesn't care what color you are, or if you like men or women. He created every last one of you. I will work for all people. Hell, I'll even work for the Democrats amongst y'all!"

And so it went for the rest of the evening. Ron's prediction came to pass. Every policy proposal, every way forward according to Stacey, involved some sort of additional legislation and funding. In their closing remarks, the contrast between the candidates was stark.

"First, I'd like to thank CNN for its evenhanded and well-run debate this evening," Stacey began. "I envision an America of caring government, an America where Washington will look after you whenever you need it. My America will be one that welcomes our immigrants with open arms, whether you arrive legally or not. For too long, so many of our minority groups have struggled and have been denied their rights. I will correct this injustice and walk them into a new dawn of justice for all." Her speech ran on in a similar vein until its conclusion. Applause ripped through the audience with some shouting "Stacey!" or "You go, girl!"

When the moderators had calmed the crowd, Ron began his closing remarks. He had not rehearsed this to word perfection as had Stacey, but he had jotted down key points throughout the debate that he now addressed. "America, my opponent paints a dismal picture of us all, one of an oppressed society, a nation of disenfranchised individuals who've spent their lives being mistreated and downtrodden. Her solution to this terrible existence is to say, 'Don't worry. Big government is here.' But let's remember, folks. It's big government that has put these people where they are. Our soon-to-be retired commander-in-chief has managed in less than eight years to drive up unemployment claims astronomically. Labor participation is at an all-time low. Welfare initiatives such as food stamps are the highest ever, burning through billions and billions. Our deficit has never been higher. And why is this? It's because big government loves control. More government means more control and these people," he pointed across the stage at Stacey, "these politicians thrive on control. They live for keeping y'all in check so they can line their pockets and keep the membership of their club exclusive. The Democrat model for our nation is no different to that of countless socialist states, and we all know how wonderful life is in places like Venezuela or China. When I'm elected, I promise you that I will gut our political fat cats. We don't need more government. We need much, much less! I intend to unleash the inherent greatness in each and every American whether he's white, black, or green. I don't care if you identify as a boy or girl. I want all of you to thrive and prosper, and the key to this policy is to get government out of your way so you can achieve whatever you want. Thanks, CNN. I'm looking forward to hearing what vile, hateful rhetoric I've just spewed on tomorrow's news."

"Kick the bums out. Kick the bums out!"

The debate closed with the moderators closing out the evening over the steady war cry of the "Suits Me" crowd.

As predicted, the next day's news extolled the Democratic vision of a caring society, contrasting against Ron Suit who doesn't care about minority oppression and rights. Polls gave a clear advantage to Stacey because obviously they had been skewed to favor her.

Ron took it all in stride. His strategy was simple: provide a small government vision headed by an outsider compared to more of the same headed by yet another insider. Ron was aiming for more than the traditional Republican base; he realized that the key to winning was to snatch Democratic votes. While that party seemed intent on slicing and dicing the electorate down to infinitesimal minority groups, Ron's aim was simple: go after the working-class voters. If he could get a decent-sized bloc of these folks to get behind him, he'd win.

His touring campaign thus focused around population centers in blue states that had been particularly hurt by the past eight years of Ludwig's progressive politics. Rust Belt towns, flyover areas, shuttered manufacturing hubs, all these areas with their disgruntled potential voters were his target. Simultaneous with his "Suit Up for America" circuit, his social media campaign made the same groups its target.

The weeks passed, and while the popular polls continued to show Lincoln comfortably ahead, Ron wasn't worried. He was interpreting his own data, gathered by the team, and it was clearly showing that he was gaining support. Some old-school Republican pols even began to tentatively accept his candidacy, although though they didn't like it—or him. Others remained anti-Suit in all aspects.

Here was a man who was threatening to uproot their rightful places in Washington, a man who could shine light on the many shady dealings of their everyday political lives.

"Our data is indicating that Mr. Suit might have an outside chance of getting elected," Milos said at a clandestine secure videoconference meeting of the Group. "While this is still remote, we should support our candidate however possible. It would be appropriate to begin leaking some of the information we have on him. A concerted negative publicity drive should push his numbers down. Let's use our media companies to initiate this new approach."

The smears thus began. With the election some two months away, Kunis had seen analysis of some polling data that concerned him. Apparently, Suit was gaining support in certain areas that held inordinate influence for electoral college votes. The overwhelming majority of America believes it lives in a democracy; after all, every four years, the populace gets to vote for a new president. In reality, this is not the case. In order to prevent a large state from exerting undue influence over the nation, the brilliant electoral college was devised, originating from the Constitutional Convention of 1787. Under this system, state population size is a factor, but it cannot dominate. Our glorious nation presently enjoys 538 electoral college votes. This number comes from three parts; the number of senators, plus the number of house representatives, plus—in a sop to the whining folk of Washington—a few for the District of Columbia. It is these relatively few votes that determine the outcome of any presidential election. For instance, California may have the nation's largest population, but its influence is muted by the fact that it has only two senators—same for all states—and fifty or so representatives. So, a state with more than 12 percent of the country's population gets less than 9 percent of the electoral college vote. It works in the other direction too. Take for example, our smallest state. Wyoming has less than 0.2 percent of America's population—but almost 0.6 percent of the electoral college. It's a fantastic equalizer in many ways, and those candidates who get hung up too much on polls can lose sight of the fact that it's not just counting heads that's important; it's where those heads live. The Suit campaign was using this as an inherent part of its strategy, and Kunis was beginning to latch onto this fact. Even though such an approach was not sufficiently proven to be superior to a more conventional methodology—and it certainly was not sufficient reason to modify the Lincoln campaign—it bothered him slightly. It was time to get dirty.

❦

Maury was sitting inside the coffeehouse. The Manhattan weather was foul, and he'd nearly fallen on his ass while navigating the Meatpacking District's slippery cobbles on the way to his regular meet-up with Joe. "Hey, man," he said as Joe arrived. "What up, dude?"

They drank their cappuccinos and chewed on sandwiches, occasionally looking out through the condensation-streaked windows. "I'm telling you, Maury, the jigsaw pieces might just be fitting. So, it turns out that the biggest auto recycling center in Trenton is about a forty-five minute drive from where Lincoln was hit. Also, it turns out that a process worker at the plant next door said he'd seen a car with only one headlight drive by as he was on his way home following his shift. The timing fits, man."

"So, who runs this recycling place?" asked Maury.

"Some Mafioso-type guy, shady dude. His background shows lots of run-ins with the law, but no convictions—he always comes up clean. Still … man, this is some good shit," he said as he gulped down his sandwich.

"So, how come the cops didn't make these connections, Joe?" asked Maury.

"Well, for one thing, the guy who saw the one-light car has

a record, and the law assumes he's lying and just trying to get his fifteen minutes of fame. For another thing, how in the hell are you going to find a crushed car in a couple-hundred acres of crushed cars? Of course, the police's unbelievable lack of curiosity in this case doesn't help either."

"Have you talked with LA about this?" Breitbart's head office was based in Los Angeles, and Maury was interested in seeing their level of interest in this investigative piece.

"No, Maury. It's way too premature to make this a real article. I'm just putzing around with it in my spare time."

"Well, gotta go, Joe. See you later this week?" Maury stood up to leave.

"Sure thing, Maury," replied Joe.

They left the café and went their separate ways. As he walked back to his apartment, Joe mused on something he hadn't told Maury. *The recycling center is next to a big processing plant, and that plant is owned by Milos Kunis. Kunis was the brains behind Stacey Lincoln's successful bid for the governorship. That is too much of a stretch, isn't it? Then again ...*

THE FINAL COUNTDOWN

Each time Stacey entered a hall or arena to give her stump speech, Helen Reddy's "I am Woman" rang out over the sound system. She gave pretty much the same talk each evening, always beginning by saying, "Isn't it time we had a woman in the White House?" That was always met by rapturous cheering.

Unbeknownst to Stacey or the crowd, scattered throughout the audience at every speech, a group of paid workers was making good money simply to yell and hoot and holler any time the woman on stage paused. It was pretty effective; *Homo sapiens* is a herd animal, and if one begins to bleat, others will join in. The more that bleat, the more will join in. It's the same at any TV show: a warm-up act gets the audience in the mood and raring to go so that when the star arrives, they'll adore him at the drop of a hat.

Stacey's traveling roadshow got tons of coverage on TV and in "serious" newspapers such as the *Times* and the *Post*. This coverage was invariably and inevitably favorable. "Lincoln Presents a Bold Plan for a Compassionate America" was a typical headline. Things were looking good for her, and Stacy was feeling pretty confident about her chances in November.

Milos saw no need to tell her about his upcoming smear

campaign against her opponent. Instead, he continued to support and encourage her, both psychologically and financially.

Over at Team Suit, Ron continued his loose approach to speeches. The rigidity of a set-piece sound bite-laden recital that was repeated ad nauseum at each stop was not for him. His years as a talk show host had trained him perfectly for ad-libbing repartee. "We Won't get Fooled Again" blared out each evening as Ron ascended to the stage. As the music died down, a unison chant of "Suit Up, Suit Up" rose to deafening levels, interspersed with "Kick the Bums out."

"Hello, audience! What a beautiful day in America. Now, let's find out if tonight's thoughts suit you!" Ron paused for some time, looking around at the crowd in front of him, even turning to nod and wave to those crammed on the stage behind him. "Now, I'll run through all my mandatory-listening serious stuff in a minute, but I need to start with a piece I've just read in *Politico*."

Some booing could be heard from the crowd at the mention of that hated media outlet.

"It says that they have video of me smoking dope and getting drunk with a bunch of strippers after one of my late-night shows a few years ago. Isn't it funny how this comes out now? I mean, really, no coincidence here, is there?"

The crowd cheered.

"Well, I'm here to tell you that it's all true. I have smoked weed, I have got drunk, and I have hung around with a load of scantily clad ladies … and it was awesome!"

A wave of noise rose up from the audience, and wild cheers and chanting erupted.

Ron waited until things had settled down a little. "No, seriously, I have done all of those things at some point in my life. Does that make me a bad man? I guess I'll be finding out come November. Just remember this though, no one is perfect, we all have our flaws, and that's what makes us who we are. If you are appalled, disappointed, or disgusted by these so-called revelations, that's your prerogative and you don't have to vote for me. I'm just saying, let those without sin cast the first stone, etcetera, etcetera. I'm pretty sure that there'll be other shocking news about me dropping between here and November, and some of it might even be true—but if you want change in Washington this election, I'm your man, warts and all!"

"Kick the bums out. Kick the bums out!"

Ron went on to riff on the key topics of his campaign: small government, less legislation, lower taxation, and giving everyone the opportunity to succeed. After closing out the speech, Ron, as he usually did, moved down and through the crowd, shaking hands and posing for selfies as XTC's anthem "Peter Pumpkinhead" rang out, the song enjoying a surge of popularity due to its use on his campaign trail. As always, the speech was rapturously received by his ever-growing fan base.

Every stop was the same: a mixture of stream of consciousness stirred into an optimistic recipe for making America a great place. That renewing freshness was what kept the crowds so massive.

Over in Stacey's camp, did you really need to go see her when the things she said were more or less repeated word for word in her endless interviews? Even the television ads sounded almost monotonous, slamming Suit for his loose character, or unpreparedness, or whatever negative issue could be highlighted.

It was early in Ron's speech. He was up in Michigan as a part of his team's focus on the traditionally blue and blue-collar state focus.

"You know, audience, an October surprise sounds good, doesn't it? It's like a surprise birthday party or something like that. Well, my October surprise is not nice, not nice at all. Our friends over in the Lincoln campaign have managed to dig up some woman who is claiming that she had sex with me. She's actually quite attractive, so I suppose I should be flattered, but you all know my wife, Megan. Why in hell would I want to cheat on a gorgeous, clever, and rich woman like her. I mean, please …"

The crowd roared, chants of "Suit Up" beginning along with some cries of "Lyin' Lincoln, Lyin' Lincoln."

Ron continued, "In a way, I'm actually pleased to see all of this crap coming out because it means we've got them scared! It means they know that we—you, us—are a threat to their status quo. These scumbag politicians are doing their level best to derail this campaign, but I'm telling you now, I'm in this to the bitter end. They can dig up anything they want on me, but I'll keep on going. I'm the Energizer Bunny!"

"Kick the bums out. Kick the bums out!"

Following his usual lengthy trawl through the crowd, Ron was driven to his hotel. Megan was waiting for him. She accompanied Ron on much of his tour, although work commitments sometimes precluded it, as did her own separate campaign trips in support of her husband. "So, you bonked this bimbo, did you?"

"Darlin', don't be ridiculous. You know they're just throwing everything they can at us." Ron began getting ready for bed, he was worn out from this nonstop effort.

"I know, but it would be nice if you could just tell me you didn't," Megan said as she joined him in bed.

Ron shuffled over to her, wrapped an arm around Megan's shoulders, and whispered, "Why on earth would I want to cheat on someone like you? You're the best thing to ever happen to me. Now, early start for me tomorrow, and you've got to get out to the airport for your LA flight." He kissed her on the cheek and rolled away.

The smears continued: "I was at an after-show party with Mr. Suit, and he grabbed my hand and shoved it into his pants."

"Ron Suit drugged me and raped me while I was unconscious."

"Suit was drunk-driving and hit my baby."

"Mr. Suit has evaded taxes for twelve years."

For each claim, the mainstream media indignantly demanded his immediate withdrawal from the campaign. "How can such a corrupt and morally bereft person remain in the race?" was the general gist of the headlines and commentary.

By then, however, much of the right-wing media had "Suited up." The writing was on the wall. This guy was the Republican candidate. He was not embarrassing himself out on the trail; in fact, he seemed to appeal to a large swath of the public. Whether for pragmatic reasons, or for actually believing in him, he was now being defended and supported, giving counterpoint to the left's rhetoric. Each nasty claim was investigated and disposed of, although Lincoln's team continued to spread them and deny the truth that they were salubrious and false claims.

"Tell a lie for long enough and it becomes the truth" was a mantra followed by the Group, the architects of all the smears, and Stacey's supporters unwittingly followed. They just hated Suit and would believe anything bad about him.

⚶

September morphed into October. Polling data still showed Stacey with a comfortable lead, and both candidates continued their nonstop cycle of speeches and interviews.

Up in the Meatpacking District, Joe Trubek was on the phone to his Breitbart contacts in Los Angeles. He was trying to convince them that his story about the untimely death of Tom Lincoln was ready to run. "Look, so after Lincoln died, it just struck me as odd that the whole issue was basically ignored. So, I followed up and am pretty sure that I've traced the vehicle."

"Okay, Joe, what have you got?" The editors at Breitbart needed solid reporting before they'd consider publication.

"Well, a plant worker just outside of Trenton saw a car with only one headlight turning into Lombardi Recycling about forty-five minutes after the incident. The timing fits. I looked into Lombardi's business. He's a pretty sketchy guy, mob links and multiple police investigations, although no convictions."

"So, you found the car?"

"Nope, my guess is that it was crushed the minute it drove into that yard, and there's no way anyone could ever find it now. But here's the really interesting part. The lead detective on the case seemed to lose interest pretty damn quickly. He essentially closed the file within weeks. I dug into this guy, he's a longtime cop, nothing unusual, but I managed to get a look at his finances, and he lives well above his station. The guy is on the take somehow. I'm sure of it."

"Joe, as much as we would dearly love to find something on Stacey Lincoln, what you're presenting simply isn't factual enough to publish. Oh sure, you could probably take it to somewhere like TMZ who don't give a shit about truth, but for Breitbart to put this out, we need more background and fact-checking. Sorry, Joe."

After the call, Joe dejectedly adjourned to the coffee shop to relay his disappointment to Maury. "I know there's something in this, man. It pisses me off that they want more, but I get it. That's life, I guess. More digging required? More digging will be done. But first, fluff pieces to write, gotta pay the bills somehow."

They split, and Joe headed up to his apartment to get back to work.

In mid-October, Joe finally found what he'd been searching for. That lead detective had an offshore bank account. *Now why in hell would a cop need that?* Lots of digging, much of it illegally, had unearthed his Cayman Islands account. Weirdly, two months after Tom's death, a quarter-million bucks had landed in it. There were too many firewalls for Joe to figure out the source of the money, but this proved to him that something smelled rotten in Trenton. He met up with Maury as usual.

"So, this is the smoking gun you've been looking for, is it?"

"Damn straight," replied Joe. "I'm calling LA soon as we're done here; they've got to let me run this now."

As the two parted company, Joe yelled, "Hey man, don't forget we've got tickets for Velvet Rope tonight."

"C'mon Joe, you know I haven't forgotten. I'll swing by your place around nine. You can update me on your call too."

Around nine thirty that evening, Maury hustled down the streets, making his way to Joe's apartment. He called him, but it went straight to voicemail. "Oh, hey, Joe. I'm running late as usual—see you in a few."

Maury slogged up the creaky stairs to Joe's tiny, run-down studio. The door wasn't locked, which was nothing new, and he went straight in. "You ready, man?" Maury asked as he entered. "It's going to be crowded if we don't get a mo—"

He stopped dead in his tracks.

Joe was hanging in front of him, his feet at about Maury's waist level. An extension cord was wrapped tightly around his neck, tied off to one of the rusty old ceiling girders that was a feature of Joe's studio. The body was swinging ever so slightly, twisting gently back and forth as it swung.

THE BIG DAY

As always, the "Tuesday next after the first Monday after November 1" was the big day: Election Day! Years of effort—much of it futile—culminates in a single day of reckoning. Endless candidates' hopes and dreams are crushed on the long road to this climactic moment. For a select few, there is the thrill of anticipation, a tingle of possibility that in twenty-four hours, they might be the most powerful person on earth.

For Stacey, it was her destiny after a long journey. She had worked so long for this, and now, with the help of her team, she was confident that her rightful place in life was about to come true. A female president was long overdue, and the exit polls were confirming this fact. All data was indicating a comfortable victory.

The Atlantic City Convention Center had been made ready, trimmed out with countless banners and bunting, "We're with Stacey," "Madame president," and so on. The media had been alerted to the timing of the victory celebration, and they would all be attending to witness and participate in the breathless adoration of a new, female president.

In Stacey's war room, her team huddled around TV monitors, tracking the polling, following the early results, and generally slapping each other on their backs in anticipation of an easy win.

With all the powerful media moguls backing Stacey, a bottomless campaign fund courtesy of Mr. Kunis and his associates, and the numbers on their side, how could they not enjoy a little early celebration?

∽⊙⋐∾

In Houston, Ron sat with his team, monitoring results. It was clear that if they had listened to the popular TV stations or cable news, there would be good cause for feeling down in the dumps. However, Ron knew that their research indicated that there was a chance of success; a few wins in key states could tip the scales in his favor. Still, listening to the talking heads gleefully spouting the exit data did not make for happy viewing.

Interviews with members of the public as they left polling stations did not help either. Invariably, when asked who they voted for, they answered, "Stacey, of course!"

Ron had booked the Marriott downtown for his celebration/ concession speech, and it was absolutely packed with supporters even this early in the evening. There was a festive feel in the ballroom. People were happy, and regardless of whether he won or not, at least their Ron had shaken things up. He had "got the politicians scared." Even in losing, surely the nation's future would have been improved by Ron's campaign, which had woken so many to the self-serving elitism of DC? Besides, Suit made folks feel good and optimistic about their country—and what's not to like about that?

Both teams split their time between CNN and Fox as the early results began to come in. "With 30 percent counted in New Jersey, it looks like a romp for Lincoln." The reporter could barely contain his excitement.

"Well, duh!" Ron said as he stared at the screen. "If she doesn't win her home state, the world's gone mad."

And on it went, partial results from the first dozen states were giving Lincoln the win. All the CNN experts were predicting a historic victory. The convention center crowd was abuzz; our woman has won! We beat that bastard!

Over on Fox News, a more somber tone prevailed. Their analysts were parsing the data and essentially saying that it was far too soon to be making any predictions over the outcome. Caution was the watchword for now.

Around ten o'clock, Team Suit began to notice a slight shift as the flyover states began to file results. Ron was picking up votes, and Stacey's lead over him was shrinking. CNN dismissed this shifting trend as an anomaly, a minor bump in the path to America's first female president. But as if they were a set of scales, the two teams' moods began to change: Ron's going up as Stacey's sank down. This seesaw effect was mirrored on the TV screens; the Fox reporters became more buoyant as the CNN crowd became more concerned. It was a beautiful sight to behold: the blowhard CNN heads slowly deflating as a creeping realization entered their biased minds that, holy crap, Suit could actually take this! Ron's Marriott crowd was getting rowdier and rowdier; they too could sense that the tide was turning, while in Atlantic City people were looking at each other in disbelief, frown lines of worry etched on their foreheads.

It was around three o'clock in the morning when the awful truth became apparent: Ron Suit looked to be the next president of the United States of America. CNN showed images of a disbelieving roomful of Lincoln supporters. There was no boisterous celebrating here; just a subdued hush as small groups gathered to console each other, arms wrapped around shoulders. Some simply were sitting at dining tables with vacant looks on their faces, not speaking and just staring into their phone screens as more and more horrible news spewed forth. Compare and contrast with events in Houston. By then, Ron, most of his team, and Megan had arrived—and the party was in full flight. "Hail to the Chief" blared over the PA, along with "We Won't Get Fooled Again," and "Peter Pumpkinhead."

Television reporters made futile attempts to speak over the din as they were jostled by a boisterous horde of Suit supporters. What a night! We did it—we did it!

The governor of Texas walked up to the podium. He had been strongly in favor of Suit, declaring his support early in the campaign when everyone else still thought of Ron as a novelty.

"Okay folks, settle down, settle down. I'd like to introduce y'all to our newest president, Mr. Ron Suit!" The crowd erupted, and a rhythmic chant of "Suit up. Suit up!" began, not ebbing until Ron—with Megan at his side—approached the microphone.

After soaking up the atmosphere for some seconds, Ron said, "Well, well! What a long, strange trip it's been! I want to thank you all and all of my team. They never lost faith, and they never wavered—even when I was so worn out or pissed that I was ready to quit. We ran a strategy based on careful analysis of data melded to a strong social media presence, and I'd like to thank the folks who handled those key parts of the campaign Of course, I want to thank everyone out there in our glorious nation who voted for our vision of what America should be." Ron paused to look around the room. "Funnily enough, I also want to thank my soon-to-be predecessor, President Ludwig. If it hadn't been for his disastrous policies, his incompetent administration, and his toadying to other world leaders, I might never have gotten angry enough to set out on this journey—and you might not have been angry enough to vote for me. Don't worry, America. We've caught the rot in time. We will no longer be a nation in decline. We're going back up to where we belong: the best goddam place on earth!"

Long cheers broke out.

When the cheers died down, Ron said, "I promise you that everything I've said I'd do I am damn well going to do it. The rats in DC are, I'm sure, already scurrying off looking for safe places to hide. Some of them will doubtless disguise themselves as friends eager to help while they wait for a chance to stab me in the back. But fear not! I have a strong bullshit detector that's been honed and fine-tuned by my many years around Hollywood types. And speaking of Hollywood, I particularly want to thank my beautiful bride, Megan. She has worked her ass off throughout this campaign, and she is a big part of why we won. I love you, hon." Ron turned to Megan and gave her a long, wet smooch.

The assembled crowd wolf-whistled and cheered.

"Now, let's all get shitfaced America—we deserve a party!" He stood back from the podium and descended into the crowd, instantly becoming lost in a sea of adoring fans.

The call came at about ten the next morning.

"Mr. Suit, I'm calling to congratulate you on your election victory," Stacey began, the words sticking in her craw. "We both fought hard, but it was your party that prevailed. I'm about to go on air to make my concession speech, but I wanted to speak to you first."

"Well, thanks, Stacey. I appreciate that." Ron looked around for somewhere a little quieter so he could hear the call better, his party still in full swing. "Good luck in your future endeavors, and I'm sure you'll continue with your life in politics."

"Well, Mr. Suit, goodbye." Stacey hung up and prepared to go in front of the cameras.

In Washington, crowds of people were assembling. Mobs of mostly women milled around chanting their support for Stacey and hatred for Ron. A Fox cameraman zoomed in on one such person; she was on her knees staring up at the sky as light raindrops landed on her glasses. A guttural scream rose up from deep in her throat as she cursed to the heavens. "No!" she yelled. An "I'm with Stacy" badge hung forlornly from her jacket. It was the perfect image for a perfect day. Elsewhere on the mall, groups of Suit supporters partied, ignoring the Lincolnites who screamed invectives at them or threw their Lincoln placards into them.

"Who cares? We won. Let's party!" was the mood of their day.

The days following the election saw any number of pundits and experts analyzing this surprising outcome. While this public display of self-flagellation continued on the nation's television screens and newspaper pages, the Group carried out their own postmortem via secure videoconference.

"We had good polling, a strong candidate, and the ear of most media—it should have been ours," remarked one of the members.

Kunis was his usual stoic self, saying, "I think that we did not sufficiently take into account one crucial aspect of this election, and that cost us our victory: We relied on the public to vote correctly." He leaned back into the comfort of his overstuffed sofa. "The voters obviously kept their liking for Suit to themselves. Perhaps they were ashamed to be seen supporting such a candidate. Perhaps they simply didn't like to answer polling questions. Perhaps the questions asked by the pollsters were wrong. For whatever reason, however, they did not telegraph their intentions to us. Future elections must be maintained under our control—we can no longer trust the people's free will."

The tech members of the Group immediately began brainstorming ideas about how future voting could be manipulated or steered to better ensure the desired outcome. "We have four years. It should be possible to develop applications that meet our needs."

Although obviously disappointed by the shock of the loss, all Group members were used to playing the long game. They could afford to wait, but the lesson was learned: you simply cannot trust the populace to do the "right" thing.

An amusing aspect of Ron's win was the number of doomsday advocates who came out of the woodwork to opine about the future under a Suit presidency. Pulitzer winners and Nobelists all chimed in with dire warnings about the collapse of our economy and America becoming a fascist regime run by a bunch of right-wing fanatics. They were all wrong. In the weeks following the election, markets soared as businesses realized they were getting a president who would unshackle them from the ridiculous burden of pointless legislation that Ludwig had imposed upon them.

As for right-wing hate groups roaming the country, Suit supporters were just so pleased that they had won; they basked happily in their success. It was the left-wingers, the Lincoln supporters, who began to riot. Marches were held, and civil disobedience became common, especially among the female Lincolnites. TV and movie stars and pop idols all raged over the injustice of the election, ranting that Suit must be thrown out of office—even though he had not yet taken it. A lot of this behavior was quietly or openly encouraged by Democrat politicians as they realized that life under a Suit administration was going to be hard. The Republicans had taken both houses comfortably, and Suit's agenda was not going to be good for them. The wilier politicians kept quiet, however, awaiting the opportunity to oust him within the first few months. Less-bright Democrats openly called for his impeachment. "The man has no morals and is not fit to lead our country!" they cried, oblivious to the inconvenient fact that he had been legitimately elected and was the people's choice.

Lame-duck President Ludwig made good use of his remaining time in office: "Let's leave President Suit some Easter eggs, a few surprises." That was his directive.

His inner circle quietly went about sabotaging and setting up hidden problems for the next administration. They changed secrecy levels on national intelligence networks that allowed certain foreign governments to enjoy increased access to the nation's secrets. They planted misinformation throughout key departments, issues that could quietly lie unknown until needed for a smear campaign.

Ludwig met with a small group of lifelong government employees who had been promoted to high-level positions throughout the government—IRS, FBI, NSA, CDC, NIH, and CIA—and all of these entities had senior personnel who were brought into the protection of Ludwig's inner circle. These self-serving career bureaucrats pledged their loyalty to the cause: remove or restrict Suit!

Ludwig established a nonprofit, the Project For America, or PFA, who's stated aim was to help keep alive Ludwig's liberal visions by enabling those with like views. Its real mission was to stymie and obstruct the new administration in any way possible. "If things go our way, we'll get rid of him long before his term expires," Ludwig explained to his team. "He'll be impeached, or he will resign. At the very least, a campaign of obstruction and interference will prevent him from implementing any substantive policies, and that should make him a one-term president."

Kunis was listening. "Mr. President, I commend you for this initiative. While your team carries out its plans, my Group is also working on something that will ensure Suit is one term only. Of course, I will keep you updated on our progress; at some point, we will almost certainly need your input and assistance."

"That's good to hear, Milos. Damn, we almost had it, didn't we? Stacey's a good woman. She's not done yet. She has a great future in the party," Ludwig remarked as they closed out the meeting.

As Inauguration Day approached, Ron made his mandatory rounds of the Sunday talk shows.

"So, President-elect Suit, it's been traditional for presidents to release their tax returns. You have failed to do this, and the American people deserve an explanation as to why."

"Well, Chuck," Ron replied, "I ran on a platform of less government, but here you are wanting the government to intrude into my privacy—and it's not only my privacy. Megan and I file a joint return, so you'd be seeing both of our data if I released the records."

"But surely you need to demonstrate to the public that you received no contributions or have financial involvement with certain parties who could influence your policies?"

"Chuck, how about you releasing your tax returns? I think there's a snowball in hell's chance of that happening. Doesn't the viewing public deserve to know that you are not in the thrall of evildoers?" Ron asked with a twinkle in his eye.

"Mr. Suit, I don't imagine that the public has any interest in my financial affairs. You, on the other hand, are about to become the most powerful man on the planet. Don't we deserve to know as much as possible about you and your background?"

"Chuck, I liked it better when you were calling me president-elect, but no matter. Look, the voters didn't know my tax details when they elected me, so they certainly don't need to know them now. Now, I know you won't believe me when I say this, but I have nothing to hide. My objection is entirely based on the fact that I don't believe any government has the right to pry into its citizens' affairs. It's as simple as that. Now, repeat after me: small government good, big government bad." Ron beamed at the presenter and rocked back in his chair.

"Thank you, President-elect Suit. After the break, our panel will examine whether the traditional electoral college system should be updated to reflect a more modern most-votes election."

The lights dimmed as Ron rose from his chair. He was enjoying poking the eye of the left-wing.

The next week, it was the same hostility, just a different channel and host. "Mr. Suit, as I'm sure you've seen, all across our country, women are demonstrating. They claim that your election will set back women's rights by decades. How do you respond?"

"Martha, firstly, your colleagues on other channels call me President-elect Suit, so they win more brownie points. Now, when I look at these countrywide demonstrations, you know what I see? I see a coordinated campaign, not a spontaneous protest. I see footage of perhaps a dozen women in a few towns chanting and carrying placards. I don't see a massive uprising, despite TV stations attempting to portray it that way. I'm pretty sure that the American public see through these deceptions, especially the ones who voted for me."

"So, what do you say to those experts who have expressed the view that you will ban abortion and take away other women's rights?"

"Well, if you'd paid attention to my campaign, you'll know that my position on this topic is clear, Martha. I'm pretty sure I saw you at some of my speeches, were you not listening? I am against abortion, but I am also a pragmatist. My view is that when the baby is viable outside the womb, aborting that child is the same as killing a person. Before then, however, if the fetus can't survive independently, then the parents have a right of choice." Martha began to speak but Ron silenced her and immediately continued talking. "Martha, let's get serious. We have an epidemic of killing in this country. Well over six hundred thousand per year. You might think that's a high murder rate, but it's actually the annual number of abortions carried out here in America. For every single murder in the USA, there are more than thirty abortions. It's become a form of contraception. That cannot be right. There's so many alternates for contraception today—why pick abortion?"

"So, you do intend to restrict abortion rights? What gives you the prerogative to impose your will on America's women?" Martha sounded more shrill than usual.

"Martha, that isn't my view—that's the view of the voting populace. They elected me knowing exactly my position on this issue. Their votes mean they agree with that position, so as I've promised throughout my campaign, whatever I said I'll do, I'm damn well going to do it."

"Thank you, President-elect Suit. We are now moving on to ask our roundtable to debate what we just heard from Mr. Suit."

"Welcome to *State of the Union*. Tonight I'll be talking with Ron Suit, the surprise winner of our recent presidential election." Turning toward Ron, the host said, "Mr. Suit, by anyone's assessment, you were an outsider, a rebel, you might say an anti-candidate. Why did you win?"

"Jake, thanks for inviting me to this hard-hitting, fair and balanced deep dive into the news." Ron had a broad grin on his face. "I won because America is sick and tired of politics as usual. Our voters are far brighter than you people give them credit for, and they've finally seen through the media bias and selective memories of our elected officials. You know, you're right, I am the anti-candidate—and that is exactly why I won."

"Mr. Suit, you've often made the accusation of media bias in mainstream news, including charges against this network. Can you substantiate any of these charges?"

Ron laughed out loud. "What?" he said incredulously. "I thought we only had six minutes for this interview! I'll need a three-hour special if you want to hear everything! Look, Jake, for the past eight years, journalism has been in an induced coma, sleepwalking its way through the Ludwig administration. The only time networks such as yours wake up is to damp down any fires that might have jeopardized his agenda. You run insightful cutting-edge pieces about improving school meals, or helping more drag queens do public outreach in libraries, but you ignore an issue such as Ludwig flying cargo plane-loads of *cash* to the mullahs. You turn a blind eye to his policy of flooding our southern states with illegal immigrants, but my god, you can use all of your resources to seek out and destroy a baker in the Midwest who didn't want to make a cake for a gay couple, who I might add are big-time activists who staged the entire event."

Jake paused slightly but responded with an edge in his voice, "Mr. Suit, I stand 100 percent behind my network's reporting and its veracity."

Ron rolled his eyes. "Look, I know that news sources such as yours have a long tradition of liberalism, and I'm good with that. A country needs opposition to provide balance. The problem is that the Republican Party's long tradition has been to roll over and play dead in the face of all your one-sided hit pieces. Well, not anymore, Jake. This president will push back." He tapped his finger into his chest. "I'll expose all the fake stories you run, and I will provide an honest rebuttal to the BS that gets spewed out masquerading as news."

"Time will tell, Mr. Suit. Time will tell." Jake closed out the segment.

As they cut to ads, Ron stood up and unclipped his mike. *Shit*, he thought. *I'm going to enjoy this!*

⌘

Maury walked in through the creaking glass door, its old green paint flaking into oblivion, and he sat down at his usual table.

"Hi, Maury," Sue said as she approached. "I haven't seen you since Joe, since, you know … anyway, the usual?"

"Thanks, Sue. Yup, it's been a while. Still all seems unreal. One minute we were planning to go clubbing together, the next minute, he's gone."

"Here you go, Maury. I'm so sorry that you lost your friend. Joe was a nice guy." Sue set his drink on the table. "Why did Joe decide to kill himself?"

Maury remarked. "It made absolutely no sense: He was on the verge of breaking a good story, and his other freelance work was keeping him busy. Hell, he had nothing to worry about. Why suicide? The police investigation concluded that Joe was suffering from depression, and that was his motive to end it all. They found a note on his MacBook to that effect. Sure, one of Joe's cousins committed suicide, but so what? Did that make him genetically disposed to off himself too? Highly doubtful. It just doesn't add up, but death seldom does, does it? People die all the time for no reason."

Sue shrugged her shoulders and moved off to deal with other customers

Maury sat in a funk, drinking his coffee and staring blankly out of the café windows. "Thanks Sue," he called as he rose to leave. "I'll try to get back into old habits and come see you more often." He wandered back to his office-apartment. He had apps to develop, and they wouldn't write the code themselves.

HAIL TO THE CHIEF

January in DC is usually cold, and it's often wet. This day was no exception. Regardless of the weather, however, millions thronged the mall and surrounding streets and parks. They had twofold purposes; one group was there for the "Million Woman March," an organized protest against the nasty misogynistic new president, and the others were there to celebrate and witness a new era in politics: the inauguration of a president who would break status quo, a man who would truly represent the people. Added to these two main blocks was a motley assortment of agitators: the Occupy crowd, Black Lives Matter, anarchists, religious sects, and every fringe group imaginable had organized something to commemorate, for better or worse, the inauguration ceremony.

Ron and Megan had used their contacts throughout the entertainment industry to ensure that the whole day would have a party atmosphere, one of celebration regardless of the manufactured outrage being perpetuated throughout the media. Marching bands from each state of the union were invited; a massive fireworks display was ready; and, following the serious business of actually swearing in President Suit, a huge outdoor concert was to be held on the mall featuring a mix of pop, rock, country and western, and classical performers. Of course, the pop and rock representation was a little sparse; most of these idols had enthusiastically jumped on the Suit-hating bandwagon. No matter, the day promised to be a big one.

The two sat in the back of their limo as it slowly made its way to the Capitol.

"Who'da thunk it, Megan?" Ron asked as he stared out of the window and saw the street heavily lined on both sides by throngs of people. Some were cheering and waving American Flags, and some waving placards that declared "Suit is not my president."

Megan stared out wide-eyed. "It's like a giant red carpet event in LA, except that there, we wouldn't be looking at a bunch of haters." She pointed out to a block of obviously anti-Suit people, all yelling and booing as the limo slowly slid past.

"I think I'll stretch my legs," Ron declared as he opened the vehicle's door and got out onto the damp tarmac.

"What the fuck, Ron!" exclaimed Megan. She reluctantly joined him outside while his large security posse was thinking exactly the same as Megan: WTF!

Ron immediately walked across to the hater group. "Hi, folks. Welcome to America, where you can express your views without fear."

The protestors began a chant of "Not my president. Not my president!"

Ron wrapped his arm around Megan's waist in front of them and began taking selfies, using the haters as a backdrop.

His security detail was scrambling to ensure that this scene didn't end in violence or thrown placards.

"C'mon, darlin'. The stage is not too far. Let's walk the rest of the way."

Arm in arm, the couple strolled toward the Capitol, frequently stopping to chat with supporters or take selfies with them. They didn't ignore the protestors either, walking up to them with broad smiles on their faces.

"Not my president, not my president" was the common chant.

"Oh, but I am, folks—at least for the next four years!" Ron replied with a grin.

Ron and Megan finally took their seats to await commencement of the swearing-in ceremony. On their left sat Joyce Flowers and her husband. Joyce had been Ron's pick for vice president. She was an experienced senator, and Ron considered her as one of the rarest of the rare: a politician with integrity who'd led an unblemished career. He had picked Joyce for one reason and one only: he needed a guide through the morass of sleaze that is Washington, and who better than her, someone who had kept her head above the mire all these years? The media had made much of his pick, taking the approach that he was simply toadying to women in the hope of getting their vote. Ron and Joyce knew better however; she was to be his guide through the jungle.

Shortly after being seated, the Joint Services band struck up, and everyone rose to welcome the outgoing president.

Peter Ludwig, and his wife, Fatima, approached and sat to the right of the Suits.

"Hello, Mr. President," Ron said airily as he shook his hand.

"Mr. President," replied Ludwig solemnly.

They sat back down, and an uneasy silence ensued. Both parties were aware of the fact that the nation's media would be filming this awkward confrontation.

Ron looked out at the masses in front of him, waving to the crowds and beaming. "I see you got a good turnout, Peter," he said.

"I'm not sure what you mean, Mr. Suit," replied Ludwig.

"Sure you do, Peter, all the protestors. I know you're behind all this nonsense, you and your PFA." Ron's smile was still on his face, but there was a steeling of his eyes as he looked directly into Ludwig's face.

"Hmm." Ludwig shrugged and broke eye contact.

"I've enjoyed our transition discussions, Peter," continued Ron, "and I'm looking forward to the final batch of rock-solid handover advice I'm sure you'll be giving me in the coming days." Ron was back to his sarcastic self. As president-elect, he'd already held several handover meetings with Ludwig and other members of the outgoing administration. They had not been impressive, and Ron was frequently of the opinion that he and his new team were being set up and deliberately misinformed. *No matter—it is what it is,* he thought.

"President-elect Suit, as I've already advised you, there are a number of ongoing issues that will require your immediate attention. I'd be happy to continue to offer guidance; some of the problems are quite urgent." Ludwig was almost gloating.

While this tense exchange was going on, the two First Ladies were chatting quite happily. Fatima seemed fascinated by Megan's Hollywood friends, and she asked endless questions about her favorite idols.

Through it all, Megan tried to find out how the White House domestic side was operated. "I guess I'm going to have to learn how to be a housewife," she said ruefully.

The Chief Justice arrived, putting an end to all the chitchat.

Just a few minutes later, Ronald George Thomas Suit was sworn in as the most powerful man on earth. Hail to the chief! His speech was solemn, invoking political idols such as Reagan and Churchill. For once, it was a scripted and well-rehearsed oration, no puns, no ad libs. Ron had recognized the weight of the occasion and acted accordingly. It was received as might be expected: cheers from his supporters and boos from his detractors. The festivities commenced.

The next morning, after their first night in the White House, Ron grabbed the stack of newspapers that had been laid out for him next to breakfast. "Let's see what today's lies are," he said to Megan as he unfolded the *NYT.* "Suit Aides Grossly Overestimate Crowd Size at Inauguration" screamed the headline. "More Against than For" was the *Wapo's* lead. The *NY Post* was obviously more upbeat. "What a Party!" its banner said, describing the day's festivities. The left criticized the flat tone of his speech, and the right praised its solemnity. The left made fun of the hokey marching bands, the fireworks, and the country music. The right loved the event's focus on American ideals.

"Ron, what have we gotten ourselves into?" asked Megan.

"Well, in the words of Bette Davis, fasten your seatbelts, ladies, it's going to be a bumpy ride!" Ron scanned through the overwhelmingly negative press coverage. "Don't worry, hon. We've got this. I'm Texas tough—and I'm going to kick their asses!

THE FIRST HUNDRED DAYS

Ron's new administration was assembled from all parts of his sphere of influence. Guided to an extent by a combination of his family back in Texas and the vice president's trusted circle of friends, it comprised a diverse array of specialists, with somewhat of an emphasis on Texas people and a lack of career politicians. His fifteen cabinet positions were thus well equipped to handle their roles, all having experience in their relevant fields, but hopefully without a taint of political cronyism. Ron followed a mantra he'd obeyed throughout his career: hire the smartest people you can and listen to them. As was expected, the mainstream media excoriated Ron's picks, citing a woeful lack of competence and predicting gloom and doom for the nation.

It was inevitable that throughout the new administration, many of Ludwig's clandestine PFA members remained in their positions. DC has more than three hundred thousand government positions, all paid for by us, and to completely change old for new is an impossibility. This is a problem for any new administration; it's hard to make sweeping changes when there is so much inertia, so many career bureaucrats, thousands upon thousands of individuals who have spent their lives doing what they wished, regardless of what party is in power. Ron's promise to clean things up was to be no easy task.

A taste of what was to come arrived early: "They've pulled all the frigging Rs and Ss from the keyboards!" declared one of the incomers as they settled into their offices. It was to be downhill from there.

Ron stared out across the Rose Garden. The enormity of his position was beginning to dawn on him. It had started out as an almost academic exercise, a vanity project of sorts, a personal response to what he'd perceived as the worst president in his lifetime. "Sure, I'll run myself. I can't win, but at least I will have done something" had been his initial position. Yet here he was, reflecting on the two years of effort that had brought him to the Oval Office. *Who knew? We did it. But maybe Megan is right. What have we brought on ourselves?* Ron was beginning to feel weighed down by this new position, and the only thing buoying him up was the knowledge that enough citizens out there had supported him. They'd placed their faith and trust in his ability to change things. He couldn't let them down. *Sure, it will be a tough road ahead, but fuck it, they believe in me. It's time I believed in me too.*

Ron laid out his strategy at the first formal cabinet meeting. "America likes a split Congress—we all know that—and I think it's likely that we have two years before the midterms, with its possibility that we'll lose one of the houses. So, the question is, what can we achieve in those two years? I want to target three signature achievements. Ideas?" He looked around the room for input. Ron knew exactly what he wanted to get done, but he also wanted input from the team, to see if there were any new ideas that might be better than his own.

VP Flowers said, "Well, the key elements of your campaign were less government and more freedom, so everything we do should fall into one or both of those categories."

Murmurs of agreement could be heard from everyone in the room.

"A no-brainer in the 'less government' basket is to give everyone a good tax break," said Ron. "That means we need to reduce government spending to offset the reduced revenue from taxes."

The treasury secretary said, "Mr. President, cutting taxes will stimulate the economy and result in more revenues even at lower tax rates. That's classic Reaganomics."

"Agreed," said Ron. "Nevertheless, we have to slash government spending. Every frigging year, it goes up, and the people don't get anything more for it—just more debt."

One of the many crazy aspects of Washington's fiscal policy is that even a frozen budget is actually an increase. In classic politician doublespeak, a party can say, "We are not increasing our budget," while hiding the fact that an annual hike is baked in every year. Thus, even a frozen budget still means more this year than last.

"Now, I know that this is unheard of, but how about each department carrying out a zero-baseline budget exercise? I hate the way it's done now, where everybody just piles more money on top of last year's number. We need all key departments to budget from scratch, to justify every cent, and to question every single aspect of their department's needs. I know we'll catch shit from the Dems about a big tax cut, so our response has to be ready. We need to be able to say we're giving the people back X billion dollars and this is covered by reducing the government's budget by Y billion."

Joyce said, "Getting a slew of bureaucrats to reduce their own fiefdoms will be tough, and of course, it's Congress that ultimately sets the budget."

"Yes, but we issue the presidential budget outline to get the ball rolling. Imagine their faces when they see how big our proposed cuts are!" Ron was desperate to show the swamp he meant business. Boldly slashing Washington's money stream was a statement of that intent.

By the end of their first session, there were three key issues:

- massive tax cuts offset by massive government spending reductions
- no new regulations without first eliminating a minimum of five existing regulations from the books
- renegotiation of all existing trade agreements to make them more in favor of the USA

A bold agenda indeed!

The PFA team and the Group were not happy. Both had been told by their moles of Suit's agenda, and neither was pleased with his plans. For Ludwig's PFA, it was apparent that many of the signature social programs enacted under his administration were going to be slashed or eliminated. His raft of restrictive regulations introduced over the past eight years in the name of saving the planet were also at risk. Ludwig's entire legacy could be in jeopardy.

For Kunis and the Group, renegotiation of America's existing trade deals was bad. The basic philosophy of the Group was one of globalism: For these people, America was not the be-all and end-all of life. They had their fingers in pies around the world, and all the current weak trade deals allowed them to go about their business of lining their own pockets and controlling global commerce without fear. If an agenda of "America First" was successfully implemented, their wealth and influence would be stunted. Both teams agreed that Suit needed stopping.

"Put Suit in a Prison Suit" became the clarion call of the Democratic Party hacks and their compliant media associates. This early into his presidency, Ron had done little to cause legitimate concern among his opponents, but that didn't stop them. They had enough hidden surprises to make life difficult for him.

CNN broke it first: "Unnamed sources in the White House have told CNN that the surprise win by Ronald Suit was, in part, due to election interference by a foreign power." Of course, the *New York Times, Washington Post,* and all the other usual left-wing media jumped on the bandwagon. Soon, the airwaves and news pages were awash with unnamed sources citing this or that, all of it designed to undermine the administration.

In this divisive and corrosive atmosphere, the daily White House press briefing became a free-for-all. Journalists grandstanded, vying for airtime while all the while citing "unnamed sources" to ask gotcha questions. It was a tough environment for the press secretary; what had traditionally been a low-key daily event devolved into a rowdy sparring match.

Ron said, "They're controlling the narrative too easily. We have to bypass those lying SOBs and talk directly to the people. I know exactly how to do it too," he confided to Joyce after one particularly nasty exchange between his press secretary and a CNN journalist who had claimed to have seen a leaked report that proved Suit was in cahoots with the Russians.

A few days later, during the daily briefing, President Suit entered the room. "Good afternoon, everyone. I'm not here to answer questions, but to make an announcement."

The room fell silent.

"As of this briefing, I'm suspending these daily press sessions. It's quite clear to me that you people," he pointed at the throng of journalists crammed into the small room, "mostly have no interest in hearing what is actually going on in our administration. It's also remarkably clear that the majority of you have zero interest in reporting actual facts to the American people. You're having too much fun inventing stories and making up fictitious inside sources. So, I'm going to have some fun too. Starting tomorrow, I will commence broadcasting a nightly briefing live from the Oval Office. Now, all you folks know my background as a talk show host, so I'll be playing to my strengths. The nightly briefing will be sort of like a late-night show, featuring guests who viewers will actually be able to see instead of all your invisible sources. I may even invite some of y'all from time to time. That's it, carry on. I look forward to reading about my announcement in your fact-driven and unbiased news coverage."

As Ron turned to leave, the room erupted. Every reporter present began shouting "Mr. President!" to gain his attention. Some yelled, "Do you think it's fitting for a president to be a chat show host?"

As he went through the exit, Ron turned around briefly and gave the Nixon victory salute to irritate the mob and give them a good photo op. He was enjoying this.

As might be expected, the news was met with despair by most members of the Republican Party and with derision by the Democrats. Many GOP representatives saw this move as a cheapening of the office, and the opponents said it only confirmed that Suit was incompetent: a man incapable of running the nation who was reverting to his old job. Ron didn't care either way; he needed to talk directly to his people, and he felt that this was a good solution, or at least an experiment worth trying.

"Good evening, America. Welcome to the first broadcast of *Daily Briefing*, coming to you live from your Oval Office. You know, when I look back at the golden days of television, I think of someone like Johnny Carson, who hosted a show that would have you falling out of your chair with laughter—yet never once would he show any political bias or prejudice. I also think of Walter Cronkite who could tell you the news as it was, without bias or prejudice. But look around at our media today, and you'll see information that's always squeezed through a filter before you get to see it. That filter might be hard left, or hard right, or somewhere in between, but you're never getting the truth—only a slanted version of it. The truth is skewed to suit the agenda of the person presenting the news or as dictated by the heads of the network in question. We all know where to go for left-wing slant and right-wing views, and frankly I'm tired of this division in our media. It's time that you hear what is actually happening and not what certain people want you to believe is happening. The *Daily Briefing* is my vehicle for talking directly to you. You know me; I'll tell it like it is. I won't lie—that's why you elected me. You'll be able to form your own opinions rather than having them fed to you. No doubt my detractors will say I'll just be spreading government propaganda. They'll claim that I'm lying or hiding facts, but at least now can hear it from the horse's mouth and make your own judgments."

Ron went on to explain how viewers could tweet or text questions during the briefing. He noted that each night he'd feature a member of his administration being interviewed or questioned and how certain sectors of the public would be featured whenever warranted, for example, acts of good after a disaster. It was to be classic Ron Suit talk show format and fodder, a mix of serious and lighthearted. Opening night took advantage of its anticipated high viewership by being the platform for Ron and his treasury secretary to outline their plans for tax cuts and budget reductions. This first airing indeed reached a record number of viewers, and figures remained high in subsequent weeks and months. Ron was changing the narrative, and the media was pissed.

❧

"So, Maury, did you watch our president's new talk show last night?" Sue had brought him his usual cappuccino, and business was slow, so she had time to chat.

"Yeah, I saw some of it. Suit is good. I guess that's why he lasted so long on TV. But the real question is, should our president be running a TV show? Seems like a pretty lame concept to me." Maury sipped on his coffee.

Sue was a purple-haired girl with many, many tattoos and piercings, but her looks belied her politics. She was as conservative as they come, and she was studying political science at NYU.

"I don't know, Maury, it makes a lot of sense to me. This is the only way he can get his agenda out. Those lying bastards at CNN spin every single thing he says against him; this way, he gets to talk directly to us."

"We've devolved into two tribes, Sue," Maury relied. "and you know what Frankie Goes to Hollywood had to say about that."

They both chuckled at the eighties reference.

"I wonder what Joe would have made of all this?" Sue asked ruefully.

"Speaking of Joe, I'm no investigative reporter, but something doesn't sit well with the whole thing about his death. I've been digging around in my spare time, and you know what? Shit doesn't add up."

Sue sat down at the table, eager to hear what Maury had uncovered.

"For example, we're in New York City, but the cop who ran the investigation is from the New Jersey PD. Why would that be? Anyway, I've got too much on my plate right now to spend more time digging, but once this coding crunch eases up, I'll do some more nosing around."

"Maury Helzburg, ace detective." Sue smiled as she arose to greet two new customers.

"See ya next time, Sue," called Maury as he left the café to get back to his computer.

THE SPECIAL PROSECUTOR

The market continued its steady rise as unemployment continued its steady fall. Even just a few months into his term, it was obvious that business liked the Suit presidency. Meanwhile, the *Daily Briefing* continued to be the most-watched show in its segment. This was disastrous, that is, if you got your information from the mainstream outlets. Per their frenetic reporting, Suit was steamrolling the Constitution, gutting departments like the EPA, and making America a laughingstock. The facts belied the rhetoric however; he was slashing regulations to unleash businesses and allow them to breathe. While the talking heads preached gloom and doom, the nation began to thrive—and its populace could sense this.

The PFA crew were particularly unhappy. Okay, the Group was not too pleased either, but since Suit had not yet kicked off his "America First" agenda, globalists like Kunis had no real reason to complain yet—other than at the mere presence of such an abominable figure sitting in the White House.

Ludwig convened a strategy session. "We need to stop this man in his tracks," he stated to the assembled team. "Suit is undermining our policies, and he's loosening government control of so many areas. There must be a silver bullet to take him down."

The House minority whip said, "Well, Peter, he is still not fully supported by his own party. There's a lot of Republicans who feel like us—that the man is demeaning the office of the presidency—and they're concerned that too harsh of a light is being shone on Washington's business. The GOP may have a majority in both houses, but I think we could get a chunk of them to cross the aisle over the right scandal."

"Time to increase the pressure," said Ludwig. "I think that the best squeeze point is foreign interference in last year's election. We've already got a good narrative established about that. There's enough smoke that it would be pretty easy to make it look like a full-blown dumpster fire." He proposed that extra effort be made to further spread the claim that a Soviet group had actively assisted Suit during the election campaign and perhaps had even interfered with actual voting processes. A report prepared by a Soviet specialist was available that listed many interactions Suit had had with Russian operatives, and now would be the time to release it rather than just leaking parts to favored news outlets.

"Look, Peter, there are enough RINOs on the hill that I believe a vote to appoint a special investigator might just pass. And of course, we've also got our guys in DOJ and FBI to help—not forgetting a *friendly* attorney general."

It was decided: Suit had been elected under nefarious circumstances using the aid of a foreign power, and he must be impeached and removed. Sure, that would mean Joyce Flowers assuming the presidency, but, one step at a time. The news cycle became incessant. Suit was helped by the Russians, or the Ukrainians, or some other shady soviet quasi-governments groups. Former and current figures in the FBI, CIA, and DOJ rose up from the swamp and declared their suspicions, in print and on the screen, becoming overnight experts in all things Soviet. The left's talking heads all agreed that there was enough suspicion to necessitate an inquiry.

Ron's response to all this was predictable: "Look, folks, y'all know this is a load of BS, smoke and mirrors to distract and demean the good work we're doing."

Pressure mounted, however, culminating in the attorney general himself going on record to note his concerns about possible election interference. Simultaneous with this, the House passed a resolution demanding that an investigation be launched. If President Suit had nothing to hide, surely he would welcome an independent review? The AG, ex-Senator George Poll, was a long-standing and well-respected member of the Washington political class. His name had come up early in the administration's term, and despite Ron's misgiving over using a career politician in such a position, he agreed to the appointment. After all, he had bigger issues to address.

AG Poll set up a working group to begin the investigation. Thus began a relentless two-year investigation that delved into every hint of impropriety before, during, and after the election. The focus was 100 percent on certain members of the Suit team and of course, Suit himself. The entire investigation took on the appearance of a circus show. Star performers would be trotted in front of cameras to cite their unnamed sources who'd told them of trips to Kiev, shenanigans in hotel rooms, and malarkey in the way Suit's team worked. It was a crass display of partisanship and further cemented the divisive two-tribes atmosphere of the country.

Throughout it all, the president maintained a consistent position: "I have no desire to intervene in this ridiculous investigation," he would respond to journalists. "My AG is doing a good job, I'm doing a good job, and I'd rather focus on bringing America and its people back to the top of the world than waste any life minutes worrying about this investigation nonsense." Inside, Ron seethed in the knowledge that this entire shitshow was being orchestrated by Ludwig and his henchmen. What could he do, though? Any public display of such suspicions would be immediately seized upon by the mainstream media as an admission of guilt or at the very least a cheap shot at a former president. He just had to grin and bear it and let the circus play out while he fixed the country.

A key weapon in Ludwig's arsenal during the investigation became Stacey Lincoln. After all, didn't she have a legitimate beef, losing to Suit in a rigged election? Stacey became a regular on all the usual shows, wrote endless op-eds and hit pieces in the newspapers, and generally became a thorn in Ron's side. Following her election loss, Stacey had heeded Milos's advice and taken a sabbatical. During this "time in the wilderness," she focused on her foundation's work and spent time with her children. Meanwhile, the Kunis team was rehabilitating her image after the humiliating defeat. It had been Kunis who'd persuaded her to step back into the limelight. "You must join Peter's team in this impeachment effort," he advised. "We have some interesting thoughts for the next election, and you are an important part of them.

"Oh no, Milos," Stacey replied. "I am not running again. The entire primary process is too grueling. I don't want to ever again have to talk nicely to some hick prick in Bumfuck, Iowa. Been there, done that."

"My dear, there are paths that offer many solutions to your way forward. At the very least, you can raise your profile and improve your public persona by joining in the attack on Suit. Imagine, you'll be able to declare yourself the moral victor, robbed of a historic victory by the illegal election tampering of your opponent."

The temptation proved overpowering, and Stacey signed on. Ludwig's team had other more subtle and insidious assets too.

"AG Poll, nice that you could make it," Ludwig said as he sat in his private jet on the apron of Hart Field.

"Peter, good to see you. I'd much prefer it if we communicate only by secure phone; a face-to-face seems risky, especially for me."

"Don't worry, George," Peter replied as he poured them both a whiskey. "You saw for yourself that we're tucked away here in the corner of the world's busiest airport, no one will see us. I'm on my way to a conference, and you're returning from depositions—nothing unusual here. Even if we were spotted, we're old friends just catching up after not seeing each other for a while."

"Okay, Peter, cut the crap and get down to business. Why did you need to see me?" Poll was clearly not put at ease by Ludwig's reassurances.

"You've been doing a fantastic job so far with the inquiry, and things are moving along nicely. The popular press and network outlets are pushing a common narrative that's being received well by the public—"

"And? If things are going so swimmingly, Peter, why am I sitting here?"

"It's time to ramp up the pressure, George." Ludwig leaned forward in his seat, as if he was getting ready to pounce on Poll. The two could not have been more different. Ludwig was a tall, blond-haired, and trim man, almost of classic Aryan looks. Poll, on the other hand, looked like an insurance salesman, a wrinkly oldie with silver hair, an ashy complexion, and watery, beady eyes.

"We will shortly be releasing some interesting information to the media. It will be shocking, and will provide proof positive that Suit's campaign was in bed with the Russians. There'll obviously be a robust defense of these allegations from the administration. So, I need you to ensure that the information gets credence. I need you to bring this to a close and get an impeachment rolling." He handed Poll a manilla envelope containing the dirt.

"Mr. President, you know as well as I do that it's not up to me to institute impeachment hearings." Poll leaned forward in his seat now, so they sat almost nose to nose. "I am risking my good reputation enough already by being complicit in this venture. Okay, it's a worthwhile risk if it gets that terrible man out of the White House, but I feel that I'm already exposing myself unduly with this investigation. You need to place all your efforts in getting the houses onside."

Peter pulled back and said, "They will be onside, George, once they see this new information, but it's your job to make sure it's perceived as credible. I know you can do it. I mean, you pulled off the impossible with keeping the Senate in line during some of my crises. You can do this, George."

Poll leaned back in his seat a little. "Well, Peter, I'll try. You know me—I always do what I believe is best for the country. But, as always, there'll be consequences. I'm getting on in years and have a large extended family to take care of. These responsibilities take time and a good amount of money."

"Understood, George. Now, don't you have a flight to catch?"

⁂

Sue and Maury were outside today, Manhattan's weather having taken a turn for the better.

Business was slow, and Sue could afford time to hang with Maury. "What's the latest, Holmes?" Sue asked, tongue in cheek.

"Remember the detective who ran Joe's inquiry? He was from Jersey, and he had no business looking into Joe's death?"

"Of course," Sue replied. "A jurisdictional issue. You should contact him and ask what the hell he was doing in NYC."

"Well, that won't happen, Sue. Not too long after they closed out Joe's case, our detective was killed in an automobile accident."

"Jeez, Maury, seems like anything to do with investigating the Lincolns ends up in death. You should watch your back." Sue giggled as she stood up to serve a new customer. "And I'm only half joking!" she called as she walked back into the café.

AN INDEPENDENT COUNSEL

"Attorney General Poll, you have been asked here today to brief the house on the state of your investigation about alleged foreign interference on our election process."

"Thank you, Mr. Speaker. I should like to begin by addressing recent new evidence made available to the Department of Justice. I'm aware that some members of the House already know of this information; unfortunately, there have been several internal leaks that resulted in certain members of the press being given access to parts of the information." AG Poll sat before the House committee. Behind him was a dazzling array of journalists, photographers, and others. "I have received a report from a Russian whistleblower that provides conclusive proof of their meddling in our last presidential election. This was accomplished by a massive social media campaign, coupled with attempts to infiltrate our voting processes. Furthermore, there are indications that such interference was specifically designed to favor Mr. Suit's campaign—and to disrupt Mrs. Lincoln's campaign. The information further provides some evidence that members of President Suit's election team were actively cooperating with the Russians throughout their efforts."

The committee chairman said, "Does this report provide definitive evidence that the Suit team was actively engaged in these efforts?"

"We continue to look into that possibility," Poll replied. "To this end, I believe that there is sufficient cause for concern that I have appointed a dedicated Independent Counsel who will be 100 percent devoted to this investigation. I have instructed him to complete his work with all haste and to prepare a report for presentation before this chamber. It goes without saying that all of my department's resources will be made available to assist in his work. I am appointing Daniel Links as the IC, effective immediately."

This was the true beginning of the assault on the Suit presidency. Dan Links was a career bureaucrat who had spent his life in the shadowy branches of government: FBI, CIA, and NSA. He was well regarded among those who knew him superficially and was, at least on the surface, a nonpartisan who would go wherever the evidence led him. Both Ludwig and Kunis were pleased with this appointment. They both knew the real Daniel Links: a man who had quietly lined his pockets throughout his career, trading information for cash or power. After retiring several years ago, Links had immediately set up a consultancy business where, for a massive fee, he could get his clients access to the right people who would fix whatever problems they were having. Links carefully maintained and massaged his wide internal network of contacts; knowledge is power, and for Links, knowledge was wealth too.

In the White House, Ron was furious. "What in hell is going on, George?" he asked after summoning Poll to the Oval Office. "The first I heard of Daniel Links is when I saw his name on TV. You're not keeping me in the loop, George."

"Mr. President, as you know, I must maintain my independence. There have been rumors circulating that I am in your pocket and that I am influencing the investigation in your favor. For both our sakes, I simply can't allow any hint of impropriety—so an independent counsel was the best solution. Dan is a good man. You have nothing to worry about."

"Shit, all the great things going on in our country these days, and I'm still tainted by bullshit accusations? Imagine how we'd perform if we didn't have all this animosity against us." Ron was holding up under the nonstop left-wing onslaught of rumors and lies, but he allowed himself to be frustrated from time to time. "Well, George, it is what it is, I suppose. But please try to keep me in the loop a little more."

I wasn't too long after the appointment of the IC that Vice President Flowers approached Ron with disturbing news. "Mr. President, I've been advised that AG Poll met with Peter Ludwig some weeks ago at a secret location. I don't know what they talked about, but isn't it odd that they'd meet at all?" Joyce was clearly unhappy with this new information.

They discussed options; they could simply ask Poll what he was doing meeting Ludwig, they could dismiss him, or they could maintain a discreet, watchful eye on him. Ron chose the latter.

"You know, Joyce, this latest snippet of news about Poll goes onto my growing list of reasons why I'm beginning to mistrust the man. That—and his sudden appointment of Daniel Links as independent counsel."

"I'm so sorry, Mr. President," Joyce replied. "I know that you took my recommendation for George to be AG. As for Links, his public persona is that of a straight shooter, but in my time on the Hill, I've seen enough of him to suspect that he's in it for himself. Links would not have been my first choice for an independent counsel by a long stretch."

"Great," said Ron, "double the reason to worry! My problem is that I have to stand back from this investigation. The media rides my ass enough as it is, and they'd have a field day if they saw me poking my nose into Links's investigation. They're already bitching about me influencing Poll's work."

The Washington swamp continued as ever, sucking down dreams and principles into its sticky blackness, aided and abetted by most of the media. CNN and the *Times* broke the story in unison: "Sources within the Links team have disclosed that there is credible proof of active collusion between Russian assets and the Suit campaign team in the months leading up to the election."

Other outlets quickly joined the bandwagon, and soon they were all singing from the same hymn sheet, declaring that what had always been suspected was now proven beyond doubt: Suit had stolen the election with the help of Russia. Stacey played her "victim" role perfectly. She appeared everywhere, declaring that she knew she had won the election—and that it beggared belief to think otherwise.

"Lester, I'm looking forward to the release of IC Links's report to Congress, where I believe that I will be totally exonerated. The American people will finally know the truth that there should have been a woman in the White House and not a talk show host!"

One word hung now on the lips of every talking head in the nation: impeachment!

Ron's loyal base was, of course, outraged by the rumor mill running at full speed; they were also motivated and animated. Across the country, rallies began to be held in support of President Suit. Ron started attending many of them, supplementing his *Daily Briefing* appearances with long, ad-libbed speeches in sold-out stadiums around the nation. This infuriated the left even more. How dare these unwashed morons be on the side of a colluding buffoon? The two tribes each dug in further, and their hatred of each other intensified.

The publication of the Links Report became the most-anticipated event of the year. In the months leading up to its release, Poll, Ludwig, and Kunis all quietly collaborated to ensure that the pot was kept boiling. With midterms approaching, all agreed that the report should be issued in October to ensure maximum impact ahead of voting.

A few of Suit's campaign team members were arrested on ridiculous process crimes such as perjury or irregular use of campaign funds. Even though such arrests had nothing really to do with the supposed collusion, they helped keep the heat on and provide fodder for the insatiable media machine. Another fan-fared event was the issuance of arrest warrants for a group of Russian nationals who had run media ad campaigns in support of Suit or against Lincoln. A couple of alt-right sites analyzed the offending ads to find that in fact the amount of money spent on these attack campaigns was actually pitifully small, amounting to a fraction of 1 percent in comparison to that spent by the Lincoln and Suit election teams, plus their associated PACS. How could such a tiny effort have made any difference to the way people vote? Furthermore, dispassionate analysis of the content of the "Russian influencers" showed that it favored neither candidate, but attacked both Suit and Lincoln in equal measure, mostly to foment unrest between parties. However, since none of these facts fit the overall mainstream narrative that Suit had colluded with Russia, the stories sank without trace.

In the Oval Office, Ron and VP Flowers were in an intense discussion about the attorney general. Since that initial talk when he'd heard of the Poll-Ludwig meeting, Ron had put together a small team of trusted nonpoliticians and had charged them with finding out what they could about both Poll and Links. "So, it's like this, Joyce. I believe that our Mr. Poll is in cahoots with the PFA, although that would be impossible to prove. As you first told me, we know that he's talked with Ludwig. We also know that he and Links go back a long way. They've had their fingers in many pies over the years, and money has been made by both of them on schemes that are brilliantly complex and difficult to figure out. None of this would stand up in court, of course. However, I'm convinced it's all true; my problem now is, what do I do about it? We're only weeks away from the report's publication, and timing is critical."

"Mr. President, as I understand it, it's not just Poll and Links who are working together; quite a few of the people who report to them seem to be mixed up with the PFA, aren't they?"

"Yes, Joyce, the rot goes pretty deep." Washington was living down to all of Ron's expectations. "I knew this place was a morass of ugliness, Joyce. Perhaps it's time to get the broom out and clean up our intelligence agencies?" Both agreed that the timing could be bad for such an initiative, but they eventually nailed down a strategy.

"So, what are our prospects, team?" Peter Ludwig asked at a planning meeting a few weeks before the midterm elections.

The minority whip said, "Well, as you know, Mr. President, we've got all House seats up for grabs—plus a third of the senate and a group of governorships. To get both Houses, we need to win twenty-six House seats and six in the Senate. The media buzz around the Links report is a tremendous help. That, plus the fact that Suit has lowered his profile recently in response to all the negative press he's getting. I think we're in good shape."

Peter said, "So, what is the optimum timing for release of the report? We initially thought that dropping it before Election Day would be the nail we need in Suit's coffin, but it may distract from our people's campaigns. Also, we need to start thinking beyond the midterms. Even if we succeed with impeachment, Suit will still be president. Maybe we should slow-walk the whole deal a little, continue with the drip, drip, drip of leaks and rumors, and then go full-blast nearer to the presidential race?"

Agreement was reached to delay the report but increase the media blitz.

Up in the White House, Ron was feeling truly embattled. While he maintained his upbeat façade on his nightly show and at all the arena events, there was a weariness inside. Could he continue to pull this off? How long before one of the pieces of shit being constantly thrown at him stuck? It had been relentless; the left-wing had kept up a nonstop assault on every aspect of his administration, public, and private life. This latest investigation had cost some of his friends and supporters their freedom. They'd been held on trumped-up charges relating to the whole Russian collusion conspiracy. He felt terrible about it, but he was helpless to react. "Megan, right now, I feel like I'm in a whirlpool, slowly spinning round deeper and deeper into a black hole."

They were in their apartment, trying to catch up with each other. Megan had adapted shakily to life as First Lady, and she deliberately kept a low profile. It was so unnerving to go from being a celebrity, loved by all, to the wife of Ron Suit, a man who inspired division and hatred. Her friends had mostly deserted her; in the entertainment industry, it did not pay to be a conservative. Those few who supported Suit's efforts did so at their peril, and a low profile was the norm for these people too.

"Damn it, Ron," Megan said. "You gave up so much to become president. I gave up so much. Now isn't the time for introspection and backing down. You've got to seize the initiative and get back on message. Get out there and kick some butt!"

Ron knew she was right, of course, but did he have the stamina?

THE SUIT STRIKES BACK

In a perverse way, the midterm results gave Ron the boost he needed.

"Well, folks," he announced on the *Daily Briefing*, "it looks like we lost the House to our Democratic colleagues, who've managed to carve out a slim majority. I'm so sorry that I didn't keep the trust of some of our electorate. On the plus side, we kept the Senate, and we have turned a few more states red. These results will in no way affect my sworn agenda to get government out of our lives and to kick the bums out of this swamp that we call our nation's capital."

Ron continued to other issues relating to the midterms, including claims of vote rigging on both sides of the aisle. For the featured hero of the day, he interviewed a police officer who had run into a nightclub, which was the scene of a mass shooting, and taken down the shooter, ignoring all danger to his own life. As Ron was wrapping up, he stood from his desk and approached the camera until his face filled the frame. "Oh, and one last thing before I say good night. A few of you might know that there's been an ongoing and interminable investigation into Russian interference in the elections. 'A few of you'—that's what's called irony, folks, as I think that probably 90 percent of the networks and cable news outlets have talked about nothing else for months now. Perhaps this had an impact on the midterms—or am I being cynical? Anyway, I just want to announce to everyone that earlier today I asked my attorney general, Mr. George Poll, to resign. I'll be appointing a new AG shortly. Meanwhile Mr. Poll's deputy will step in. An explanation of this move will be forthcoming. Good night America—and God bless!"

Ron stepped out of camera frame as the program ended. He felt strangely invigorated, a bit like his old self, ready for battle again. *I'm gonna nail you bastards, all of y'all,* he thought as he made his way to the presidential apartments.

As expected, the news outlets were ablaze with righteous indignation. "Suit's Last-Ditch Attempt to Stymie the Investigation" was a typical headline, or "Suit Perverts Justice Once Again." The theme of the narrative was that Suit had got rid of Poll because he knew his goose was cooked and that Poll's work was circling in on his misdeeds. This was clearly the last desperate act of a man who knew he was a long way down the inevitable road to impeachment.

The left's wrath was only tempered by increasing buzz that the Links Report's release was imminent. Back at team PFA, the news of Poll's firing was an unexpected surprise. After holding an emergency session, it was decided to bring forward the Links Report's publication in order to build on the hype over Poll's axing. Getting the public boiling mad was the intention. Links's document had been essentially ready for some time anyway, so with Poll gone, better to get it out in public before his successor could start interfering.

Except that … the report was not released! The interim AG was quickly replaced with Ned Odom. Mr. Odom had been a deputy attorney general way back in the eighties under a prior Republican administration. He had long since retired, but by using Ron's family influence, after much persuasion, he was talked into stepping back into the morass. Ned was a crusty old dude, well into his seventies, but with a sharp mind for the law and a fearless belief in justice. He was a perfect choice. Following Suit's recommendation of him, the

Republican-held Senate moved to ratify his appointment—but not without much complaining from the Democrats, of course.

Throughout the appointment process, Ron and Ned met on a regular basis, and the vice president sat in on each meeting.

"So, that's where we are, Ned," Ron said after running through all the details of Poll's relationship with Ludwig, and Links's longtime friendship with Poll, which went as far as working together on consultancy projects and quietly making a ton of money together. Ned and Joyce had been colleagues for many years, and while even he was little leery of President Suit, given his unconventional approach to governing, Ned trusted Joyce completely. He knew that much of the investigations into Poll and Links had been ramrodded by her, so Odom was comfortable in accepting the information at face value, and he agreed with their suppositions and conclusions.

"Mr. President, this old dog still has a few tricks in him. I've seen some of Links's draft report. It's breathless and accusatory, but it's lacking in any real substance. If you'll allow me some leeway, I believe I can help set things straight. What these people are trying to do to you is an absolute travesty." AG Odom had been around the block many times in his career; he wasn't afraid of anything, and despite his reservations about Suit, he could see that the man was clearly being unjustly persecuted.

"Ned, it's all yours," said Ron. "I've got a ton of shit on my plate, and I need to keep my distance from this whole mess as much as possible."

The three of them shook hands as Ned left the Oval Office to implement his plans.

The two men sat facing each other in the AG's office.

"So, Dan, it's like this. I'm not one to assert influence over anyone, especially an independent counsel such as yourself, but I've read your report thoroughly, and I must say, I'm, er, surprised at a couple of things. Firstly, it seems light on facts. There's so much hearsay evidence, there are many implications unbacked by facts, and nearly all of the evidence is single source without our department's required secondary corroboration. It's not even subtle that you're doing a hit job on our president. I've made some suggestions and comments on this marked-up copy." Ned pushed a folder across the desk to Link.

Dan took it up, flipping through it as he quietly scoffed. The report was covered in Post-It notes and deletions.

"Now, Dan, I know what's going on. You've got masters to satisfy, and I get that, I really do, but I can't allow you to publish anything that is not true."

Links looked puzzled. "What do you mean by *masters*, Mr. Odom?"

Ned leaned back in his chair and folded his arms behind his head.

"I could slide another folder across this desk for you to look at, Dan. It will show that you're part of a team working for Peter Ludwig to discredit President Suit. It will provide phone transcripts of your calls with George Poll. It will show a history of colluding with him for illicit monetary gain. It will even show bank records giving details of how much money you've received over the course of this whole investigation. Now, I get it, you are an avaricious son of a bitch." Odom's voice got louder, "You are one of the reasons Suit was elected—because people are tired of all the corrupt bullshit that goes on in Washington."

Odom stood and began pacing slowly around his office. He sat of the edge of his desk in front of an uncomfortable Links and peered into his eyes. "So, here's the deal. Your people want blood, but I won't allow that. I want your ass in prison, but that would be a long, drawn-out process. Disastrous for you and your family, of course, but the country doesn't need yet another sleazy scandal. So, I have an offer for you. Make my amendments to the report before publication, and speak only to the facts at any future hearings, and I'll let your impropriety slide. Don't worry, even with my changes, the report will still cause a stir, and should keep your masters at least somewhat satisfied. So, what's it going to be Dan?" Ned patted Links on the shoulder as he returned to his seat.

⤜⬥⤛

D-Day! The Links report dropped! Journalists and other media representatives lined up like children before an ice-cream truck, waiting excitedly to receive their copies of the heavy tome. Hearings were scheduled for two weeks following the report's release. This, of course, gave the media ample time to parse and interpret every single word of Links's document. Once again, an alien visiting our planet during these two weeks might have thought that there were two entirely different reports. The left-wing view was that it confirmed Russian interference in the elections; that the Russians had colluded with Suit's campaign; and that members of Suit's election team had gotten dirt on Stacey Lincoln from the Russians. Meanwhile, over on Planet Republican, the consensus was that there was no "there" there; the report did not provide any proof that Suit had colluded with the Russians in order to skew the election; his team had in fact rejected overtures by them; and that there was certainly nothing impeachable about the way he had acted both before and after his election. Out in real America, all this breathless commentary didn't move the needle one way or the other: To the Suit haters, there was enough dirt to hang the bastard; the whole document was confirmation that Ron Suit was not fit to hold office. Meanwhile, those who had "Suited-up for America" were unmoved. It was all hot air—so much bullshit that proved nothing. Suit's approvability ratings didn't move a point one way or the other.

The PFA were naturally disappointed, and in a video debrief with Links and Poll, they expressed this view.

"Well, Mr. President," replied Poll, "I can assure you that the document was much more hard-hitting prior to my departure."

Links said, "Guys, Odom was very firm in his support for my work provided that it could be 100 percent backed by multiple sources, per DOJ guidelines. I had to water down some of the report in order to pass the department's peer-review process."

Ludwig sat pensively for a moment and then said, "Gentlemen, we'll have to work with what we've got. There's still enough smoke in the report to build an impeachment bonfire. Let's mobilize our media and get to work."

Links inwardly breathed a huge sigh of relief. He had gotten away with it, the PFA didn't suspect anything of him, and he would not be going to jail, courtesy of AG Odom. Maybe it was time to take his money and lie low?

VP Flowers was extra busy in the weeks leading up to the Links Hearings. Working discreetly with certain Republican members of the Judiciary and Intelligence Committee, she primed them all to ask specific questions of Links that would put him on the spot. With the Democrats holding the House, however, they were running the show and would obviously have more say in the hearings than the GOP.

The chair of the committee was a longtime representative who looked like Tweedle Dum from *Alice Through the Looking Glass*: short, round, and almost as wide as he was tall. He called the hearing to order, and the show began. While the media's talking heads had been all agog for two weeks, devoting every second of airtime to frantic speculation and accusation, the nation had long since tuned out. This was not a hearing for the American public; this was merely an opportunity for a group of partisan politicians and media darlings to bloviate and strut their stuff.

As at any such hearings, the chamber was packed with politicians, aides, and media, all of them jostling for the best viewing point, making sure that they'd be in the camera's viewing range as the broadcast was aired. In the social media universe, celebrities opined on the shocking fact that Suit was still in office. How could such an evil man lead our country?

As expected, the Democrats' questions focused on Russia's attempts to undermine the election process and Suit's collusion with them. They questioned Links at length about how one specific member of the Suit election team had actually told an undercover FBI agent that he'd been in contact with someone who claimed to have damaging information on Lincoln. Supposedly, that someone was a Russian agent. The day dragged on with endless speechifying and self-aggrandizement by member of both parties.

"The chair recognizes the gentleman from Alabama," Tweedle Dum announced.

At last! Time for some Flowers-directed gotcha questions!

"Mr. Links, when you state Russian election interference, you specifically are referring to their social media campaign, headed up by those parties who were subsequently indicted during the investigation, is this correct?"

"Yes, sir, that is correct."

"And if I was to total up the amount of money spent on this 'substantial misinformation campaign' by the Russians, how much would that come to?"

"I don't have that information at hand, sir." Dan shifted a little uneasily in his seat; he knew where this was heading.

"Well, I can help you there, Mr. Links. Throughout the entire election season, these Russians spent a total of approximately $600,000 on all of their social media efforts. Does that surprise you, Mr. Links?"

"I will take your word for it, sir." Dan was feeling just a little hot under the collar now.

"So, this massive investigation of yours over so many months and with so many resources resulted in finding that the Russian election interference amounted to less than one-tenth of 1 percent of the money spent by the leading candidates on their advertising and social media efforts? I don't think that 0.001 of a media blitz is going to give anyone much influence, is it? I yield, Mr. Chairman."

As expected, the next representative guided Links back on message, asking questions to mitigate his Republican colleague's previous interrogation. Later in the hearings, another Joyce-primed Republican got his chance to dive into Links.

"Now, IC Links, I see from this report that one of President Suit's junior team members was approached by an undercover FBI agent, and this aide disclosed that he had been offered damaging information on the Lincoln campaign by someone who the agent believed was a Russian FSB operative, is that correct?"

"Yes, sir, we have tapes that clearly show this conversation. It is incontrovertible that there were communications between the Suit team and Russian undercover operatives." Links was feeling more at ease with this line of questioning.

"So, it strikes me as odd that the FBI was apparently surveilling the Suit team, even to the extent that conversations with an American citizen were being recorded without his knowledge. Does that seem odd to you, Mr. Links?"

Dan felt the color drain from his cheeks. He shuffled in his chair and glanced around the room, as if looking for help from someone, anyone. After a long pause, he said, "Sir, I headed up the investigation under the direction of then-AG George Poll. It was my duty to gather, interpret, and analyze all pertinent information pertaining to the investigation. However, since I was not involved in authorizing any undercover activity, I can't speak to your point."

"Mr. Links, did you also know that this Russian agent was actually working with the FBI, setting up a trap for this junior member of the Suit team?

Links sat up with a jerk. "Sir, as I told you, I was not involved with certain aspects of the AG's work, but I find it outrageous for you to suggest that our FBI would cooperate with a foreign actor in the manner which you suggest."

"I think I've made my point, Mr. Links. I yield my remaining time."

And so it went. After showing outrage over the very implication that American intelligence would be in cahoots with Russian intelligence, the Democrats continued asking their softball questions. They led Dan by the nose with their inquiries, walking him through points that cemented the main theme that Suit had colluded with the Soviets and was therefore an illegitimate president. Meanwhile, other Republicans got some shots in, pointing out the vapidity of the case and building up a narrative that the investigation had been implemented on a bogus basis and carried out using questionable if not downright illegal surveillance tactics.

On conclusion of the hearings, the media retreated to their lairs to feed red meat to their hungry viewers, readers, and listeners. Both tribes had plenty to work with.

The biggest surprise of the hearing actually came two days after it finished. On this particular night, Ron's *Daily Briefing* chief guest was AG Odom who, although uncomfortable with the format of the program, had been persuaded to use it to make an important announcement.

"Following a long and costly investigation by my department into our most recent presidential election, a number of issues have arisen from the release of Independent Counsel Links's report. While there is some evidence that foreign actors attempted to influence our election, of more concern to me is the fact that certain methods used during the investigation to gather evidence clearly violate US law. Of greatest concern is that our own intelligence agencies appeared to surveil President Suit's team before, during, and after the election. Illegitimate surveillance is a serious matter, and so I am initiating my own investigation into the entire 'Russian interference' narrative. Thank you."

Milos was not pleased. His initial misgivings about the final format of Links's report and the man's disappointing performance at the Hill's hearings were rising again. *Odom was no fool; what might he find once he starts digging into things?*

⌘

Sue was super excited when she heard Odom's announcement. As a regular viewer of Suit's show, this new development was encouraging. "The whole thing is bogus, Maury," she said as they chatted outside of the café. "Ludwig has been trying to take down the president ever since he kicked Lincoln's ass."

"Maybe," said Maury. "I've never been a big fan of Ron Suit, even when he had his late-night TV show."

They chatted about this and that, and then Maury declared, "Well, Sue, you're going to really hate me now. I've just taken a consulting job with the Democratic Party. I'm part of a team developing software to analyze voting data and such. Should keep me in cappuccinos for a while."

"Don't worry. I forgive you, you son of a bitch! Kidding—a man's gotta work. Any progress on poor old Joe?"

"Sorry, girl. I've not had much free time—so no progress. I wish I could find out what Joe had dug up before he died, but the cops took everything: his computer, his phone, the lot. It might be on a cold case TV show sometime at this rate."

They said their goodbyes, and Maury headed back to work.

TRADE

Milos was not pleased with what he was hearing. He would normally never dream of listening to a Ron Suit broadcast, but here he was, in a rare idle moment, sitting in his New York penthouse staring at the massive television screen before him. His suite was in one of those pencil-thin condo skyscrapers that line the southern rim of Central Park. The view north was stunning, across the park and up into Harlem, with the Met and Guggenheim clearly visible. To the east, the now slightly passé-looking UN headquarters and below it the magnificent deco crown of the Chrysler Building, now Chinese-owned like much of Manhattan. Off to the south was the Empire State with One World Trade Center in the distance and a hazy Statue of Liberty beyond that. To the west, Hudson Yards glimmered in its chrome-glass glory with the river behind and Columbus Circle in the immediate foreground.

All fabulous views, but Milos rarely took them in. He spent perhaps four weeks a year here, mostly one or two nights at a time as he was on his way to or from another continent, doing business, working his moneymaking magic. The high-end fitted German kitchen had never even been used; Milos ate out when in town, usually with business contacts or members of the Group. If he needed food, the Russian Tea Room was close by and would, by special arrangement, deliver anytime, night or day. No, this mega-million-dollar residence was simply a stopover to Kunis, a place to stay on his way somewhere else.

The evening that Milos watched, Ron was continuing his rebound and was as upbeat as he'd ever been. He had good reason too. While there was still much noise about Russian collusion, the wind had gone out of the Democrats' sails in this matter. The Dow, which had had surged on his election was now flirting with twenty-five thousand, a historical high. Meanwhile, jobs were so abundant that it was becoming difficult to fill positions. Unemployment down, wages up, and a scandal behind him—what's not to like?

Until now, all of this had been an irritation to Kunis, but it had not had any real impact on him. The Group and the PFA were developing strategies to ensure that Suit would not get reelected. The failed impeachment attempt was a setback, true, but with almost two years to go, Milos was confident that he'd be impeached or ousted one way or another. As with all things, Milos played a long game. It was Ron's opening monologue that stung so much.

"Well, folks, our friends on the other side of the aisle, you know, the donkey party, continue to make life as difficult as possible for us, but I'm happy to report that our country has never had it so good. Even if you're not in the stock market, I bet part of your pension is, so everyone, Democrat or Republican, is benefitting from our booming economy. Jobs are everywhere, even for you minorities who probably didn't vote for me. You'll remember that Peter Ludwig lectured us about how America's best days are behind us, how we are no longer the dominant nation, how we must accept a reduced role in the world, and blah, blah, blah. Well, we're back! Our nation is as great as ever, greater, even. We are once again the country that other countries look up to. And certain other countries sometimes use our good nature to take advantage of us. Do you know, the other day I was looking through some of our spending data, and it struck me that America is a benefactor to the world like no other nation on earth. We give hundreds of billions in aid; we contribute more than anyone else to questionable organizations like the UN, NATO, and the World Health Organization. Yet, we're treated like crap by everyone. Oh, yes, everyone hates the USA, but they hate us with their hands held out. Not anymore, folks. Our team has initiated a sweeping review of all our global aid with the aim of slashing it. Why give these ingrates money when all they do is run us down and oppose us?" Ron moved across to his desk and sat down behind it.

Milos was still only half-listening, but his ears pricked at the next announcement.

"And another thing, folks. Over the years my predecessors have signed off on many terrible trade deals with pretty much every global power. We are being screwed, folks! In every single international trade agreement that we've signed, the scales are weighted bigly in favor of the other country, never in ours. So, while we're looking at all our charitable activities, I've also put our trade partners on notice that a renegotiation of all deals is about to begin. Ha! Trade *partners*? I should say trade *masters*!"

That got Kunis's attention, all right!

Ron continued, "Anyway, tonight's guest was supposed to be AG Odom, but he told me sternly that he will have nothing to say until completion of his investigation into the Russian nonsense. So, then I asked Misty Moistly to come along. You know, she's the stripper who's claiming to have been my main squeeze for years. If you watch or listen to or read anything these days, that's all you'll hear about, isn't it? Russians didn't take him down—maybe a stripper can? Funnily enough, Misty declined to appear tonight too. So, let me bring out our amazing vice president, Joyce Flowers, to talk about the working budget and the impact it will have on our fat and bloated government."

Kunis was furious. If Suit began ripping up existing trade deals, it could hurt his global business dealings. He had been using such one-sided agreements to his advantage for a number of years now, most recently with a series of acquisitions and partnerships in China. Changes to the existing US-Sino agreement could seriously compromise his position in Asia. Time to get serious. It's one thing to keep up a steady flow of sleaze and innuendo in order to distract Suit, but stronger measures were now obviously called for. He picked up the secure line to arrange a meeting. Maybe he'd need to stay over in NYC a little longer. "Hello, Stacey, I hope you are well. I'm in New York for a few days, and I thought we should get together to discuss your future with the party. I'll be inviting Peter too."

They met for dinner at Eleven Mad, one of Milos's favorites. Placed discreetly in one corner of the art deco elegance of its dining room, the three got down to business as an extravagant tasting menu slowly unfolded before them over the course of the evening.

Kunis said, "Stacey, we have learned from your loss. The next elections will be controlled so much better than the last. I have a team developing software that will be able to gather, analyze, and present votes so much more efficiently than the current systems. Its first real test of course will be the primaries. We are already seeing candidates coming forward, and some of them are not to our liking, but … of course, democracy must be allowed to play out."

Ludwig said, "Exactly, Milos. Our primary system is a chaotic mix of caucusing and voting. It's been an undisciplined mess for the past several election cycles. We need to grab the bull by the horns and push through this new streamlined application. To do that, we need a strong chair of the DNC. I would like that person to be you, Stacey."

Stacey stopped eating and sat back in the banquette. While she remained certain that she didn't want another run at the presidency, this offer seemed like a big step down for her. "Look, I've done my time in the wilderness, but the impeachment effort brought me back into the public's eye. I'm now doing very well with speaking appearances, TV interviews, and the like, but more importantly, my foundation is raking in cash. People around the world know that I can still open doors, and they're willing to pay for it. Why in hell should I bother becoming a fucking paper pusher for the party?"

Peter and Ludwig exchanged swift glances.

Ludwig said, "Stacey, being chair isn't pushing paper. It wields significant influence, and with the plans we're putting in place, it will wield even more. The chair of the DNC will control everything in our party going forward. I really hope that you will consider the position."

Stacey picked at her foie gras. "But, Peter, the chair is elected by the committee members. Who's to say I would get the nod even if I wanted the job?"

"You don't have to worry about that my dear," said Kunis. "If you want the chair, it's yours. Tell me, are you familiar with the Mexican elections of 1988?"

Stacey confessed that she was not.

"For the first time in its national elections, a computer system was used to tabulate votes. Traditionally, early voter returns in Mexico would heavily influence the overall outcome because news media would report on them while outlying provinces were still voting. Well, in 1988, the computer that tabulated results was *adjusted* to favor one candidate even though he was not actually in the lead. So, he looked to be ahead in early results, the media reported this throughout the country, and this discouraged opposing supporters. They saw their candidate as a lost cause and didn't bother coming out to vote. Ultimately, the trick computer was discovered and eventually everyone knew that the vote had been rigged, but by then, it was too late—and the *leading* candidate succeeded." Kunis slid closer to Stacey and lowered his voice. "Stacey, we need someone who can manage the process. It is a vital role. Oh, I accept that the best candidate should win the primary, but as we know from bitter experience, it doesn't always work that way. You will be key to ensuring the right candidate to beat Suit is selected."

"So, okay, I take on the job. What makes you think that our

'best candidate' will beat that bastard in the actual election?" Stacey remained skeptical.

As the courses came and went, Milos and Peter outlined their various options to compromise President Suit in the run up to the election.

"So, Stacey, are you with us?"

"I guess so," she replied after a long pause. "Anything to hurt that asshole."

The wonderful meal finally ended, and the three parted company.

Stacey left with a feeling of resignation; she was not at all pleased to be taking on this role in the DNC, but she trusted Kunis, and as she had done on so many other occasions, she accepted his recommendation.

Ludwig climbed into the back of Kunis's Maybach, and Milos said, "How is George Burton doing?"

Ludwig was a little surprised at the mention of his old VP. "Well, as you know, George stepped down from public life when we left the White House. That's probably a good thing too; he is not the ball-busting Burton he used to be."

"Oh, that's disappointing to hear," Kunis said. "I saw him on a fluff-piece interview recently, and he seemed okay. Why do you say he's not the man he was?"

Peter paused slightly to gather his thoughts. "He's slowed down, Milos. The man is well into his seventies, and he's just not as sharp as he used to be. It happens to us all, I suppose. I think that deep down inside, he knew that he's not 100 percent anymore, and that's why he decided not to run for president." Peter looked out of the car window and added, "Plus, he was in politics for a very long time—a lifelong career politician. I suspect that he thought he was stretching his luck; we all have skeletons in the closet, and old George decided to quit while he was ahead."

"Peter, as you know, I've been studying the likely runners

for our upcoming primaries. I'm not convinced that any of them can beat Suit. Oh, I know we hope to get rid of him before the election, but it pays to be prepared for any eventuality. Early days, I know, but these current frontrunners are all too far left. We need a moderate, a steady hand—that's how to beat Suit. The country is tired of all the drama of Suit's presidency, and they long for a return to normalcy."

They arrived at Peter's hotel, and the limo sat idling as they continued their conversation. The sidewalks were crammed with people—tourists, workers, bums—all rushing to be somewhere, even at this late hour. New York's bright neon lights reflected in oily puddles on dirty streets. A cacophony of taxi horns, street vendors' calls, and police whistles pierced the night, but inside the Maybach, all was quiet.

"You think George would be a good candidate?" asked Ludwig. "Surely, you're not serious, Milos. The man is past it!"

"Just a thought, Peter. Enjoy the rest of your night. I must leave for Beijing first thing, so I need to get back to the condo."

The two parted company, leaving Ludwig puzzled by Kunis's sudden interest in George Burton. Peter had not really kept in touch with the man since they'd both left office. It had never been a close relationship; oh, sure, their public persona was that of a dream team, fighting the injustices of the world, and making it a better place, but in reality, Ludwig had not rated Burton highly—he had been an establishment pick for VP, someone from the old political class who had his tentacles in so much of Washington, and for this, he had been useful when persuasion was needed. But Burton's style didn't sit well with Peter's; George liked to glad-hand people, slap them on the back, and make vacuous small talk, while Ludwig was an elegant orator who was inherently superior to the masses around him. Yet, if Kunis had an interest in the man, perhaps it was time to touch base? Ludwig took out his phone. Burton's private number was still in his contacts list. "George, is that you? It's Peter, Peter Ludwig. I was just thinking we haven't talked for some time. I'm heading back to DC tomorrow—how about we meet up for breakfast or coffee?"

༄༅

A handsome face atop a perfectly suited torso was on the screen. "I will prove that my client, Miss Moistly, was in a sexual relationship with the president for a number of years, and that her silence was bought off using Mr. Suit's campaign finance monies. As you all know, this is a felony." Nick Ferrari was giving a press conference on the steps of the LA Courthouse before a throng of eager reporters. Nick was a sleazeball lawyer who'd made his name and money from working with high-profile clients in sensational cases. The common denominators for any case he took were that it must involve sex or murder, and it absolutely had to garner a massive amount of media coverage. Misty's case was well and truly in his sweet spot.

While Maury was lazily half-watching the Ferrari press conference in NYC, more important eyes were intently following it in DC. Peter Ludwig and a few of his team were tuning in. They had essentially "shepherded" Misty to Nick for the purpose of hurling yet another grenade in Ron's direction.

"Useful idiots," said Ludwig. "With people like Ferrari, we'll always have ammunition against Suit. The guy is a total waste of space, but opportunists like him are perfect for us; wind him up and off he goes, hot on the trail of the president, another shitstorm for him to deal with!"

The PFA core team turned their attention to a more important topic. The failed investigation into Russia needed something substantial to bring it back to life, and Peter thought he had the answer. The conspirators sat in a corner room of the grand old Bradley Manor estate house, looking out on immaculately groomed lawns. This room had once been the house's dining room, but now it was Ludwig's office-cum-war room. As the team planned tactics within, armed guards and agents patrolled the grounds without, Ludwig's post-presidential lifelong protection.

"We have a loyalist who's working in State at quite a high level," Ludwig said. "I activated him and requested proposals for a new attack on Suit's legitimacy. He's already come up with a pretty solid plan, so let's workshop his idea to see if we can improve on it."

The team discussed the pluses and minuses of the mole's idea, tweaked it here and there, and finally agreed to press forward.

"We're agreed then; QPQ is the way forward," Ludwig said. "I'll get back with my man and get the operation underway. We'll need to discreetly put the judiciary chairman on notice that this is coming down the pipe so he can be prepared too."

All faces around the desk were smiling; it seemed to be a solid strategy.

"Mr. President, do you still want to push on with the Twenty-Fifth Amendment attack too?"

"I think so," Peter said with a smirk. "The man is obviously certifiable. Let's keep leaking the rumors—most people will buy into that immediately."

The PFA team dispersed. All in all, it had been a very satisfactory meeting.

⁓⊙⥾⌁

Blissfully unaware of the fresh mountain of crap that was about to be piled on him, Ron was en route back to the USA from his summit meeting with the Chinese leader, Xi Jinping. He strolled easily down the aircraft's aisle to the press section of Air Force One and began to address the group of journalists who had, up until then, been enjoying Air Force One's excellent free food and drinks.

"Well, I must say it was a very productive day with Premier Xi. I didn't pull any punches, but I told him that this massive imbalance in trade must be rectified. I also put him on notice that his continuous stealing of American intellectual property must stop. I mean, surely even CNN can agree that we've been screwed over by the Chinese for years?" Ron looked at the CNN reporter, but she remained silent.

The Fox representative said, "Mr. President, given that the current status quo has existed for so long, how do you propose to make changes? The Chinese government grows more powerful each day, and it's projected that within just a few years, they will outstrip the US in terms of overall economic power. How can such a major entity be persuaded to change?"

"Good question, John. It's very simple. We either amicably redress the imbalance—or I implement sanctions and tariffs. I've already had a team drafting up a declaration to this effect."

The CNN reporter said, "You mean you are about to start a global trade war? Isn't that an extremely high-risk option that could jeopardize our nation's security?"

"Well, Erin, I'm sure that's how you'll be reporting it tomorrow, but the truth is that my predecessors always accepted any deal they were offered—and that's why so many of our trade agreements suck. You've got to remember that they can do damage to us, but we can do just as much to them—if not more. It's sort of like MAD, you know, mutually assured destruction. For the first time in years, the US is going to stand up to the Chinese, and we'll win because they know they've had a good run for their money: Backing off their current position will be a no-brainer for them. Now, we'll be landing in a few hours, so I'm going to go watch a few reruns of my old TV show. Good night, all." Ron went back to his quarters, chuckling to himself over the certainty that at least one of tomorrow's headlines would be along the lines of "Vain Suit likes to watch himself on TV."

A summary of the Suit-Xi meeting quickly reached Kunis's ears. He was not happy, and he immediately placed a call to Peter Ludwig.

"All in hand, Milos," Peter said. "In a few weeks, Suit will have so much else to think of that trade deals will be on the back burner for quite some time."

Kunis hung up, a little reassured, but not satisfied.

⸙

"So, you see, Sue, this new software will transform the way the Democratic primaries work. It will be *so* much better. We'll get results almost instantly and won't have to rely on blue-haired ladies counting pieces of paper. It's been such an interesting project for me."

Maury was as excited as Sue had ever seen him.

"Well, of course I'm not happy that you're helping the Dems, but at least you're working, and it sounds like you're enjoying things." Sue sneaked a sip of Maury's cappuccino. "Hey, did you hear about Dan Links? Poetic justice at work if you ask me. He just dropped dead with a stroke. I heard it on the news earlier today. That'll teach him to mess with President Suit."

Maury grimaced. "That's not exactly the nicest thing to say, Sue. Maybe Ron ordered his assassination?" Maury giggled at the look on Sue's face when he said that.

"As if," Sue said as she stood. "Although it wouldn't surprise me at all that it was divine punishment for not nailing the president. Anyway, I've got tables to bus. Take it easy." She waved as she walked into the café.

Maury got up and went back to work; he needed to finish running through the beta and checking the code for errors.

Now why is there a back door? he asked himself some hours later as he sat in front of his laptop. Although Maury was involved in only one part of the DNC program's development, specifically some of the macros for collating and sorting votes, he nevertheless had access via the network to the entire beta version's code. After checking through his sections, he'd begun to look idly around the whole package, and he had discovered some weird shit. Buried deep within the code were some hidden links to something outside of the main program. Maury's initial conclusion was that a virus or malware had somehow infected the beta, but further discovery and testing disproved this theory. This mysterious part of the code's algorithm was quite deliberate.

Oh well, he thought. *At least my input is perfect.* His phone rang, and after a lengthy conversation with a friend, Maury began to stream some TV—and the strange anomaly in the program was relegated to the back of his mind.

IMPEACHMENT

Ron and his team had long since concluded that their best campaign strategy for the upcoming election was to simply do good work. Keep focusing on the promises made at the last election—and keep honoring them. This was proving to be a successful strategy; unemployment continued downwards toward historic lows, personal incomes sat at all-time highs, and the economy remained strong.

Despite all of the left-wing media's hysterical rantings about how bad everything was, most normal folks in America could clearly see that things were actually fine. Oh, sure, our president is unconventional, can be a sarcastic asshole, and is constantly displaying his lack of political skills, but it works—the country is booming. The Democrats could see this too, and they knew that if Suit's administration continued to perform so well going into the election, they had no chance of seizing power. "It's the economy, stupid" was a truism of one of their revered own, and it looked like these prophetic words could spell four more years for the GOP.

Alarmed at such a prospect, Ludwig initiated Plan QPQ.

The story dropped first in the *New York Times*. A lengthy piece by their leading political reporter kicked off the rumors: "After an unsuccessful attempt to link president Ron Suit to the Russians' interference with the last election race, special investigating counsel, Daniel Links, died tragically of a stroke just months after his shocking report was issued. Some say that the newly appointed attorney general's mismanagement of his investigation may have placed inhuman levels of stress on Links that hastened his demise. Now, the *New York Times* has found new evidence that reportedly shows President Suit attempting to influence Soviet domestic policy by using a quid pro quo in his dealings with Ukraine's newly appointed prime minister."

The article went on to outline how a State Department whistleblower had decided to step forward upon seeing Suit's flagrant disregard for policy and the law during his dealings with Ukraine. The revelations spread like wildfire across the mainstream media, and within days, it even threatened to eclipse all other news.

Ron followed the breaking news with a mixture of disbelief and anger. *Here we go again,* he thought. *Don't those sons of bitches ever give up?* He met with AG Odom to be briefed on the status of his investigation into the Russian fiasco and to ask about this latest assault.

Odom assured Ron that a lot of wrongdoing had been perpetrated during Links's work, specifically that the FBI had been either used as a tool to illegally spy on the Suit team or had been actively involved with the illegal activity.

"Mr. President, you cannot wiretap someone without cause. You cannot set up a trap for an individual and catch him a fabricated situation. All these things happened. All of this will be proven. But, if we go off half-cocked, the Democrats and press will have a field day. I'm simply trying to make 100 percent certain that we've crossed all the T's and dotted all the I's before we go public. It's essential to follow protocol to the absolute letter on this one, sir."

"Okay, and what about this Ukraine nonsense?" Ron asked.

"Well, as we already know, every part of this administration is riddled with moles and spies. The White House has been leaking like a goddam sieve since the day you took office." Odom was clearly agitated. "We're slowly weeding out disloyal operatives, but obviously there's someone close to you who is still working against you. Regarding the nub of the *Times* claim, I think you're fine; all your official conversations are recorded, so when this mysterious whistleblower finally gets around to actually saying what he heard, you'll be able to deny it. Hell, there were probably dozens of people listening in on that call, weren't there?"

"There sure were. Okay, let's see where this trail takes us." Ron ended the meeting feeling reassured, but still pissed.

"Hello, America. Welcome to tonight's edition of the *Daily Briefing*. I have a bit of a coup with my guest tonight, but we'll get to that later. I wanted to start by making a quick recap of progress we've made in the judicial branch of our government. It's clear to me, and probably to you, that justice in America is often distorted, and that sometimes plain wrong judgments are handed down. A perfect example was the Russian witch hunt where, until AG Odom came along and sorted things out, the investigation was clearly a partisan attempt to impeach me. Imagine if we'd held both Houses in the midterms, but no! The left's media blitz and baseless accusations did our administration significant harm, and that probably resulted in the loss of the House. We now know, of course, that it was all BS—but the damage is done. It's water under the bridge now, isn't it? I know that AG Odom is well into his investigation of the investigators, and I'm looking forward to the day when his findings are issued. But, back to justice," Ron was pacing around in front of the camera, thinking on his feet as usual. "Since my election, we've appointed hundreds of new judges: Article III judges, District Court judges, Appeals Court judges, and most importantly, Supreme Court judges. The days when Democrats can shop around to find a judge who'll give them the verdict they want are dying. Oh sure, there's still some holdouts, some districts where a left-wing special-interest group can file a case or successfully appeal one of our administration's rulings, but it's getting harder and harder for them." Ron moved to his desk. "Now, in a perfect segue, I'm excited to introduce my special guest. Nick, come on out!"

A chiseled face in a five-thousand dollar suit walked out and sat in the chair next to Ron. "For the one or two people who don't know who this chunk of sartorial elegance is, it's Nick Ferrari. Y'all may know him better as the guy who tried to bring down our last Supreme Court nominee—or perhaps as the man who is currently trying to get yours truly in trouble." Ron smiled broadly as he said this. He then turned to Ferrari and fixed his gaze upon him.

"Nick, when I got the idea to get you on the *Briefing*, my team said I was crazy, that you would never in a million years agree to appear. But I knew better; if there's money or media exposure involved, you're going to be there, aren't you, Nick?"

"I wouldn't say that at all, Mr. President," Ferrari replied, looking comfortable in his surroundings. "I wanted the opportunity to confront you about your behavior with my client, Miss Moistly."

"Don't worry, Nick. We'll get to that, but first I need to know why you cannot hang your head in shame over the appalling way you attacked Supreme Court Justice Smith during his confirmation hearings? I mean, in a way, I should thank you for turning so many independent voters into Republicans because of your vicious attacks." Ron was losing the friendly tone. "To attempt to destroy an honest man's reputation with the shameless and sleazy claims that you made is unforgivable!"

Nick remained at ease and said, "Mr. President, you have to remember that it wasn't me doing anything. I was merely representing my client. Every person deserves the right to representation, and I was fulfilling that right for Miss Kowalski."

Ron dialed back his ire and said, "Nick, she was an obvious liar, she had a muddled accusation that constantly changed, and she had not one single person, friend or family, to support her outrageous claim that Justice Smith had repeatedly raped her at frat house parties during his time in law school. Hell, she didn't even live in the same town as him! How could you in good conscience take on such a ridiculous case?"

"Mr. President, I thought that you of all people would know that when a lawyer represents his client, he takes their assertions at face value and presumes that they are telling the truth. That's certainly been my credo throughout my career." Ferrari felt like he'd gotten one in on the president.

"And Mr. Ferrari, I thought you of all people would know about the presumption of innocence," Ron shot back. "But let's move on to your latest 'defense of the downtrodden,' Misty Moistly."

"Sure thing, sir." This was the main reason that Ferrari wanted to come on Ron's show—plus the massive exposure he'd get from the appearance.

"I do know Miss Moistly," Ron continued. "She appeared on my talk show around fifteen years ago. A good-looking girl and with a head on her shoulders too. But here you are, using that one appearance as the basis for all these stupid claims that she's been my lover, that I fathered a child with her, that I introduced her to drugs, and blah, blah, blah. I mean, really, Nick, are all these her claims—or are they coming from you in your never-ending search for fame?"

"Time will tell, Mr. President, and I look forward to our day in court when I'll be able to substantiate all of Miss Moistly's accusations." Ferrari was looking directly into the camera as he talked.

"Me too, Nick, me too. Oh, and good luck proving any of it. I'm afraid that's all we have time for, Nick, so good night and please send my regards to the PFA."

⟡

Tweedle Dum was in full flight. He was ranting about President Suit's abuse of power and specifically his collusion with Russian operatives to influence the election. "I recognize that the independent counsel's investigation failed to definitively prove some of the accusations, but my office has now received a statement from a concerned worker in the State Department—you might call him a whistleblower—and once again, we see the president abusing his office for political gain. As chair of the Judiciary Committee, I am commencing an investigation into these latest abuses, and I expect to hold hearings in the near future."

Here we go again! Journalists crushed around him after he finished his announcement, pressing him for details of the whistleblower.

"Obviously, the identity of this individual must be kept secret in order to protect his safety. I should also point out that I myself have not met this person. I prefer to keep a distance in order to maintain the integrity of my committee's inquiries."

In the Oval Office, Ron was essentially resigned to these latest developments; they'd been in the pipeline for some time, so there was no surprise over Tweedle Dum's announcement. He asked for Ned Odom to come over and brief him on the situation. "So, Ned, do we know who this mysterious whistleblower is—and what he is going to say?"

"Sir, my understanding is he'll probably state that during your call with the Ukrainian prime minister last month, you said that he would not get the planned shipment of surface-to-air missiles until he had unearthed who was behind the dirt that was dished out during the Russian collusion investigation. As for who he is, we don't have any idea as of yet; my guess is that he's probably an embedded Democrat with ties to Ludwig and the PFA."

"Son of a bitch," declared Ron. "They don't give up, do they? Why don't we just ID the bastard and unmask him and his ties?"

A long debate ensued on this very topic. The AG was of the view that any such unmasking would be detrimental; his advice was to let the circus perform, and meanwhile, he would be setting some things up to discredit the whole sham. "Mr. President, I took care of things during the last fiasco, and I hope you can trust me again with this one."

So, it was agreed that Ron would stand above the swamp as the whole charade played out, and Odom would do more digging and hopefully get a satisfactory resolution to this latest fabricated scandal.

Tweedle Dum began his investigations inside a secure office of the Capitol. He was joined by his partner in crime, Tweedle Dee, another Democrat House representative and member of the Judicial Committee. Given that their party held the House, these two felt empowered to dictate whatever terms they desired for their inquiries. The contrast between the two could not have been greater. Dum was a walking bowling ball who waddled his way around the Capitol, always accompanied by his posse of sycophants, and Dee skulked about on his own, a painfully skinny loner who looked as if he'd been the model for those old "ninety-pound weakling" adverts. The two of them set rules for the initial meetings that essentially excluded any Republican from asking questions—and even limited their attendance. It was a wholly partisan effort, complete with strategically timed leaks to waiting members of the press. The outcome of this initial work was clear; the whistleblower had devastating information on President Suit that was the very definition of quid pro quo. Interestingly, as their work progressed, the two representatives began to modify their description of the heinous deed, using the phrases "tit for tat" or "you scratch my back." This was because the PFA, who were deeply involved in the whole show, were concerned that quid pro quo was too lofty a phrase and needed dumbing down in order to connect with their base.

Following the initial meetings, it was obvious that the next move would be a full House inquiry, hopefully leading to yet another impeachment attempt.

Odom, in addition to his ongoing investigation into the Russian collusion narrative, was digging into the whistleblower, eventually gaining a good idea of his identity. He kept this to himself at first, however, saving the information for an appropriate moment.

The House Judiciary Committee convened its full series of hearings.

"Ambassador Neglund, you were on the call between President Suit and Ukraine's prime minister?" Tweedle Dee's goggle eyes roamed around the chamber, seemingly independently of each other.

"Yes, sir, I was." The ambassador had been a Ludwig appointee and consequently was considered a "friendly" witness, at least by the Democrats.

"And can you tell us about the nature of the call?" The ambassador went on to explain how Suit welcomed the PM in his new role and how he seemed particularly interested in the origins of the damning report that had surfaced from Russia during the previous investigations.

"So, did President Suit say that he would be withholding our military aid until the prime minister had determined the origins of the report?" Tweedle Dee was abuzz with excitement over the answer he was about to hear.

"Sir, President Suit certainly did not forward the arms when promised. I believe there was a six-week delay."

"So, you could characterize this as a tit for tat?"

"Well," replied the ambassador, "it certainly seemed that way to me, and many of the aides listening on that call thought so too."

Game, set, match for quid pro quo!

As with the collusion hearings, several of the Republican representatives had been briefed ahead of the day, this time by AG Odom. One of them got to go next. "So, Ambassador Neglund, you say that the phone call seemed like President Suit was setting up a quid pro quo?"

"Yes sir, that was my impression."

"Okay, did the Ukrainian PM ever know that the arms shipment was being delayed? Did President Suit advise him of this?"

Neglund shifted in his chair, "No sir, he did not."

"So," continued the GOP representative, "the prime minister had no idea of any link between President Suit's quite legitimate questions about Russian election interference and the withholding of arms?"

"Umm, no, he didn't." The ambassador plainly did not want to answer that question.

"Seems like the weakest attempt at tit for tat in the history of tit for tat—when one party is blissfully unaware of the pressure being placed upon him. I yield."

A long string of aides and minor State Department folk were trotted out over the next two days. All of them were 100 percent certain that the president had been trying to blackmail the Ukrainian into getting information in exchange for weapons. However, not a single one of the accusers had been on the call.

As more and more questions were answered, it became apparent that the quid pro quo issue was in fact a rumor initiated by a person or persons unknown that had spread like a disease throughout the people who were now assembled for their depositions. Each time a Republican member asked when the mysterious whistleblower was to be questioned, the answer was always that this individual's safety was paramount—and that bringing them to the hearings was far too risky. The absurdity of not being able to question or even meet the very person who had initiated this whole shitshow was not lost on the red side of the aisle, while the blue side and all its compliant media were benignly indifferent to it.

The final day brought a senior State Department official who had been on the call. After the Democrat softball questions had been disposed of, the Republicans were ready. "Did President Suit meet with you before the call to plan out a strategy?"

"That is correct." The middle-aged career bureaucrat had seen many presidents come and go, but this one was by far the worst.

"And did in fact President Suit state during that pre-call meeting that he did not want any implication of a quid pro quo during his discussions?" AG Odom had been doing his homework.

"I'm ... er ... not sure I recall that, sir," the squirming bureaucrat responded.

"Well, luckily, I can help with that. I have here a transcript of your conversation with the president. As you know, all State meetings are recorded, and the exchange goes exactly as I've just implied. The president specifically said there must be no hint of quid pro quo by him or any other person on the call. He instructed you to relay this order to your team. Do you remember now?"

"Well, if you say it's in the transcript, then apparently, he did say it, although I have no recollection of that."

The GOP representative said, "I love it when I hear the word *recollect* because, as a lawyer myself, I know that word *recollect* is usually code for 'I do remember, but I don't want to come out and admit it.' I have no further questions and yield my time."

Well, what a way to end a hearing! Of course, the Tweedles summed up by emphasizing the myriad voices who'd said there had been a quid pro quo, but they specifically railed against the accusation that the State Department aide had lied—or at least been economical with the truth in respect to the president exhorting involved parties to avoid any hint of quid pro quo.

"I think it's quite obvious that anyone with an agenda can claim to have transcripts that are demeaning to the other side, but where is the proof of that conversation? I don't see any. Against this so-called transcript, we have the word of a longtime State Department official who has served our country flawlessly for decades."

The next day's news was as polarized as ever; all right-wing press was full of the revelation that Suit clearly had wished to avoid any hint of impropriety during his call and had instructed his team to that effect, while the left-wing press ignored this or hinted that the call's details had been faked or altered. Nonetheless, after a straight up-and-down vote, the House impeachment articles were sent to the Senate for consideration. This attempt had at least gotten one step further; there would be an impeachment.

✺

On the evening's *Daily Briefing* before the Senate impeachment trial was to begin, Ron looked at the camera and said, "Look, folks, I've talked this through with lots of people in the team, and I've received a variety of advice. As you know, there is clear proof that I was specifically avoiding any hint of quid pro quo in my discussions with the Ukrainians. Our Democrat friends say that this claim is fictitious. So, despite misgivings by some in the administration that it could compromise national security in the future and set a dangerous precedent, I've instructed my team to release the recordings in question, along with a written transcript. As I've told you so often, I'll provide the facts—and you make the conclusions."

Ron's good fortune was that the Senate was still held by the GOP. As the impeachment trial opened, America's attempt at pomp and circumstance was on full display. A robed Chief Supreme Court justice walked in slowly, part of a long line of solemn-looking senators, and led by a crier who declared entry to the chamber in order to commence the trial. Clothing colors were along party lines: red for the Republicans and blue for the Democrats.

As a precursor to the main event, the Speaker of the House had created a televisual extravaganza for the media by signing the articles of impeachment using specially made "impeachment pens," which were ceremoniously handed out to the assembled acolytes. The whole thing was a carefully orchestrated façade, a showcase trial. Every Democratic senator knew that the odds of impeachment were slim; a two-thirds majority in a Republican-held Senate was highly unlikely. This inconvenient fact, however, had not prevented the PFA and members of the Group from pulling out all stops in an attempt to sway the vote. Favors had been called in, and threats had been made. It was a tough task, but with luck and a following wind, Ludwig and Kunis had guarded optimism that they might just pull it off.

As promised, the phone call's details had been made public, and this caused a stir. Even the CNNs, *WP*s, and *NYT*s saw that this was effectively a slam dunk. As with any issue that did not match their agenda, the chosen course of action was to mostly ignore the call and transcript. Whenever this topic was raised in discussion on their shows, the lead anchors made much of the few redactions and tape edits that had been made in order to protect the names of certain individuals on the call. Their message was consistent: obviously the deletions and amendments had been made to change the tone in the president's favor.

The biggest bombshell came in the final stages of the trial. The Republican senate majority leader addressed the assembled throng and said, "As you can see, I have arranged for a slideshow as a part of my closing argument. I'd like to show you several pictures of members of the House Judicial Committee in conversation with a certain individual."

The screen flashed on to show long-lens shots of a group of men in a park, deep in conversation.

"Now, most of you will recognize everyone there except perhaps the gentleman on the right." He pointed to the image with a laser. "I am not going to name this person, but I can assure you that he has been identified as the *whistleblower*. It strikes me as odd that our Democratic friends have been on record many times saying that they do not know who the whistleblower is, and that they have never met him. These photographs belie such statements. I welcome our friends across the aisle to deny or disprove the truth of what I've just said, and I expect that some of them will do exactly that. However, we have ample evidence to back up my statements; perhaps the old adage that when you're in a hole, stop digging is worth listening to in this case."

Once again, the media launched into a feeding frenzy. Fox News had been quietly tipped off about this sensational disclosure ahead of its release, and they had already carried out a massive investigation into the man ID'd as the whistleblower. Legal issues prevented naming him, but it was remarkably easy to paint a black picture of him. He was a longtime State bureaucrat, had been involved in the Ukrainian negotiations and call, and had decades-old ties to the Democratic Party. Myriad photographs began circulating, showing him at DNC events or sitting at a donor dinner next to Ludwig. There was no question of his origins or loyalties. Alt-right sites were not as afraid as Fox; they named him, digging into his past and hammering out every smallest negative detail about him.

Meanwhile, the mainstream media chose to completely ignore this last-day revelation. As far as they were concerned, Suit was guilty and must be impeached. No mention was made of the blatant lies told by the Democrats.

As expected, the Senate vote didn't come close to reaching sixty-seven votes. Three Republicans defected, either because of an inherent hatred of Ron—or because the dirt Kunis or Ludwig held over them was too nefarious to risk being leaked. Impeachment's over, folks. Let's get back to the primaries!

❧

Maury was making his regular visit to the café. "Sorry, Sue. I'm won't be here again this week; got a boondoggle to DC coming up."

"Oh yeah, diving into the swamp, eh?" Sue replied.

"Yup, the software team is having a launch workshop at DNC headquarters ... should be cool." Maury was looking forward to the trip; it would make a nice change of scene from Lower Manhattan.

"Well, tell those scumbags to lay off our president," Sue said. "They've tried to get him twice and failed both times. They just need to accept that he is president and get over it."

"Y'know Sue, I don't think that's likely to happen anytime soon." Maury got up to leave. "I'll bring you back a present from Washington—maybe a Democratic Party T-shirt!"

"Sure, I could use that for work—to wipe the tables with!" she yelled after him.

PRIMARIES AGAIN

"**A**nd so, my fellow Americans, I can declare that the state of the union is strong!"

Ron looked around the chamber. Behind him was seated his vice president, Joyce Flowers, and to her left was the House Speaker—let's call her Widow Twankey (look it up). She had a contrived look of disinterest on her face and had spent hours in front of a mirror practicing this because she knew that millions of eyes would be on her during the State of the Union address. What a spot! Seated above the despicable Suit in full view of the nation. Other visual effects had been planned by her too in order to belittle Suit and minimize the impact of what would be his inevitably upbeat speech.

Ron began to reel off a list of his administration's accomplishments: record-low unemployment; record high wages; record low food stamp and entitlement claims; record high stock market performance. Every point raised was met with the same response—loud cheering and applause from the red side of the aisle and folded-arm silence from the blue. Silence, that is, except for a group of newly elected progressives, who sat en masse, all dressed in white. This uber-left wing of the Democratic party yelled insults and expletives every time Ron opened his mouth.

"You lie!"

"Racist!"

"Shut the fuck up!"

It perfectly displayed who these people were: disruptors, even among their own party. Thankfully, about two-thirds of the way through the SOTU address, the Mob rose up as one and stormed out of the chamber, a move intended to show their disrespect and hatred of the evil President Suit.

"Well, thank goodness," Ron remarked as this event unfolded. "I thought they'd never leave!"

Speech over, Ron stood at the podium for some time to absorb the lengthy rounds of applause and cheers from his party's representatives. Behind him the sour-faced Widow Twankey began her final visual stunt; after applauding him for a few seconds in a weird duckbill hand-clapping gesture, she stood up and with great pomp and deliberation, ripped up her copy of Ron's speech. "There, that's what I think of you and your speech," was the intention. To avoid any possible misstep, the Speaker had carefully ripped the speeches pages ahead of the SOTU so that her public act could be easily accomplished. Unfortunately, the display only made her look like a petulant, spoiled brat who'd not gotten her way.

Ron ignored her stunt and worked his way through a sea of supporters to eventually leave the chamber. *Beat that, Dems*, he thought on his way to his quarters.

In parallel with the latest attempt to impeach Suit, Democratic presidential hopefuls had begun assembling, and now that impeachment was over and done with (for now), a weary nation once again was subjected to the drip, drip, drip of election torture. Although still many months off, media content was already full of speculation over the candidates. Of course, given Suit's enduring popularity, the Republican ticket was likely to be him and him alone, but over on the Democrat side, a motley crew was assembling that had declared or expressed interest in the world's most powerful position. This wasn't surprising; Stacey Lincoln had categorically stated she would not make a second run for the presidency, and VP Burton was missing in action, so it was a wide-open field. Initial skepticism about Stacey's refusal to run was replaced with surprise when it was announced that the DNC had elected Stacey as its chairwoman, and this quickly shut down all wishful thinking of another Lincoln-Suit grudge match. Nonetheless, pundits were ecstatic about many of the candidates, a fascinating mix of the usual boring politicians stirred in with wildly progressive socialists. The season was looking promising, if not to the public, then to the myriad talking heads and expert consultants who could smell money in all the commentary they'd be asked to give.

A gaggle of has-beens began their campaigns as they had in past elections; these were familiar faces who had failed before, and were likely to fail again, but hope springs eternal in the minds of such egomaniacs. Much more interesting were the newbies: a trio of young, progressive liberals. They shared common themes; that the Democratic Party was filled with old white guys who needed to retire; that the nation needed a socialist base where government was the answer for every question, and that big business must be punished at all costs. Add to this a sprinkle of eco-alarmism, and their platform was the ideal talking point for mainstream media, who embraced these candidates and their ideals with open arms.

Another name had begun circulating in the early days of primary season; would George Burton come out of retirement to make a run? This rumor had actually been quietly planted by Kunis's people. Burton was tracked down and questioned over the issue. "Vice President Burton, we understand that you are contemplating a run for the presidency?" was a typical query.

"What? I don't know who told you this, but that idea couldn't be further from my mind. I'm happily retired and enjoying my wife, Maria's, company."

Interestingly, Maria was the name of his sister; his wife was called

Martha. No matter, Burton firmly denied any plans for candidacy, and his possible candidacy was thus squashed for now. In this matter at least, he was being truly honest. Following his dinner at Eleven Mad with Kunis in New York, Peter Ludwig had met with Burton several times, but he had always avoided raising the possibility of a presidential run. Every meeting with George convinced Peter more and more that Burton would be a disastrous choice. The man was old, white, and distracted. He'd expressed such views to Milos on more than one occasion, and Kunis had taken his comments with a nod. "Thank you for the update, Peter," he would say. "I appreciate your candor. Time will tell if we need to revisit this topic."

The furthest-left of the unholy trinity of young progressive candidates soon became the media's favorite: Shawanda Durelle was a first-term congresswoman from San Francisco. She had blown up the House of Representatives by teaming up with other radicals and was informally leading this group in open defiance of the Speaker. This group of young women had quickly been named "the Mob," and they soon became a thorn in the side of the Democratic Party in general. All were first-time representatives who'd been elected by wide margins in targeted districts. A shady PAC had bankrolled their campaigns, and each candidate had been picked solely on the basis of their radical views. It was as if the PAC was deliberately aiming to disrupt the establishment, and indeed, they were. When you are a globalist who believes that big government is the key to control, progressive views fit perfectly with yours. Get more social programs, get more dependency on government, and presto, a compliant populace! Furthermore, when a nation is tightly controlled by a small body of people called "government," there are fewer people to influence or coerce when things need "changing" to suit your goals. The PAC's work had Kunis's signature all over it.

Shawanda was a master of social media, being young enough to have grown up using it as an everyday tool and not as a novelty. She would regularly stream videos of her off-the-wall viewpoints. "So, here I am in my kitchen, and if you look at the vegetables that I'm chopping" pans phone camera down to show the vegetables," you can see in them the sacrifices and backbreaking work that poor, undocumented laborers have poured into their production. We are living in an oppressive regime where big business controls every part of our lives—even these vegetables. It's time to put the power back into the hands of the people. Our House Speaker *must* introduce legislation to help the poor and undocumented. Give them the money and support they need! Take the money from the billionaires and redistribute it to our oppressed minorities!"

The irony that she had been elected with the help of one of those very billionaires who she detested so much was completely lost on Shawanda; not for her the reality of life, her mission was change, change, change. Let us take care of you—the government is your friend! Such a view resonates with a chunk of our population, specifically the young, broke millennials and post-millennials who have entered adult life woefully unprepared for its realities. This demograph is burdened with student debt, hold degrees that typically have no practical means of monetizing into a career, and have grown up with the sure knowledge that the world was dying because of old people's mismanagement of the earth. The one thing this part of society has, however, is a loud voice. When you work in a lousy, boring job, any chance for excitement is quickly snatched up. Demonstrations, marches, rioting, all these things break up the routine, and if only for a while, they make you feel better, that you are making a difference. Shawanda is our mouthpiece, she has the power to change things, and we can help her win! No surprise that initial polling gave her a solid place in the pecking order.

Overseeing the party's motley crew of hopefuls, Stacey was settling, if a little uneasily, into her new role as DNC boss. Her job description could be easily summed up: strategy and money. Her strategic role was to guide candidates through the election process in a manner that was compatible with the party's goals and ideals.

Of course, to truly be effective at this, a bucketload of money was required for national and targeted local advertising and candidate support.

One additional item on her job description was shepherding the introduction of "VoteNow!" The newly developed software had been designed for collecting, collating, and presenting primary votes and caucus results. On a typically cold and miserable day in DC, she convened a three-day workshop to review the status of the package and launch it across the party. Developers, key DNC members, and selected electors from several states all were in attendance to hear about this new miracle app that would ensure swift and accurate presentation of the primary results. It was a productive time, and in wrapping up the workshop, Stacey even felt a little bit of pride for a job well done.

Some weeks later, she was enjoying a one-on-one dinner at Annabelle with Milos.

"My dear, how are you settling into your new role?" Milos asked following their initial small talk.

"Well, Milos, I'm still feeling like it's a job way below my pay grade, but the voting app workshop went well. At least that was a few days of doing something real." Stacey ordered another Blanton's.

"I heard that it went well. The attendees seemed pleased with the outcome, and that's important; it won't be too long before we'll be using it in our first primary contests. These things are always quite messy, such a needless mix of pledges and votes. Anything to simplify them will be of great value. Any issues come up?" Milos asked.

"No, Milos, things went well. So, what are your thoughts on our candidate pool?" Stacey was seeking the sage wisdom of Kunis. "I must say, I'm not particularly impressed; they're a strange mix of radicals and oldies, at least 'Bedtime Burton' doesn't look to be joining the race, which is a good thing."

"Bedtime Burton?" Milos exclaimed, "I have not heard this nickname before. Why so?"

"Ha! In the old days, it was because he was always trying to drag you into bed, but now it's more like he just wants to go to bed and sleep!" Stacey laughed out loud at her own description of the VP. "Tell me, Milos, I heard from Peter that you were quite serious about getting George on the ticket. That can't be true surely?"

Milos was happy to expound a little on this topic. "Well, Stacey, he would be far from an ideal candidate, but you only have to look around at the present field to realize that none of them have any chance of beating Suit. In today's polarized environment, perhaps a safe pair of hands would be the best choice?"

The dinner and conversation went on until they had to part ways. As Kunis waited for his limo to appear, Stacey opined that she'd walk home; her place was close, after all. "Good night, Milos." She kissed him lightly on the cheek.

"And to you, my dear. Keep up the good work." Milos's eyes were searching for the car, and Stacey felt a little awkward about leaving before his vehicle arrived.

They stood quietly for some moments, and then she said, "Oh, you know there was one small wrinkle at the workshop. Some New York Jewboy software developer brought it up under any other business at the close of the workshop. He said that there seemed to be an embedded algorithm in the code that no one could figure out the purpose of. All the other geeks seemed totally uninterested in his point, so it got dropped. Weird, huh?"

The limousine drew up to the curb.

"Well, good night again." They two parted ways.

For a fleeting moment every four years, Iowa becomes of interest to the nation. The first primary has been held in this state for the past fifty years, and all participants maximize their fifteen minutes of fame accordingly. So it was this time, as Democratic hopefuls began their rituals of town halls, breakfast meetings, and pretending to be nice to the Iowan hicks. "You are the salt of the earth," "the very heart of our nation," "the real America," etc. Anyone with brains can quickly see that, especially in the case of the Democrats, this is all hot air, empty rhetoric. Blue districts are usually urban areas, not the rural communities that make up most of Middle America. Why is that? Well, most country people are independent, not relying on handouts but, in times of trouble, preferring to find their own solutions. This is antithetical to the Democratic credo that government will take care of you: "No thanks, we can take care of ourselves." Nevertheless, Iowa and the like are important for elections because votes are votes. Plus, a good win at this first primary can be parlayed into continued success.

Ron had effectively preempted the Democrats by commencing a series of "I Love America" rallies across the Midwest, focused strategically on swing states, but also timed to take the wind out of the sails of any Democrat rally. He was essentially taking his *Daily Briefing* show on the road, presenting a feel-good atmosphere with a mix of politics and ad-libbed brain dumps. This format reached out to potential supporters, propped up his base, and maybe most importantly, allowed him to bypass the biased mainstream media and send his message directly to the people. Attendance at the rallies was big; adherents and curious alike would line up for hours, waiting to get into the invariably packed arenas.

At first, the left's media machine covered such events, passing them off as cult gatherings or decrying the morons who attended, but they quickly changed from looking-down-their-nose reporting to ignoring them completely when it was obvious that turnout for Ron's events far exceeded that for even the most popular Democrat candidates. Their focus turned exclusively to the left's runners. As expected, AM radio and a certain cable news station did the opposite, covering every "I Love America" rally in adoring detail while demeaning and criticizing the Democrat candidates' every word. It was business as usual on both sides.

Stacey spent time in Iowa, getting VoteNow! ready for its first, albeit small, test. Thankfully, this time around, she did not have to interact with the locals too much, letting her assistants take the brunt of that.

Meanwhile, Shawanda Durelle had taken a leaf out of Ron's old playbook and was concentrating somewhat on Ames. This was a smart move; she was well aware of her special appeal among the younger crowd and could therefore easily mobilize a big following in this university town. Her campaign team established this model throughout its primary push: get crowds of young, restless folk to work their asses off for free and spread the gospel of Shawanda with a zeal that was truly awe-inspiring. No moderate voters for them. Primaries would be won by massive enthusiasm and carpet-bombing tactics, and for this, who better that a bunch of unpaid zealots?

The day of the quirky Iowa caucus arrived. No trip to a voting station to cast a ballot for Iowans. No, these folks gathered in churches, town halls, libraries, and houses across the state to speechify and cajole others into picking their preferred candidate. A painful series of counts are made. Each round realigns the count and makes "committeds" into "uncommitteds" and vice versa until finally, when all are on the point of exhaustion (or boredom), a final count is taken.

Some have described the Iowa caucus as quaint, but most call it a hot mess, full of errors and often managed by partisans who can skew outcomes to their preference. However, with VoteNow!, the plan was to keep the quirkiness while having a comprehensible outcome. At all the gatherings across the state, key people had been trained in its use, and expectations were high that, for once, there would be clear, collated results quickly delivered that would not be endlessly challenged by the losing candidates. Alas, it was not to be; trying to get septuagenarians to understand the workings of smartphones and laptops was a daunting and ultimately impossible task.

As Stacey sat in Campaign HQ in Des Moines, it quickly became apparent that things were not going well. "Goddam it," she yelled to no one in particular. "It was perfect at the workshop. What in hell is happening?"

Back in DC, members of the PFA huddled around a desktop, peering intently at the screen. "We keep losing the link," said the frustrated man sat at the keyboard.

"Shit!" Peter Ludwig said.

Each time they were almost in, the screen would freeze.

"This is not a very auspicious debut." Kunis had been invited to witness the first use of VoteNow! His secure mobile rang.

Stacey said, "Fuck, Milos! What are you doing back there? The whole fucking system keeps crashing. People here are getting pretty pissed off, and I'm looking like a goddam idiot!"

"My dear, I understand, but each time we go in to massage the numbers, there is a micro-interruption of our signal, and this locks up the program. I assure you that we are working hard to resolve this."

The man at the keyboard said, "That's it—it's crashed.'

"Stacey, unfortunately I think we need to end this trial. Agreed?" Milos was looking over at Ludwig when asking this.

Ludwig nodded dejectedly.

"You need to instruct everyone to use the backup paper counts, and I'm afraid we'll just have to see where the chips fall."

Stacey hung up, passed on the instruction to go "paper," and closed the door to her office.

In DC, the tech gurus were at a loss to figure out what had gone wrong. After hours of running diagnostics, they concluded that the firm that had installed the high-speed fiber-optic line specifically for the VoteNow! hub had been shoddy, hence the repeated breaking off of connectivity. It was a company run by friends of Fatima's who had assured them they knew what they were doing.

"We live and learn," Ludwig said, trying to hide how pissed he was with his wife and her useless pals.

Status quo was maintained; the Iowa caucus was its usual chaotic mess, and the media had a field day. "Crash and Burn" was the New York post's headline with a story below that compared VoteNow!'s launch with the horrendous website introduction that Ludwig's administration had launched for its "socialist" health care initiative (also developed by Fatima's friends).

The *New York Times* and others downplayed the entire fiasco, citing "teething troubles for the new process." Almost as much was written about VoteNow! as was about the primary's landslide winner; Shawanda Durelle had taken more pledges than the other candidates combined. Apparently, these Midwestern farmers had a real taste for radical-left policies—or perhaps Shawanda's strategy and planning had simply been vastly superior to her opponents?

The decisive victory by such a radical was cause for great concern among the PFA and the Group. Oh sure, her ideals fit perfectly with theirs—total government control and dependence—but a giant question hung over her. Could she beat Suit?

Ludwig and Kunis were in agreement; she could not.

❧

Back at the café, Sue was enjoying a bit of a gloat at Maury's expense. "I'm sure it wasn't your fault, Maury, but it looked like a real shitshow with your software."

Maury squirmed a little. He had closely followed the first use of VoteNow! and was horrified when it failed so completely and so publicly. "I just don't get it, Sue. The workshop was perfect, and then it all goes poof? I wonder if it was that weird algorithm hidden in the program. I brought it up at the workshop, but no one seemed interested. Maybe it had something to do with the crash, who knows?"

"So, how was Mrs. Stacey Lincoln? Did you get to meet her? Talk to her?" Sue was trying to steer the conversation away from the software disaster, which was obviously a touchy subject for Maury.

"She seemed nice. She ran the workshop well, very professionally, although she was a bit testy at times." Maury drained his coffee cup and stood to leave. "Ciao. Probably see you tomorrow."

Sue went about her day, dealing with the steady trickle of regulars and tourists visiting the Meatpacking District. At the end of her shift, she strolled along to Brass Monkey, her favorite local bar. Sitting at the regular place, she ordered her usual draft IPA and began chatting with Lou, the bartender, which had been an almost-daily ritual for Sue since moving to the neighborhood. It was one of the things she loved about the area; in the middle of a giant megapolis, it was like a small town down here, insulated from the rest of Manhattan and full of quirky places and people. As she sipped her beer, Sue stared idly at the big TV behind the bar, alternating between that screen and her phone.

"Breaking news here on Fox Five," the reporter announced.

Sue was scrolling through her Facebook page as she sipped the IPA.

"Yes, Michelle, I'm here just below the High Line, close to the Whitney Museum, where a man has been shot in what looks like a robbery gone wrong."

Sue began to pay attention now; that location wasn't far from the bar.

"Witnesses reported seeing a masked gunman approach the victim and engage in a short conversation before shooting him in the chest at point-blank range. The gunman then rifled through the victim's pockets before running off to a waiting car that quickly left the scene. Police have informed us that the victim was deceased at the scene. They have identified him as twenty-nine-year-old Maury Helzburg, a computer specialist and software developer who lived not far from the crime scene. We'll update you with more information as we receive it. Back to you, Michelle."

Sue stared agape at the screen. Tears began to roll down her cheeks as she softly muttered, "No, not you, Maury?"

"You okay, Sue?" Lou asked when he noticed her wet cheeks.

"No, Lou. No, I'm not." She ordered a double tequila shot.

WHITE KNIGHT TO THE RESCUE

ollowing Iowa, the rest of the month had a hundred more delegate votes to offer in New Hampshire, Nevada and, most importantly, South Carolina. Whoever took the lead in these early stages would surely go into Super Tuesday with a huge advantage. This was the window when the deadbeats, also-rans, and fringe candidates would begin dropping out of the race. Come the end of March, the chosen candidate was oftentimes obvious.

Shawanda was looking strong going into New Hampshire, which was giving the Group and the PFA ulcers.

"We've no chance of getting a new candidate on the ticket in time for the next primary, but maybe Nevada is doable?" Ludwig said.

VP Burton was urgently summoned to the PFA war room.

Kunis said, "George, you've seen where the party will head if we don't intervene. It's going radically left, and this is not a winnable situation. We need a moderate who can bring us back to center. That's the only way to beat Suit." He was sweet-talking Burton with the aim of getting him to declare his candidacy.

George was, as always, reluctant to reenter the political world. Deep down, he knew that the country was doing well under Suit; he'd be a tough nut to crack. Besides, he was tired of the nonstop give-and-take of an election campaign. Would he be able to stay the course? Plus, a life spent in DC meant that George had many skeletons buried; if any of them were unearthed, it would be bad news for him and his party.

"Gentlemen, I'm flattered that you think I'm the man to beat Suit, but I truly don't see how that's possible in the real world. I mean, the party has tried to impeach the man twice now, and he comes up smelling like a rose. He's like Ronald was, made of Teflon, nothing sticks to the man. Besides, who's to say I'd even get the DNC candidacy, coming into the race so late in the game?"

Stacey joined Peter and Milos, and three of them outlined their strategy for the coming weeks and months. It took a couple of hours to wear him down, but George finally caved to the pressure and said he'd be willing to give it a go.

"You've made the right decision, George. With our team and the tricks we have up our sleeves, there's a strong chance of kicking that bum out in November." Ludwig cradled Burton's shoulder as he talked.

Stacey and Milos looked relieved.

"Well, I'm up for it if you are, Peter." George began to walk out to his waiting vehicle. As he climbed into the back seat, he turned to the three of them and said, "Let's do this thing! Goodbye, Peter, goodbye Minos, and of course, goodbye Sally."

The SUV drove out of the mansion, and the three stood on the doorstep, looking at each other with puzzled faces.

Using the media might of the Group, headlines across the country began shouting "Burton Declares!" If you only read and watched the mainstream news, you would assume that this old man was the beloved savior of the nation, a man who could oust the corrupt Suit and return the country to business as usual. What had been a nondescript eight years as vice president magically became, at least in the eyes of the left, a golden age of politics when the Ludwig-Burton team transformed America into a haven for the oppressed, and where the USA's world standing had been elevated to that of guardian of the earth. The various scandals that had occurred throughout their time in office were quietly swept under the carpet—to be replaced with a sanitized version of history where Burton was a champion of women, a man who reviled callous big business, and was surely the best pick to bring the nation back from the brink.

Buried amongst all the pro-Burton coverage were occasional brief pieces about a mysterious sickness that was beginning to permeate the Western world. Its origins were almost certainly in China, hence the various disparaging nicknames of Kung Flu Sicken, Chinese Flu, or Mao Sick Lung.

General public awareness of it only became apparent when President Suit implemented travel bans for Chinese and Europeans. Of course, the media jumped all over this, citing it as an excuse for Suit to exercise his xenophobia and expand his policy of racism.

Meanwhile, the rebellious "Live Free or Die!" folk of New Hampshire were becoming the center of attention. The next primary was to be held there, and candidates with their entourages flocked to the Granite State to woo the populace. Thanks to its lax ballot access laws, the PFA, working in conjunction with Stacey and the DNC, had managed to get Burton on the ballot. How would George perform against the large field of rivals? The team knew the answer to that already. Besides being an easy place to get on the ballot, the Granite State is also a user of electronic voting, and Stacey's team had been diligently working to blend VoteNow! with the state's "Accuvote" system (unbeknownst to the world at large of course).

⟳⟲

Ron couldn't resist the opportunity to do a bit of Granite State campaigning of his own while poking a stick at the Dems. He arranged for a rally to be held in Manchester in the week of the primary. As with all his rallies, it was essentially the *Daily Briefing* on the road, and massive crowds flocked to the SNHU Arena, filling it with eighteen thousand adoring souls.

Over on the Democrat side, Shawanda was pulling in crowds too. Although not anywhere near as big as Suit's, she nonetheless had a dedicated and crowing following, mostly younger. Poor old George, however, was giving speeches in echoing empty rooms, a few dozen here, a score there, interest in his reemergence had been touted by the media, but reality was showing a severe lack of interest in the man. Perhaps this was a good thing? Every time Burton rose to speak, his handlers tensed, waiting and wondering what in hell might come out of his mouth. Despite their best efforts to groom George for his new role as leading candidate for the presidency, the members of his election team could never guarantee that he'd stay on message—or that he wouldn't just plain screw up. It was as if he was distracted, his mind elsewhere. And so it was thus, Shawanda's speeches typically went as follows;

"People, elections come, and elections go, but the revolution to transform our society never ends. Every day, every week, every month, I am fighting to build an America of social and economic equality. Our revolutionary movement is about civil rights, it's about trade unions, it's about women's rights, it's about LGBTQ rights, it's about the environment, and more than ever, it's about bringing down the capitalists and billionaires who have shaped our society to their benefit for far too long! Now, this revolution cannot just be fought by those at the top. No, it has to occur from the bottom up—from the millions of voters who want the same kind of change that I do. We aren't fringe voters, we aren't radicals, we aren't progressives. We are the people! And we can change America for the better!" She continued to list everything that was wrong in the USA and how her supporters were in the process of rectifying so many things. With president Durelle, there would be no more injustice; everyone, legal or illegal, would enjoy generous government support and aid. Student debt would be erased, health care would be handed out to anyone who needed it, and all of this would be funded by enforcing punitive taxes on the 1 percent, those selfish evildoers who thought only of themselves. "This campaign is about defeating president Ronald Suit, but that cannot be our only goal. We need to continue our bottom-up, grassroots effort to transform the country, and we must take that energy to Philadelphia at the Democratic National Convention and win the nomination! I want to conclude by thanking everyone who has participated in this campaign. Keep it up! The fight will go on. We must ensure that historians will look back on this election and see the point where the United States halted its descent into oligarchy and became a government that represents all people. Thank you and good night."

Heady stuff. Ron's Rally was different, a perfect example of compare and contrast:

"Hello, America! Well, here we are again, heading into an election, an election that will decide whether our country continues on its return to greatness, or if it will begin to transform into a socialist regime of oppressive regulation and high taxes. I know what I want—how about y'all?"

The packed arena exploded with cheers of a supportive crowd.

Ron went on to list of his administration's accomplishments: historically low unemployment, deregulation that had unleashed an economic boom, appointment of conservative constitutionalists to the courts, and implementation of efforts to stem the flow of illegal immigrants into the country.

"And you know, we've done all of this while being the most scrutinized and investigated government in history. No administration has had to work under the constant threat of impeachment, and no administration has had to work with so many rats and traitors hiding in its midst, yet no administration has achieved so much! Just think what we could do if our opponents started thinking about the best way to help our nation instead of the best way to get rid of the president? Finally, y'all know that I'm a lover of borders; we cannot have a country if we don't have borders. You'll have seen that I recently closed these borders to many of our foreign friends. If you're from Asia or Europe, you'll not be able to come here for a month. I've gotten a lot of flak from all sides over my decision, but let me tell you, it's better to be safe than sorry. The strange illness that appears to be spreading around the globe might not be anything, but the scientists within our government have got me sufficiently cautious that I've closed our borders, at least until we have more information." Suit ended the Rally and did his usual slow walk through the crowds, stopping to chat or pose as he worked his way out of the arena.

So many pundits continued to bash Suit for his racist decision to ban foreigners, but a certain member of his opposition was quietly surprised by his apparent foresight—he knew what was coming.

Meanwhile, in a mostly empty hall in Concord, George Burton was about to address his audience. News reporters and cameras almost outnumbered the attendees.

"Well, I'd hoped for more, but I guess you'll have to do." He grinned down at the people, obviously pleased with his little quip.

The audience were not amused, and a few of them got up to leave.

"Hey, don't go!" George yelled. "I need all the bodies I can get! Anyway, where was I? Our country is divided. This incumbent has managed to turn our great nation into a place of haves and have-nots, a land of the privileged where the rich folks do what they like, and the rest of us struggle to survive. Now, you know me. You know George Burton. I've spent my life helping America. During President Ludwig's time in office, we were a safe pair of hands that kept things in order. There were no scandals, and there was no division—just stability and a happy country. Let's get back to that time, to stability. We've had enough of divisiveness, enough of some talk show host pretending to be a president."

George continued talking, hitting his policy topics that walked a fine line between a moderate agenda that would suit his base and a progressive strategy that was hoped would attract new voters.

As he began to wrap up, his handlers let out a collective sigh of relief that things had gone okay.

"So, I just want to thank you all for listening to me today, and I hope that I've earned your vote." He paused to look around the room. "I'm George Burton, and I want to be your senator of the great state of Vermont!" George walked triumphantly off the stage while a bemused audience sat in stunned silence.

The collective sigh of his team morphed into a collective "What the fuck?"

Ludwig, Lincoln, and Kunis had to be discrete and subtle in their VoteNow! Manipulations. They spent a lot of time discussing what would be a good New Hampshire outcome for George that wouldn't raise suspicions or concerns about the results. It was a difficult choice, but the morning after the vote, news outlets reported how the Democratic election had now turned into a two-horse race: Durelle versus Burton. Talking heads generally went along the lines. "Despite a late entry into the race, VP George Burton showed that he is a contender. While progressive candidate Shawanda Durelle claimed victory in the Granite State, Burton ran a close second, indicating that the people want a moderate in the White House." No mention was made that, even though he was the only name on the Republican ticket, Ron had a massive turnout, just as he had in Iowa. His base was as solid as ever, and indications were that it was growing.

The Burton team was planning next steps. "We've got Nevada coming up and then the biggie: South Carolina. Time to start racking up wins."

The only fly in the ointment, however, was George himself. To be convincing, particularly in the upcoming Democratic debates, Burton needed much more coaching and—it was agreed—a means of controlling his wayward mind.

"So, here you are, George." Ludwig handed him a tiny earpiece. "You put this in your ear, and we can feed you answers—or help when you get stuck on any issue."

"You really think I need this? I've been doing pretty good without it," George replied.

The team collectively rolled their eyes.

"George, it's a heavy schedule. There's Nevada, and South Carolina, with all the debates coming up as well, plus a ton of media interviews. Any advantage is worth it—surely you know that?"

Their eight years together had taught George one thing—that Peter knew what he was doing—and he reluctantly acquiesced, placing the device in his ear.

"Don't worry, if anyone spots it, you can say it's a hearing aid," a tech remarked as they tested it out.

❧

Back at the White House, Ron had assembled a working group to evaluate the threat of the Chinese virus. It was a tough task; each day brought differing data and contradicting anecdotal information. He had to place reliance on the scientists within NIH and CDC, mostly career bureaucrats, mixed in with several Ludwig appointees. All assured Ron that the threat level was low; had he overreacted by placing travel bans?

Dr. Alan Giovanni, CDC's leading virologist, said, "Mr. President, the World Health Organization is on record as saying transmissibility is low, and outbreak locations are limited. Of course, we should prepare, but making too much of this virus could be unsettling to the public, caution is the watchword here, I think."

The president was uneasy in this new challenge; he had not signed up to be a potential overseer of a catastrophic illness. His only way forward was to place faith in the experts. "Okay Alan, we currently have cases at two main locations: New York and Seattle. Both of these places are common ports of entry for lots of Asians, and that's why I put the travel ban in place. It looks like this sickness has been around since Christmas, but it is now on a bit of a roll—not just here but over in Europe too. Do we have any treatments or cures?"

"Sorry, Mr. President. It's a variant of a common corona-type virus that we've seen many times in the past: SARS, MERS, bird flu, they've all been coronaviruses. The difference with this one is that it has double hooks, as we call them, and that's the way the virus attaches itself in the body. Now, because of this double-hook feature, it makes it essentially twice as hard to get rid of. But I repeat, the WHO is advising that it has low transmissibility, so that is a benefit. My recommendation would be to maintain vigilance, tell the public about this sickness in a unsensational manner, and watch where it takes us."

"So, no preparations then?" asked Ron. This didn't seem right to him. After all, his stated reasoning for the travel ban was "better safe than sorry." Shouldn't that also apply to the administration's response? "Let's at least make inventory of our emergency pandemic response equipment and see where we stand."

The feedback from this request was not going to be welcome.

A CHRISTMAS PRESENT

In the months before the end of the year, Milos had become increasingly uneasy about the Democrats' prospects in the coming year's elections. It was apparent to him that the field of possible candidates was either too weak or too radical to go against Suit, but more importantly, the president's track record was unassailable. Anyone who wanted to work could work, and consequently, entitlements were way down. Americans were becoming independent, thinking for themselves, which was not a good model for Kunis's ideal for a big government; free thinkers are harder to manipulate.

At a more personal level, Milos was fuming over the US-China relationship. Since his declaration of plans to dismantle and renegotiate existing trade deals worldwide, Suit had focused on China and had attacked the issue with gusto. He had had some measure of success too, with several American companies repatriating their manufacturing capabilities back to America.

On the advice of his financial team, Suit had weaponized tariffs, not just against China, but against any country that was deemed to have an unfair advantage in trade. Kunis could see the consequences of these actions in the performance of his portfolio, particularly the Asian assets. Over the course of the past several years, Milos had expanded into China with a vengeance, acquiring companies at what he considered to be very favorable prices. The Chinese model, however, never allows for outright foreign ownership, and consequently, Milos had many Chinese partners, influential people high up in the Chinese Communist Party, which controls every aspect of its population's life. Biotech, manufacturing, information technology, and all areas of industry were now in Kunis's realm. It was inevitable that he would become an advisor to the party, and its senior members soon came to rely on his counsel, feeling that he was offering an insight to the American mind-set.

The results of Ron's aggressive attacks on Chinese trade had been painful for the United States—but even more so for China. When he placed safeguards against Chinese steel dumping, they placed restrictions on grain imports, and so on. The American response was always more severe than the Chinese. It was a high-stakes standoff; who would blink first? The Chinese did. They proposed to hold talks to end the trade war, and after extensive negotiations, a new, more balanced agreement was reached. Ron's team always questioned the communists' sincerity in abiding by the new deal, but nonetheless, it had seemed like a great outcome for America.

It was during this time of the regime losing face that Kunis began his big play: a bold plan to set back the Americans on their heels and restore China and its leaders to their rightful place in the world as leaders of the new age. The idea had been brewing and developing in Milos's mind for some time. It was risky and even dangerous, but to him, that made it even more exciting, a potential masterstroke that would cement his place as the world's greatest influencer. He kept it entirely to himself, deeming it far too outlandish to be confided in anyone else. Milos recognized that implementation of his big plan would create massive business opportunities for him; imagine being the only person who could effectively see the future? He could dominate commerce!

"You see, Mr. Chairman, with today's DNA sequencing and

CRISPR technology, it's possible to tailor bacteriological and virological weapons for almost any desired purpose." Milos was walking through lush private gardens in Beijing, explaining his plan to one-up the Americans and restore China on the road to its destiny as the most important world economy. "Several of my companies here have been involved heavily in bio-weaponry research. A virus might be tailored to focus on Caucasians, or Asians, or any distinct race. Of course, when developing such a tool, it is also possible to simultaneously develop vaccines for the virus. Imagine a scenario where the US is beset with a nationwide sickness; it would be of great use to your party, would it not? Their economy would be crippled, and they would become highly dependent on China's manufacturing capacity during the crisis—and of course, it would be the American president's downfall."

"Mr. Kunis," replied the chairman, "what would prevent this weapon, if it was to be developed, from spreading outside of the United States?"

"Collateral damage, Mr. Chairman." Kunis was exhibiting his pathological nature quite openly. "It would be unfortunate, of course, but should that happen, then as with the American downfall, there would be tremendous opportunities for your country and myself, wealth and power-wise."

"And how deadly is this malady? What casualty count would be likely?" The chairman was warming to the idea.

"Sir, it would be similar to the SARS outbreak of 2002. In fact, it was that specific coronavirus that was used to develop this tailored version. Symptoms will vary from nothing, or asymptomatic, through mild sickness, severe respiratory distress, and for perhaps one in one hundred, death. Of course, the impact for those of Asian descent would be notably less."

"This is an interesting suggestion you have brought me, Mr. Kunis." They were entering a dining room where Milos had been invited for a banquet. "We should discuss this further."

In early December, teams of representatives from many of Milos's Chinese companies were dispatched to a Kunis Holdings Group conference to be held in New York City. Some flew via the Eastern Russian route, some via the Pacific, entering the US at Seattle or San Francisco. Things went smoothly enough, the trip from the corporate offices in China passed unnoticed, just another business activity for the Chinese biotech behemoths that Kunis owned.

Close observers may have noticed one unusual issue about the conference attendees; although the majority of the travelers were asymptomatic, some employees had varying degrees of flulike symptoms, but it was that time of year after all. One thing was certain: none of them had any idea that they'd been infected prior to their departure. And so, the bespoke coronavirus began its journey around the world.

There was no single "Patient One" but simultaneously hundreds upon hundreds of them. From its origins in a Level Four laboratory in central China, courtesy of commercial airlines, the virus arrived at every stopover and layover along the travelers' routes. Some spent a long weekend in Italy or London, where many of their family members were working in textiles or finance; some passed through Korea or Singapore en route, where the virus was far less effective, having mostly only Asian hosts to attack.

Over the course of several days, the staff members finally gathered in New York for their conference, their unwitting mission now successfully fulfilled. There was of course massive exposure in NYC during the conference, but at each and every stop prior to their arrival, the carriers had spread their insidious infection. Anyone who encountered these people almost certainly received a dose of the coronavirus and then took it with them wherever they were heading.

The transmission of infection grew silently and exponentially. Inevitably, infections broke out in the city where the virus had been developed, but because of its genetically engineered "friendliness" toward Asian DNA, the breakout was a more manageable affair, made easier by the Chinese authorities' ability to impose draconian shelter-in-place tactics.

By the middle of January, about a month after the workers had taken their trip to America, the coronavirus was making news in many countries around the world. The strange new infection seemed difficult to pin down, but it had severe outcomes for certain parts of the population.

Milos's bold strategy was in play across the globe.

EARLY DAYS

I n the White House, Ned Odom had some good news to share
with the president. "Mr. President, you have one less lawsuit to
worry about. Our friend Nick Ferrari has been found guilty of
extortion and will be spending the next twenty-something years
enjoying Rikers."

"Damn! Awesome, Ned!" Ron was pleased. Although this had
been a minor thorn in his side, he'd take a win on anything these
days. "How about Miss Moistly?"

"Well, sir, she claims that it was Ferrari who made up all the
accusations. She has no plans or interest in pursuing the lawsuit
going forward." Odom didn't mention that some of his men had
quietly taken Misty to one side and recommended that she should
let things drop unless she wanted an ongoing investigation into her
relationship with Ferrari as a possible accomplice in the extortion
case.

"While you're here, Ned, can you give me a briefing about the
impeachment investigation?" Ron was still seething over the fake
story of his collusion with Russia and his supposed bribery of the
Ukrainian president. He was anxious to hear of progress in the DoJ's
current investigations.

"Sir, it's an ongoing investigation as you know." Odom was

reluctant to discuss such topics until he'd gotten all of the evidence and had a slam-dunk case to present. "But I can tell you this: it has the PFA's prints all over it. If we want to talk collusion, we can talk about Ludwig colluding with certain members of Congress to push through phony impeachments. We can talk about several members of our government, including some in my own department, outright lying in order to cover up their duplicitous activities. The investigation is ongoing, sir, and I'm hopeful for a positive outcome."

The two parted, and Ron returned to his latest pressing concern: the coronavirus. The news was not promising. Following his instruction to make inventory of all personal protective equipment and other relevant items, the feedback was that the country was woefully lacking and unprepared for a major nationwide sickness. Following some particularly bad recent winters where seasonal flu had killed tens of thousands of Americans, supplies were depleted. To add to the gloomy picture, many face masks, ventilators, and related equipment had been used up in the last SARS crisis, and the previous administration had failed to restock.

Giovanni said, "We should rebuild inventory, Mr. President, but current projections are indicating that this latest outbreak will not be as severe as SARS, so I think you have time to restock."

Shortly after Giovanni's update, Ron was sitting with VP Flowers, and he expressed uncertainty over what course of action to take on this possible viral threat. "It's seems to be hitting some parts of Europe pretty hard, yet we've got next to nothing here so far. All our *experts* are contradicting each other—it's dangerous, but don't worry about it; it could become a pandemic, but might not be worse than a typical flu season. And so on. What do you think, Joyce?"

"Well, Mr. President, we both know that our intelligence agencies are, how can I put it, compromised, given their performance during the impeachment nonsense." Joyce paused to look round the room as if to make sure that no one else was listening. She leaned in close to the president and whispered, "But I've heard rumors of some intercepted chatter coming out of China that mentions phrases like 'the American Plague' and 'a present for the USA.' We know from work being done over in Europe that it's highly likely this virus originated in the Far East as they always do, so, to turn your own phrase against you, better safe than sorry?"

Ron was pissed. "Why aren't our own damn intelligence agencies being more open about things if they've heard this chatter? It's the same old crap, Joyce. They work for themselves, or for Ludwig, but never for us!" Ron started pacing around the room. "We need to get firm recommendations from Giovanni and his crew—and act on them. I'm no goddam medical expert—let's get the folks who are off their asses and earning their salaries."

So, in early February, as Democratic hopefuls crisscrossed the nation on their quest for the presidency, Ron addressed the country via his nightly televised briefing. "People, you'll know that I recently imposed travel and border restrictions with certain countries in order to mitigate the sickness that's become known as the coronavirus. So far, there's only been a handful of cases in our country, but by looking across the ocean to Europe, it seems like there could be some risk of an uptick here in America. We've therefore taken action; our supplies of personal protective equipment are being replenished as we speak. More importantly, I've established a Corona Strike Force. This team is made up of our government's leading experts in their fields. They're currently writing guidelines for the path forward, and these will be circulated to our state governors over the next few days. Folks, we live in a federal republic, so it's only right that each state formulates its own plan of response, using our guidelines as the basis of their work. Our nation is huge—over three hundred and twenty million citizens and almost four million square miles. Each one of our fifty states will have different needs and will be affected by this virus differently, if at all. A centralized response doesn't make sense." Ron moved over to a couch. "Now, to elaborate on my remarks, I've asked Dr. Alan Giovanni to join me tonight. Doc Alan is with our National Institute of Health and is considered to be one of the world's leading experts in bacteria and viruses."

The rest of the program was spent discussing what was known, what was unknown, and what the country's response might be. Throughout the talk, both Suit and Giovanni downplayed the possible seriousness of the viral threat, but some viewers were left thinking, *If it's not bad, why are they even talking about it?* In the midst of primaries and so many other recent or ongoing crises, some sort of flu was not high on the priority list of most Americans.

⚜

"Look, Martha, this president is totally unqualified—and it's shown in everything he's done since coming to office." Veep Burton was being interviewed on one of the Sunday morning talk shows. His recent "bionic ear" implant seemed to be functioning well; Burton's election team had been briefed in what questions he would be asked and were therefore well prepared, feeding responses into his ear whenever George seemed about to falter. "The man has no experience in politics, so he doesn't know how to smooth things over when needed. With him, it's always a fight. When I'm elected, we'll restore civility and normalcy to the office. It's going to be back to the way we successfully ran the country under the last administration."

"Vice President Burton, some are saying that breaking the existing way of governance is exactly what was needed and was why President Suit was elected. What say you?"

The question had been anticipated, but as he was listening to the question, Burton felt an itch in his ear and unwittingly reached up, dislodging the earpiece. He froze, his eyes darting left and right, and without thinking responded, "Goddam it, I can't hear a goddam thing!"

The host said, "Mr. Vice President, I'm sorry, Mr. Vice president, should I speak up?"

George glared at Martha. "'Course I can hear you. What in the hell is going on?" Burton felt obligated to wing it. "Well, Martha, what you said is right. Politics stinks and is corrupt. Washington keeps the electorate in the dark, but they're happy about that. Our citizens don't need to know what goes on in government. The people want to get back to the old ways, and that's what I can offer."

"I'm sorry, Mr. Burton, but that's all we have time for. Thank you for being with us."

George's face faded from screen. As Martha segued into her next segment, her look of puzzlement was clearly visible.

George stormed off the studio floor to meet up with his team in a side office where they'd been feeding him answers. "Jesus, guys, you went dead on me. I had to make shit up." He was pissed. "Lucky for you that I was quick on my feet. I think I gave a good response."

His campaign manager responded, "George, you knocked your earpiece out when you scratched your ear, and I'm not so sure that your answers were that good."

"Bullshit, you stopped talking to me."

The video playback proved otherwise.

Elsewhere that weekend, Shawanda was in full stride. She made the rounds of mainstream political shows and acquitted herself beautifully. Questions were softball and generally gave her a chance to climb on a soapbox to bemoan the terrible state of the nation and how her government would fix everything. Sure, the also-rans made the rounds too, but, ahead of the looming South Carolina primary, it was clearly going to be a two-horse race: radical versus old-school.

On *Face the Nation*, Shawanda said, "Well, Margaret, my main opponent has blanketed the airwaves, but our campaign raised almost $50 million in the past month. That's phenomenal, but how we raised it is more significant. We don't use PACs; all our money is coming from individual contributions. We don't tap billionaire Democrats for cash; we get donations from everywhere. Do you know the average donation to our campaign is about twenty dollars?

Now that's a lot of individuals who believe in me and my vision; it's the working people of America who give, and I'm so proud of that. Margaret, we are living in a time when Americans are sick and tired of the massive income and wealth inequality that exists. People are working minimum wage jobs—ten or twelve hours a day—just to make ends meet. They can't afford health care, they can't afford college, and they can't afford any of the extras that make life bearable. These people want a government that represents them and looks after them. That's why they're donating, and that's why we'll win. Our grassroots base will bring us the nomination, and we will beat Suit in November."

Every interview went the same way: a message of how terrible things are and how government will solve all the problems.

Courtesy of VoteNow!, Burton gained a slight edge in Nevada, and he headed to South Carolina as a credible alternative to Durelle. This next primary was the first state of real significance, accounting for about half the delegates from the first three primaries combined. George was confident; South Carolina was a traditionally heavy black vote state, and George knew he was beloved by African Americans throughout the country. There was actually an element of truth in this. In all his years as a politician. Burton had usually gotten high black voter turnout in any election. Would his track record stand this time around? He visited all the usual places in the days leading up to the primary: the stores, the barbeque joints, the churches, and the businesses.

As he left Nichols Chapel in Charleston, a crowd of admirers were thronged outside. George began pushing through, glad-handing his supporters, posing for selfies, and generally acting the politician. He stopped and said, "Thanks for coming, brother. Is this your church? Where do you work?"

"Yes, sir. This is my church … been coming here all my life. Right now, I'm doing real well … got me a good job making good money."

"That's great. That's great, son," George said. "But let me tell you, when I'm president, you'll do even better."

"Say what!" The guy became agitated. "You never did nothing for me. In all your years in DC, what did you ever do for us? It took Mr. Suit to make a change."

Burton exploded in righteous indignation and got up in the man's face. "What do you mean I never did nothing for you? I don't work for you, you son of a bitch. Now, get out of the goddam way before I punch you in the face." He brusquely pushed the man to one side and stormed off into the back of the SUV. This was all captured on video by the many TV news cameras that were present, but you wouldn't know it. Fox ran a piece on his outburst, but the other networks ignored it, preferring to focus on what a great president Burton would make.

"George, you can't say and do things like that." His campaign manager was reviewing video with him. "That is a bad look for us."

"I know, Bill, but these people talk about how good they've got it under Suit, and it just makes my blood boil. Now, how are we doing in Nevada?"

"George, you won Nevada. This is the South Carolina primary."

"Of course it is, Bill. Of course it is. Sorry."

Stacey and her IT team had once again worked their magic: VoteNow! had been discretely embedded, and the PFA team in the war room back in Washington was primed and ready.

Ludwig said, "Who knows—we might not even need to massage the results. George has always done well in this state."

It was not to be. Shawanda began to pull ahead early, and intervention was required. The following morning, newspapers and TV stations alike declared Burton's great comeback a sure sign that America was not yet ready for the progressive agenda offered by Durelle.

Ludwig met with Kunis; he was worried about George and wanted to express his concerns. "Milos, George is struggling. Even with us in his ear all the time, the man goes off script at the drop of a hat. He's becoming more and more irrational. I'm really worried for him; he might not last through the nomination. Maybe it's time to make overtures to Durelle?"

"Peter, I appreciate your concerns. I too have seen some deterioration in George's cognitive abilities, but let's keep at it a little longer. He is manageable, and thanks to VoteNow!, we've established a narrative for his comeback and ascendancy to the nomination. It would be a shame to abandon our efforts now."

Milos was keen on sticking to the plan.

Ludwig reluctantly agreed to keep handling Burton for another month on the proviso that they'd revisit the plan then—and make some tough decisions if necessary.

Super Tuesday is the biggest single event of the primary season. It's when sixteen states go to the polls, and when well more than a thousand delegates show their preferences. The biggest prize of the day is California—with more than four hundred delegates up for grabs—followed by Texas and Florida with more than two hundred each.

Burton's schedule became even more stressful as he jumped mostly between these three states in the few days available after the Carolina vote.

Shawanda had a crammed schedule, but her relative youth made campaigning an easier task for her. By then, many of the also-rans had dropped out of the race, and as in previous elections, they were now bargaining for some sort of government role in exchange for their paltry pledged delegates. In politics, whether blue or red, it's always about what can you do for me if I do something for you? This point was driven home by one of George's many gaffes while out on the stump. By then, his audiences were larger—and his base was more enthusiastic. During one town hall session, he was asked why money and lobbyists were such big influences in Washington.

"That's a good question, sir." He paced around the middle of a room in Los Angeles, surrounded by the crowd. His team was off to one side in an adjacent office, feeding him answers and hints whenever required via his earpiece. "Say you come to me and say, 'George, I want to give you two hundred fifty thousand dollars for your campaign.'"

"Careful where you go with this, George," they said in his earpiece.

George was on a roll. "So, I say, thank you very much, and that's the end of it. But then a few months later, you come to my office and ask for a favor. Well, of course I'm going to oblige—you've just given me a quarter mil—"

"Jesus, George, you've got to walk that back right now!" the voice in his ear was screeching.

"Err, I mean, I'd help you only if it was a legitimate request. Of course, I wouldn't do anything for you just because you'd given me money." However, the damage was done, George's true colors were on display—if only for a brief moment. As usual, Fox made much of his slip while the other media outlets covered alternate topics.

On another occasion that even the mainstream covered, Burton got into a shouting match with a man who questioned his physical and mental health. "Look, you son of a bitch," he said angrily as he prodded the man's chest with his finger, "I'm not crazy, and I'm in great shape. Let's get down on the floor right here, right now, and do push-ups, huh? You won't, will you? Maybe you want to step outside so I can slap the shit out of you?"

Right-wing news bracketed this event as a clear sign of his worsening dementia. Left- wing news proudly declared that it was "Burton showing that he's tough and has the passion that will carry him to victory."

Shawanda was loving all this; her base was young and enthusiastic, unlike Burton's, many of whom seemed to be attending his events out of morbid curiosity. "What's he going to say or do next?" She stuck to her message of more government equals good, Suit government equals bad—and her crowds grew.

Ron didn't sit on his heels either. As he had previously done, he arranged for strategically timed rallies to deflect from the keynote speeches being given by his rivals. Even though he knew there was a snowball in hell's chance of him winning California, he nevertheless held a huge rally in Fresno. As usual, it was a mix of prepared speech and ad-libbed riffing.

"Did you see old George yesterday?" he asked.

The crowd answered with boos mixed in with chants of "four more years."

"I mean, he got into it with that dear old lady. She asked him about how caucuses work, and he basically called her a liar, didn't he?"

"Four more years. Four more years!"

"What did he call her? A lying dog-faced pony soldier? I mean, what the hell, folks? I really hope he is the Dems' choice 'cause I sure would love to debate him; it would be hilarious, wouldn't it?"

Back in the war room, Ludwig was counting the hours until his deadline with Kunis came. *How could this man be president?*

The tech team had been focusing on California, Texas, and Florida, and they were ready for Super Tuesday. Finally, the day came, and results began coming in. Smaller states voted for Durelle with the exception of North Carolina, while VoteNow! made sure that the important delegate count went in favor of Burton—even though Shawanda had taken California. With Stacey's help and manipulation, things were looking good for George, and the media reinforced this opinion. Shawanda couldn't understand how a crazy old guy could be doing so well? She had suspicions that somehow things were being rigged, but any public opinion about such a touchy subject was out of the question; it would just look like sour grapes. Quietly she instructed her most-trusted campaign aide to do some digging. "I need to know if there's anything crooked going on, Josie. All of our internal polling has me kicking that man's ass, but he somehow pulls off wins when it counts. See what you can find out—please."

The week after Super Tuesday was another multiple-state set of primaries worth more than 350 delegates. Shawanda was hopeful for answers by the time the day came, but she needn't have worried. Events were about to overtake her.

LOCKDOWN

"**A**cting on the advice of our finest medical experts, I am issuing guidelines that encourage our state governors to impose a 'stay-at-home' order for the next several weeks. Now, I know this is unprecedented, and I know that it will be difficult for many of us, but current projections show that as many as two million Americans could be lost to this insidious virus. If it comes close to that number, our health care system will be overwhelmed. So, by asking you all to stay home, the hope is that, while we can't stop the virus, we can at least delay its rate of infection by slowing the spread. Dr. Giovanni calls this 'flattening the curve.' It's his advice that has formed the basis of the CDC's new guidelines. I also want to remind you that Vice President Joyce Flowers is head of the Corona Strike Force. It will be her job to coordinate our government's response to this threat and to keep the public updated. As I've stated before, we live in a federal republic, so each state will tailor its response using the CDC guidelines as a base. I hope that everyone will abide by your governors' requests. Thank you. God bless America."

Ron's address to the nation came as somewhat of a surprise, a much more severe response than some were anticipating. It was now the middle of March. In just a few short weeks, the seriousness of the virus had gone from a low threat with just a handful of cases to outbreaks in many urban centers with thousands of infections and hundreds of deaths. Suit simply felt obliged to act; his entire team was preaching gloom and doom if nothing was done. Their point of reference for worst-case scenario was usually Italy, where its aging population had been severely hit. The thinking behind the "flatten the curve" philosophy was that, even though the economic hit would be significant as America's workers took an enforced pause, the outbreak would be short-lived, and by midyear, life would be back to normal. At least this was the received wisdom Ron was getting from his experts.

Ron had overseen the biggest economic boom in America's history, and the thought of bashing the economy by halting jobs, even if only for a short time, was anathema to him, but he felt an obligation to protect the population—surely that's the most important job any president can do? Each day brought new knowledge about the coronavirus; by now, it was 100 percent certain that it had originated in China in a city that housed a level four germ warfare laboratory.

Intelligence efforts showed, as hinted at earlier by Joyce Flowers, that there was some measure of human intervention over the virus's origins. It was also certain that this coronavirus was sufficiently different to previous ones to ensure that no sure treatment or vaccination was currently available. Even more worrying, symptoms and outcomes varied widely, meaning that the mechanism by which the virus attacked a body varied widely too. From liaisons with other affected nations, there seemed to be general consensus that elderly people with underlying health issues were most at risk. This was being born out in several states where the infection rate and increasingly common deaths were often in retirement communities and old folks' care homes. The young and healthy usually brushed off the virus like a case of mild flu or a cold—or with no symptoms at all.

As might be expected, state responses were wildly different. Urban areas such as major cities had immediate lockdowns with severe penalties for noncompliance, and rural states such as Wyoming and Montana effectively ignored stay-at-home measures; after all, they had zero infections, so why bother? Amazingly, the citizens of America took the lockdown to heart, embracing the mantra of "flatten the curve" with gusto. It was bizarre to witness the people of the Land of the Free meekly sitting at home just because they'd been asked to. It was heartening too; the majority of the population was willing to undergo sacrifices themselves in order to protect the elderly and infirm.

As the contagion spread around the world, different countries varied their responses. While a majority followed the principal of lockdown—indeed, the US response was largely based on actions already implemented by several European countries—some chose the "herd immunity" route, allowing its populace to catch the infection under the assumption that the outbreak would die out naturally when a large-enough percentage had contracted the virus and thus offered no new hosts. Other nations tried a hybrid approach, with limited isolation focused on the most-at-risk demography of elderly and infirm. It was a lab experiment on a global scale, but who would get it right?

Kunis and the Chinese followed the outbreak with interest as it inexorably morphed from epidemic to pandemic. Certainly, China had not escaped sickness, but scientists around the world had observed that infections appeared fewer and milder in the Far East; they put it down to the vagaries of this curious illness. Within China, a great show was made of the impact of this new sickness. Entire urban areas were locked down using armed troops. Chinese citizens were literally padlocked into their own houses.

Behind the subterfuge, key members of the party and area governments were quietly given preventative treatment. For Milos, besides being an ideological victory that was confounding the USA, it was also a personal boon. Careful and subtle preplanning meant that he had bought into businesses that would profit from a lockdown and the chaos it wrought, while simultaneously he was divesting or short-selling entities he knew would be hit badly. Any business that was connected to e-tail would obviously benefit, whereas the opposite held true for businesses that involved crowds or extensive personal interaction such as cinemas or airlines. For him, it was a positive sum gain exercise, and he was pleased. The Chinese regime was pleased too as it had generally followed his investment advice in the period leading up to release of the virus carriers in December.

Kunis's fellow members of the Group were less pleased. For them, it was a potential catastrophe as they watched markets drop by about 50 percent over a few short trading sessions. Oh, some cottoned on quickly and minimized losses or even managed to get ahead, but this wasn't a universal outcome for them. They looked enviously to Kunis and his obvious windfall. He had done so well; how had he managed this? Pundits outside the Group, when they bothered to investigate him at all, likened his present success to the same perfect timing he exhibited when he cornered the currency market back in the day; he's just a very astute businessman was the conclusion. They of course didn't know the inside skullduggery that had taken place to allow his massive profits.

One particular perk enjoyed by both Kunis and the party was the ironic fact that the majority of the world's needs for personal protective equipment, medical testing, support equipment, and other specialized merchandise needed during the pandemic came from China. This was the perfect opportunity to bump up prices; anyone who simply had to have the equipment didn't worry about the cost. In an emergency, that's secondary. The Chinese industrial machine cranked up to meet demand from hundreds of countries. Inevitably, quality control and assurance dropped, resulting in many defective items: ventilators that didn't work; test kits that gave false results; and face masks that were nowhere close to their rated filtration. But who cares? In a panic situation, if a bureaucracy demands X quantity of something, the civil servants award the contracts without regard to cost, and the equipment arrives to much fanfare, regardless of whether it will actually work.

Across America, to varying degrees, people adapted to this novel new way of life, one of sitting at home, staring out of the windows. Some worked from home, some schooled their kids at home, and some wondered where the hell the next rent money would come from given that they'd been laid off from their nonessential jobs. As the Arab curse goes, people truly were living in "interesting times.'

❧

Sue was taking a double whammy. The café was closed until further notice, and classes at NYU were canceled. She putzed about in her apartment, taking online courses to the extent that the university had published them, streamed tons of trashy TV, and Zoomed with her friends.

It was in this time of supreme boredom that she began morbidly reviewing past events. All the death: There was Tom Lincoln first, then Joe Trubek when he'd looked into Tom Lincoln, then the cop who'd investigated Joe, then another Lincoln pops up—Stacey this time—and bingo, Maury is gone too. It was a conspiracy theorist's dream, yet in Sue's cynical mind, it was all too plausible. She only had memories of conversations with Joe and Maury to go on, but she recalled enough to know that the whole situation stunk to high heaven. *Surely, Joe had kept Breitbart in the loop with every discovery he'd made?*

With nothing much else to do, Sue began to scratch the nagging itch that had been irritating her for so long. She picked up her phone, and after a quick Google search, she dialed a Los Angeles number.

Is Breitbart an essential business? she wondered as the ring tone persisted. *Maybe they've shut up shop.*

Someone finally picked up. After a lengthy go-round of being on hold, being transferred to other numbers, and many puzzled responses from people who had no idea what she was talking about, Sue finally was connected to Joe's old editor.

"So, it's like this," Sue began. "I was a good friend of Joe Trubek, and it's always bugged me that he seemed to be right on the cusp of a really big story when he supposedly committed suicide."

"Well, we're going way back here, but, yes, we were always suspicious of the circumstances too" replied the editor. "But, what with the present state of our country, isn't that just water under the bridge now?"

"I don't know about that, but here I am with lots of time on my hands. I feel like I need to revisit the whole thing and see if I can put it to rest. Is there any way you can give me Joe's old records or communications?"

"The thing is, Sue, Joe always played his cards really close to his chest. He was old school, and he liked to be 100 percent sure of a story before submitting it. Funny thing though, with the Tom Lincoln death, he was much more gung ho than usual. I had to keep telling him to get more solid information and corroboration before we could even think of running the story. The day he dies, there's a voice mail on my phone saying that he had everything he needed—and we'd better clear off shelf space for all the awards his story was going to win. Ha, crazy guy."

Sue was disappointed. "So, you've got nothing to give me?"

"Sorry, and you know, even if we did, I couldn't give it to you anyway. You're not one of our reporters, and as much as I sympathize that you lost a good friend, that's not reason enough to hand anything over to someone I've never met. Have you tried talking to the police?"

"No, sir. No, I haven't. Besides, the lead cop died in a traffic accident not too long after he closed the case ... isn't that in itself suspicious?" Sue was beginning to feel very disheartened.

"Wow, I didn't know that! Sue, you're beginning to remind me of Joe. He was always trying to tie things together—even when they didn't match up. He was a real bright journalist, but he could be a paranoid bastard. He told me that he always kept a backup of his work hidden inside a coffee can just in case his laptop got stolen. I wonder if the police ever found that?"

"I'm sure they did. I heard that they tore his place up during the investigation. Well, looks like it's back to binge-watching crap TV shows for me. I appreciate your time—I really do—and if you can think of anything, please contact me. Thanks again."

Sue gave him her email and phone number and hung up. Ever since Maury's death, and especially since lockdown, she'd become fond of tequila; she poured herself a shot even though it was only five. Half watching the screen, half daydreaming, Sue's mind wandered. *Why had all this happened? Why isn't Joe still around—or Maury. Maybe we could have self-isolated as a group and made life more bearable, fun, even. And what about my other friends? Who knows the next time I'll see them at the coffeehouse?* A thought sprang suddenly into her head. She leaped off the couch, put on her hoodie, and ventured out into the alien world of a deserted Manhattan.

It was so strange. The normally bustling streets of New York were silent and empty, the silence broken only by an occasional distant siren, the emptiness punctuated by a sparse smattering of hobos and other people with legitimate reasons to be going somewhere. Weirdly, in the lockdown, the streets had actually gotten cleaner; there were no massive mounds of black plastic trash bags piled high everywhere or swept garbage making rainbow-colored ribbons along the gutters, as if creating demarcation zones between traffic and pedestrians, of which there now were neither.

During her brief walk to the café, Sue was stopped only twice. A bum felt the need to just talk with someone. "This is some crazy shit, isn't it? How's a man supposed to make a living when he can't even get money off of folks?" He proceeded to ask for a few bucks. A policeman seemed interested in every citizen's reason to be outside of their homes. She told him she was simply out for groceries.

She made it to the familiar shopfront with its peeling paint and milky glass, surrounded by cobbled streets. Sue had keys, and she knew the alarm code since she was often first in and last out. A wave of comfort swept over her as she locked the door behind her and looked around the familiar space. It was just as she'd left it a lifetime ago, or so it seemed, though it was now a lot dustier. She put down her bag, took off her hoodie, and got to work. Using a logical approach, Sue began at one shelf and worked her way across, then the next shelf and so on, from front to back throughout the interior. Each coffee can, percolator, and other decoration was examined carefully, and Sue dipped her hand inside where possible or peered down into the container when her hand was too big. She worked her way through the collection, a tedious task, yet one that kept her stomach in knots throughout. The steep stairs down to the bathrooms were approaching as she neared the end of her search. By now, Sue was feeling a little dumb for even having her crazy idea. On the left of the stairs hung another shelf full of coffee-related paraphernalia. A green "Wak-Em-Up" coffee can beckoned, complete with an Indian chief as its logo. Sue reached in. So far, she'd discovered only wads of dried-up gum, scrunched-up receipts, or dust bunnies, but here it was! She pulled out a USB stick and gazed at it in disbelief.

Son of a bitch, Joe. I should have looked here first; it's the perfect place to drop your "insurance" on the way to or from the toilet!

With a rush of excitement and a knot in her stomach, Sue donned her hoodie, locked up, and headed back out into the eerie silence of Lower Manhattan.

DESCENT

Daily briefings morphed into daily Corona Strike Force status reports. As more knowledge was gained, the team's actions were fine-tuned to suit, but one inescapable and depressing fact was the rising daily toll on lives. Each day saw the number of infections climb and the number of deaths increase.

Experts around the world all had developed computer models that unfortunately gave widely disparate predictions. Some claimed a likely final US death toll of more than two million, while even the most optimistic models showed five hundred thousand. The nonstop onslaught of news from both left and right increased the country's anxiety about this terrible sickness, this silent killer.

There was an initial period of national unity when the country adopted a "we're-all-in-this-together" mentality. Some likened it to a war footing: us against a common enemy. Citizens adapted to their new normal of being at home, avoiding other people, homeschooling, home working, and binge-watching. All these things were novel, and hey, it's just for a few weeks, so let's enjoy the change of pace.

However, inevitably, after a few weeks, tribal feelings began to resurface. It started in the usual places; the *New York Times* had initially adopted a stance of asking, "Why is Suit going to these lengths? Corona is just like the flu." It soon transformed into asking, "Why is Suit not doing enough to quell this terrible outbreak?"

Other mainstream outlets followed, sliding quickly from simply reporting corona-related news to sticking a slant on every piece. The administration was mostly criticized for not having sufficient equipment and for not carrying out enough testing; they shouldn't have complained about a slow response, given that they'd just been complaining about his hair-trigger overreaction when he'd implemented travel restrictions, but they did.

Ron took all this in and accepted responsibility; it was his administration after all. However, behind the scenes, a frantic scramble was ongoing to shake up the CDC and NIH. Both organizations had been woefully unprepared for the outbreak and were lumbering behemoths of bureaucracy. However, like trying to turn a supertanker, change was being made at a snail's pace.

These flawed entities were nonetheless given a public veneer of competence so as not to over-discourage the populace. Dr. Giovanni became a nightly face on the nation's television screens. He quickly endeared himself to most people, especially the media, because his persona was one of someone who didn't take bullshit from anyone. "I'm a scientist, not a politician," he was fond of saying. He seemed to almost enjoy gainsaying some of Ron's statements. When the president was asked about a possible antidote or preventative inoculation, Ron merely repeated what he'd been told: that perhaps there might be something by year-end. Giovanni immediately stood and noted that a typical treatment's development is a long and arduous task, and that two years was the likely time line.

Ron bit his tongue.

VP Flowers made some excellent decisions early in the outbreak. Seeing the terrible shortage of certain equipment and supplies, she implemented a "public/private enterprise model," whereby the government worked hand in hand with companies to manufacture needed equipment. Soon, automobile factories were producing ventilators, drug companies were making test kits, and countless clothing manufacturers were sewing face masks. Across the country, state governors too were making decisions, some excellent, some not. As expected, states with urban hubs were experiencing the worst of the virus. Unfortunately, these same urban-centric states were typically also Democratic strongholds. Thus, an uneasy tug-of-war commenced between some governors and the administration. The governors made extravagant demands for equipment, pressuring and almost goading, the Suit team to meet their needs.

"I need forty thousand ventilators ASAP!" the governor of New York yelled during his regular briefing with the Corona Strike Force.

"But, even with our most pessimistic projections, you should only need one-quarter of that!"

"Yeah? Well, my team tells me it's forty thousand."

In spite of these increasingly common outlandish requests, Suit instructed his team to comply whenever possible; he didn't need Democrats and their media friends telling everyone that the president was not being responsive to the nation's needs. Particularly in New York and New Jersey, the number of infections and deaths had been ramping up alarmingly compared to elsewhere. Once again, in order to meet the demands of these governors, the administration reactivated US hospital ships and sent them out. They even built the world's largest hospital (with three thousand beds) over a couple of weeks at the Javits Convention Center on the West Side of NYC. None of this was enough; no matter the response, new demands and accusations flew. By the middle of April, it was essentially business as usual: left against right, Democrat against Republican. To reinforce the tribal model, Fox and AM radio sang the praises of the Suit team's response, while mainstream stations pressed on with nonstop criticism that evolved quickly into outright blaming Suit for the virus itself.

All of the enforced self-isolation had an inevitable impact on the primaries that had all been postponed. Ron was no longer able to hold his big rallies, but at least he was in front of cameras every day, keeping his base happy.

For George Burton, it was a godsend; he could no longer campaign.

For Shawanda Durelle, it was a catastrophe; she had lost her momentum.

"I think now might be the time to open discussions with Durelle," Stacey said to Ludwig.

"Perhaps. What do you think, Milos?"

"We can test the waters and learn what kind of appetite she may have," Kunis said, and so it was agreed.

An offer was made to Shawanda. She must withdraw from the primary race, on the understanding that she would get the veep position. The PFA's argument was fairly powerful; no chance of campaigning or voting for the foreseeable future due to the lockdown meant that Burton's lead was cemented, and Shawanda had no chance to change that. By conceding now, she would effectively be greatly improving her party's chance of beating Suit. Every political expert had agreed that her position was too far left, too progressive to be a viable alternate to the president, whereas Burton's moderate stance was much more palatable to the public. She simply had to do the right thing for the sake of her party.

Peter said, "Of course, Shawanda, if you continue with your campaign, you will not be getting any future support—financial or otherwise—from the DNC. That will make life hard for you. You're young, and you have a great future ahead. Take the VP position; that will set you up perfectly for the next election. We all know that George is going to be a one-term president. It will be yours for the taking in four years, and we'll throw the full weight of the party behind you then. As for now, we'll obviously make sure that you get adequately compensated for your withdrawal."

"Mr. President," Shawanda replied with an angry edge in her voice, "the people are ready for my agenda. You can see that. Until this damn virus came along, my campaign was soaring. Sure, Burton pulled ahead, but do you really think he can last through November? The old man is struggling now!"

"Shawanda, we know he'll last, and we know he'll get the nomination. George is the only realistic chance we have to get back in power. Look, we don't want this to get unpleasant. I truly hope you'll see sense and make the right decision." This time, it was Ludwig who had an edge to his voice, a threatening one. "I realize this is a surprise to you, Shawanda. How about thinking things over, let things sink in a little, and then get back to me?"

They parted on an uneasy truce. Shortly thereafter, certain media outlets began running stories of how Ms. Durelle had been misappropriating campaign funds, and calls for a formal investigation into her finances began to be made.

Meanwhile, for George, the lockdown was a blessing; he could now get relief from the stress of campaigning. His team of handlers was relieved too; now they could regroup and retrain him.

Kunis instructed a thorough medical examination be conducted in full secrecy in order to find out if there were real medical issues with George, particularly neurological and cognitive problems. Following the results, a treatment plan was initiated that was hoped would mitigate some of his issues.

The weeks slipped by in isolated monotony. When it wasn't bashing Suit and his corona response, most media focused on all the good that Burton had done over his long career of public service. They ignored Shawanda for the most part, except to periodically question her radical agenda and her financial goings-on.

About one month into the lockdown, terms were finally agreed, and Shawanda announced the suspension of her campaign to much hand-wringing from the mob and the progressives. No announcement was made of her vice presidency because strategically it was deemed smart to keep this quiet until closer to the national convention. This was conventional wisdom; not picking a VP early allows a party to negotiate with several of the also-rans and pick up their electoral pledges, and of course, speculation feeds the hungry media machine.

The potential dirt on Durelle magically evaporated: no more dodgy finances, no more outlandish political positions, just mention of her strong and supportive base who were looking for guidance from her now that she was withdrawing herself. Guidance didn't take too long to arrive. In an awkward speech broadcast over the web, Shawanda explained that the only way for her party to beat the incumbent was for Democrats to unite behind George Burton, and that included her own bloc of avid supporters. It was a bitter pill to swallow for many; they'd supported Shawanda for her forward-thinking ideas—for her youth and enthusiasm—and now they were expected to get behind an addled old white guy? Fortunately for most pols, the country was still mostly distracted by the pandemic and wasn't paying too much attention to the presidential race.

Infections climbed, deaths increased, and frustration levels rose as the lockdown dragged on. By now, most people were sick and tired of being cooped up. Sure, the government had implemented historic bailout packages that somewhat cushioned the blow for those out of work and with no source of income, but a surprising truth was emerging: most people want to work and want to have purpose.

This life of doing nothing was not good for the nation's soul. Of course, the media didn't help. The usual outlets were singing the administration's praises or condemning them—even as horror story after horror story came out. Nursing homes with dead bodies stacked up in corridors; new infection hot spots where the death rate was orders of magnitude higher; the revelation that African-Americans were more than twice as likely to die from the virus. All these stories were fodder for the left, more proof of Suit's incompetence. When you are penned up with nothing else to do than watch television, the gloom and doom takes its toll; the sense of "we're in this together" slowly evolved into "when will this shit end?" To make matters worse, as the original deadline for ending the lockdown came near, many states announced an extension of the quarantine. What had been a few weeks or a month of isolation was turning into maybe two months.

Dr. Giovanni stuck to his position. "We have made good progress on flattening the curve, but we must remain vigilant. Infection and death rates continue to rise, and until we can see a clear peak and downward trend, the isolation and social distancing should continue."

Ron continued to heed Doc's advice, and he pleaded for the population to be patient. "Folks, we've come so far together. We asked you to flatten the curve by staying indoors, and you know what? You did us proud; the curve has been flattened. We enacted historic legislation to keep businesses and individuals solvent, and if we have to enact more, we shall. Trillions of dollars have already gone out on interim payments, stimulus checks, and rent supplements, but that's a small price to pay if we save tens of thousands of lives. A few more weeks can help enormously, so I'm asking y'all to stick to the plan and stay inside for a little longer."

Some journalists began to actually do their job and dug into the accumulating masses of data relating to the pandemic. A common truth emerged: every single expert had gotten it wrong. All those projections of millions of deaths were patently nonsense, and it now looked like the toll could be perhaps one hundred thousand or so.

Frustratingly though, analysis of the numbers was often difficult because of skewed data. For example, many deaths were reported as corona-based deaths when the deceased had died from other causes—but was found to be corona positive during the autopsy. The death was therefore classed as a corona death. One satirical site said, "Skydiver who forgot parachute found to have died of corona."

How inflated were the figures? No one knew, although one member of the NIH team was caught in a hot-mic moment observing that deaths were being overreported by at least 25 percent.

Similarly, as testing finally got up to reasonable rates, the number of cases increased. This was glaringly obvious. The more you test, the more you'll find—and, incidentally, the more the death rate drops—but the headlines screamed, "Coronavirus Cases Skyrocket!" The increased testing was showing that perhaps one-quarter of the population had contracted the disease but had displayed no symptoms.

The data was also showing up other weird anomalies across the country: 40 percent of the deaths were in New York and New Jersey alone, and the northeastern corner of the country accounted for about three-quarters of all the deaths. Why? Southern states fared much better; only around 20 percent of the deaths occurred there, despite, as the press put it, the lamentable recklessness of many who were flouting the lockdown and enjoying the beaches.

Not a lot of things made sense about this pandemic. Some things were easily understandable: The states that were more relaxed about lockdowns and that did not extend the deadlines excessively tended to be red states. Those that implemented deadlines well in excess of CDC recommendations tended to be blue. There was some nonpolitical logic to this; urban areas lean Democratic, and high-density populations spread the virus more easily—or was it because blue governors enjoyed wielding power over their constituents?

Regardless, all the quirks in the data made for great debates on both sides of the political divide. Unfortunately, two numbers were indisputable. In less than two months, the nation had gone from record economic performance and historically low unemployment to a stock market crash and Depression-era numbers of people out of work. President Suit's amazing record was in tatters.

❧❦❧

The excitement in Sue's head as she pushed the USB stick into the port was almost unbearable. What legacy had Joe left? Her creaky old laptop took forever to boot up, but it finally found the stick. It was password protected.

"Goddam it," she muttered to herself and she began entering possible passwords—"Joe123" and "Trubek123"—but nothing worked. In a sudden "doh" moment, Sue typed in "Wak-Em-Up" and the screen flashed up a long list of cryptically named files: "Tldeath," "vehicle," "copbank," "Caymens," and more.

Well, I've got nothing else to do, Sue thought as she dived into the masses of information.

It was a long but rewarding night. Joe had meticulously and methodically gathered a ton of evidence that clearly showed foul play in the death of Tom Lincoln. More shockingly, it seemed to prove who was behind his demise. There was evidence that traced the hit-and-run vehicle to the wrecking yard; there was strong proof that the investigating NJPD detective had deliberately buried information and cut short his investigation; offshore bank records showed how the same cop had received $250,000 via a series of transfers from offshore banks via several clearinghouses to disguise their origins; there was another hundred thousand from the same offshore account that possibly had gone to the owner of the wrecking yard too, although this had been turned into Bitcoin and was too difficult to positively trace. Sue was intrigued by the detective's name; it sounded so familiar. She realized it was the same man who'd led the investigation of Joe's suicide. Bingo, another connection!

Most sensational, however, was the folder named "Slmail." Sue opened this to find some correspondence between Joe and Wikileaks, which had apparently provided him with various email files from several people. The smoking gun message read as follows:

> Thank you for supporting me through all this. You are a true friend. I've played our conversation over and over so many times in my head, but in my heart, I know it was the right decision. Tom is gone,

and we can now move on with our plans. You are such a careful person that I'm sure there's no loose ends or things that could trip us up in the future. Speak soon, Stacey.

Holy crap! Sue thought as she finished reading the message. *This is a note to Tom Lincoln's murderer from Stacey Lincoln—who was in on the whole thing!* The email had been sent to an indecipherable encrypted address, apparently over the dark web via Tor. A few other messages to the same address were also in the folder; these covered issues relating to her successful governor's campaign. One enigmatic note referred to her eternal gratitude for helping to buy the Lodge, whatever and wherever that was.

This was explosive, and dangerous, stuff, and Sue felt a little lost in deciding what to do with the information. She picked up her phone and dialed.

"Hello, Professor Epstein. It's me, Sue Oakley, from your political science class. Listen, I know you lean Democratic in your views, but can you help this right-winger and recommend someone on the conservative side who I might be able to talk with? I've got some ideas and just want to kick them around with a like mind."

The professor gave her a contact at the Manhattan Institute. "Dr. Casey would be a good pick; he's always looking for young conservatives. I'll email him and CC you, and then you can take it from there."

Sue thanked her professor and hung up. *Now, how in hell do I approach anyone about this?* She carefully wrapped the USB stick in foil and buried it in a can of Italian coffee that she kept in her refrigerator. *Might as well keep up the tradition, Joe.*

UPRISINGS

As Memorial Weekend neared, the natives were getting restless. Weeks and months of pent-up frustration began to bubble up around the country, driven in part by a schism between states. After the initial period of enforced quarantine, many states were beginning to reopen, albeit with reduced occupancy at restaurants and the like.

While unsatisfactory in many ways, this gradual approach was at least giving people hope that a return to normal life was on its way. Other states, however, declared extensions to their quarantine time line. Their citizens looked on enviously at the normalizing situation elsewhere, and they were angry; why can't we get out and about too?

All of this frustration was exacerbated by conflicting news on the virus. The CDC continued issuing its regular statements, but now there was a subtle shift in the messaging. No longer were we sacrificing to flatten the curve—now we had to remain indoors to avoid contracting the virus. What did that mean? Stay in lockdown until the virus has vanished or we have a vaccine? That could be six more months—or even years!

Large blocks of the public began to feel as if they were being sold a lie, and the demonstrations and marches began. Citizens assembled in front of state capitols and city halls wherever an extended lockdown had been imposed. They always began peacefully, but they were in violation of the social distancing and isolation edicts, and so heavy-handed police began breaking up the demonstrations and making arrests with the obvious consequence of scuffles and resistance. Others chose to protest not by demonstrating but by simply going back to work. Why in hell can I not cut hair when the grocery and hardware stores are full of people? Even automobile dealerships were open, but my salon can't be? The inequities of the seemingly random regulations came into stark relief, and people were not happy.

The president was not happy either. "What's with the new story line, Doc? We flattened the curve, the nation responded fantastically, and hospitals weren't overrun. Geez, that monster facility in New York treated a couple hundred patients at most. The projections were way off, and we're doing much better than all the predictions. Why in God's name are you now saying we've got to avoid exposure? It's obvious to everyone that, sooner or later, folks will get infected, but so what? The longer it hangs around, the weaker this virus seems to become, and it's nowhere near as lethal as first predicted. Herd immunity seems to be working too."

"Mr. President, we have to continue quarantine. There cannot be any resurgence allowed; otherwise, a stronger second wave could break out and kill many thousands more people. Isolation and social distancing have been proven to work, so we should keep it in place."

"Sorry, Alan, but if people have to stay isolated for much longer, we'll be looking at economic ruin—and that will bring on deaths from suicide, crime, and domestic abuse."

Ron stood silently as Giovanni made his nightly update. He then approached the microphone to announce that the Corona Strike Force was going to shift its emphasis from containing the disease to rebuilding the economy.

"Folks, it's time! Time to get America back to work. Time to ease restrictions. Time to rebuild our economy. Time to let people mix and mingle again. Time to reopen our stores and factories. As a nation, we flattened the curve. As a nation, we saved the lives of countless at-risk citizens. And as a nation, we'll put America back where it belongs—leading the world!"

Some states continued their recalcitrance and kept their draconian measures in place, but following Ron's declaration, much of the country felt a shift in gears and bought into its optimistic message. Much of the nation breathed a collective sigh of relief as the months of solitude waned and a return to normal life waxed.

For Kunis, this was an expected but disappointing development. He had been hoping for a longer quarantine, more time for the US economy to truly tank, and thus more time to make money and gain power.

The Chinese were stoic. They had already been seeing developments around the Western world that indicated a weakening of the virus and its effects. The party was satisfied; Western economies had all been devastated by the pandemic. GDPs plummeted, unemployment skyrocketed, and social unrest soared. It was a good outcome for a plan to put China on top—per its true destiny.

Sure, there had been some downside. In a backlash against Chinese-made drugs and equipment that had all had their supply choked and prices increased, many countries were vowing to repatriate the manufacture and delivery of strategically important items, eliminating any future reliance of the Chinese. No matter, this was a small price to pay for what was a highly successful—and repeatable—venture.

A small consolation came in the form of a massive surge in one drug's sales. The CDC began to recommend a possible treatment using an existing antiviral drug that had not yet received FDA approval. Under emergency laws enacted, it was, along with other existing drugs, permitted for use in treating coronavirus. However, the narrative soon became one of "all drugs bad except this one," and its use skyrocketed. The manufacturer of the drug was a Kunis company with Chinese-held patents. It was a nice windfall for Milos and the party.

Milos quietly suggested to his CDC contacts that they should start placing an emphasis on a "surge or second wave" and on "asymptomatic spreaders." "Keep the anxiety levels up, keep the people unsettled," he said.

Facts were secondary to the message. several European countries had carried out studies that clearly indicated the chances of a surge or second wave were minimal—and that asymptomatic carriers actually were highly unlikely to be contagious—but such news could easily be buried, and besides, haven't the experts always been wrong? They certainly had been throughout the pandemic, issuing conflicting news on a regular basis. The disease doesn't transmit easily between humans, no wait, it's highly contagious; masks don't do anything, no wait, you must wear a mask; the virus can live on surfaces for many hours, no wait, it can't. Chaotic contradicting expert views only helped fuel the unrest that Kunis desired. The WHO added to the mess with pronouncements that asymptomatic carriers didn't spread the virus, followed within twenty-four hours be a retraction of the previous statement. The public's disdain for the WHO was cemented when it was reported that their head public relations officer was, in fact, a close relative of the premier of the Chinese Party. No wonder their initial pronouncements had declared the coronavirus as mostly harmless and of unknown origin!

In Washington, it began to be back to business as usual. Even though many House members still refused to actually come to the Capitol for business—too risky—the political machine began to lumber back to life. House Democrats proposed a new stimulus package to hand out another trillion dollars around the nation. Close inspection of the thousands of pages of potential legislation revealed many hidden Easter eggs: millions of dollars tapped for handing out to Democratic Party donors; massive expansion of entitlement programs, and most significantly, but buried deep within the legislation; implementation of a vote-by-mail initiative whereby voters need not appear at a voting station. Just fill out a form and mail it in. The Democrats said that this was a vitally important part of the bill so that voters could avoid exposure to the virus come Election Day.

Eagle-eyed GOP senators spotted the hidden gems in the bill and removed most of them prior to enactment, although there was still a massive amount of pork left in; politicians on both sides of the aisle can't help but be politicians even in times of national crisis. Of course, Democratic leaders also began to demand an urgent inquiry into the president's terrible handling of the outbreak, which had resulted in more than one hundred thousand deaths.

"Here we go again, Ned," Ron said as he was being updated on the DOJ's investigation into the Russia and Ukraine hoaxes.

"Well, Mr. President, there's been good progress on our investigation. I'm not yet ready to issue a full report, but I can advise that we know certain members of our administration, and certain members of the House colluded to build a false narrative that led to your impeachment. It may be worthwhile to encourage Senate hearings about this and shine some light into the darkness."

Ron was satisfied to hear this for several reasons. Maybe now he could get some payback for all the crap he'd been put through. Just as importantly, putting out a full report later in the year, closer to Election Day, was a good thing for his campaign. Leaks were made to a few right-wing media outlets in order to get the nation's attention ahead of the Senate hearings.

Longtime rumors of FBI and Democrat malfeasance seemed to be turning into facts: A fake set of documents with false claims had been developed by the Democrats and weaponized by the FBI in order to justify spying on Suit's campaign team and then his administration. However, despite tons of evidence proving the case, the mass media did what it often does when faced with a story that doesn't fit its agenda; it ignored the revelations. To the left-wing media, this was unimportant, and probably untrue, they upheld "truth over facts." Far more relevant to them was the need to report on the increasing calls to investigate Suit over his handling of the pandemic, supplemented by adoring coverage of George Burton's public statements on anything he wished. Meanwhile, to the right-wing media, this was vindication of all their claims that the Democrats were hell-bent on destroying the Suit presidency. The two tribes were back to their usual mudslinging and stone throwing.

⌘

Ensconced in his large penthouse condominium on Water Street in the heart of DC, George Burton could spend hours looking out across the Potomac, drinking in the beautiful view, happily isolated from the world. Unbeknownst to him, he had recently gotten a new neighbor; his future veep pick Shawanda Durelle had just begun to move into to her newly purchased two-bedroom condo several floors below George. Burton's handlers initiated a daily regimen for George, one of prepping for, executing, and "postmorteming" a webcast, whereby George opined on matters of importance. Low-hanging fruit topics were obviously the pandemic and how Suit had murdered hundreds of thousands of citizens, or how he had mismanaged the distribution of emergency supplies and equipment. These topics were the main emphasis of his webcasts—but not to the exclusion of other vital topics such as universal health care or free education.

"Look at New York," he earnestly stated on camera. "So many dead, so many of our elderly, our dearest, died because of the Suit administration's failure to respond to the needs of its governor."

This was an outright untruth. New York had received more help than any other state. Those forty thousand desperately needed ventilators were now gathering dust in warehouses around the state, about to be shipped to India in response to an emergency plea from them for assistance. Even worse, investigative reporting would prove that people already sick with the virus were actually being placed into elderly care homes, thereby ensuring a massive spread of infections in those communities with resulting spikes in deaths.

"We need a nation with a centralized universal health care system," George continued. "This would have been so useful during this pandemic. As president, I will make sure that everyone has access to good medicine. You know, our founding fathers talked about this. They said we had the right to life, liberty, and, er, you know, the, um, the, good health care."

His handlers' eyes rolled en masse; they hated it when George went off script or ignored the advising voices in his earpiece. The postmortem of the webcast was intense, with George's usual assertion that he'd done great. This was just one of a regular diet of faux pas, gaffes, and plain screwups for George. Here was a man not comfortable with new technologies such as webinars, Zoom meetings, or podcasts, yet he was being coerced into participating in them, with often comically disastrous results.

The topic of George's competence arose in the regular PFA/ Group get-togethers.

"Stay the course, Peter," advised Kunis. "The pandemic has hit Suit's campaign hard. All we need do is keep Burton on an even keel for the next few months, and we will retake the White House. The people want peace and stability, and the more we unsettle Suit, the higher our chances are of winning."

"I wish I shared your confidence, Milos," replied Peter. "It looks like the delayed primaries are going to crank up again soon, and with Durelle out of the picture, his nomination is in the bag. Plus, we should get a big bump when Durelle is announced as vice president, but keeping him coherent for five months is a big ask. It's a high risk, Milos."

Stacey gave Milos darting glances but remained silent. As they parted company, she took him to one side and asked, "Is it still on?"

"Of course, my dear. You have nothing to worry about," Kunis replied as they kissed each other's cheeks, blatantly disregarding social distancing policies.

The Senate hearings commenced to little fanfare. Over two days, Republican senators excoriated various members of the FBI and pointed fingers at key Democratic Party members, up to and including President Ludwig himself. Democrat senators defended the FBI's actions, citing a clear and present danger to election fairness because of Russian interference that necessitated investigation. No one really paid attention; the country was still hooked on pandemic news. Some listened carefully, however.

Stacey said, "I don't like it, Peter. They're getting too damn close." She had been a passive witness to the FBI shenanigans during the campaign, but she had been fully briefed on the postelection efforts to unseat Suit.

"Agreed, Stacey," Peter said. "If they continue to get closer, we'll need to do something. Time to talk over options with Milos."

Following the Senate's hearings, information continued to be dripped out to the public, punctuated by the occasional statement from AG Odom, who more and more was feeling confident enough to note that the entire Russian hoax was the biggest political scandal he could think of in his long career.

"This goes all the way to the top," he remarked on Fox News one night. "And I intend to follow it there. In this country, no one is above the law."

Fighting words indeed. It was time to fight back.

A HELL OF A DISTRACTION

Peter, Stacey, and Milos sat in the war room, dejectedly watching the president's daily briefing.

"So, following the Corona Strike Force's brilliant efforts to reopen the country, led by VP Flowers, today's labor report should cheer everyone up. Despite our media friends' predictions of 25 percent unemployment for the past month, the actual numbers show that America is hiring again. Unemployment last month saw its biggest drop in history—more than nine million jobs added!" Ron was jubilant, and he wanted the country to know that the crisis was on its last legs. "We're getting back on top, folks. I think that by year-end, we'll be back where we were before this awful catastrophe."

For the PFA and the Group, this was all too soon. They needed the pandemic to continue until November; they needed the economy to still be in the toilet; they needed the people still sitting at home and obeying their governors' edicts. Voters had to be so tired of the country's terrible state of affairs come November that they'd vote for anyone other than Suit. It was time to bring out their next weapon: a tried and true Democratic tactic.

Ironically, it began in Stacey's home state of New Jersey. The Democratic governor there had extended the lockdown longer than all other states. People were pent-up, bored, and frustrated; it was a tinderbox waiting for a spark. The spark came in the form of a drunken confrontation between a black man and a policeman. Cyril Shaw was out of prison, a beneficiary of the state's corona policy of releasing inmates from prison so they could avoid infection. He was celebrating and had overdone it big-time.

Cyril was a small-time crook—nothing bad, car theft and the like—and he was a likeable rogue who had spent his first week of freedom nonstop partying with old friends and family. This night was to be his last. Officer Symes received a call that there was a drunk wandering around in front of a fast-food restaurant, yelling various obscenities at customers and generally whooping it up.

The unit arrived, and two policemen approached Cyril. Following a fairly civil and friendly twenty-minute conversation with Officer Symes, Cyril decided he didn't want to be arrested. He lashed out at the policeman, wrestled with him briefly, and then turned and made a run for it. This fateful decision was unwise, but it was nowhere close to being deserving of what happened next. Symes briefly attempted to chase him, and then he pulled out his revolver and emptied three shots into Cyril's fleeing back. Shaw died instantly. The incident was caught on the officer's bodycam, and it was captured, as so many things are, on several phones held by horrified bystanders. No excuses could be made, no cover-up done for the terrible string of events that had unfolded with deadly consequences.

The blowback was quick. Symes and his partner were fired immediately, but it was too little, too late. Within the day, protest marches had been organized by Cyril's family, planned for the evening after his death. Following their mantra of "never let a crisis go to waste," the PFA and the Group immediately began to pour fuel on the fire by blanketing media with footage of the appalling murder. Condemnation flowed in on both left and right. How could the shooting be justified? The nation's attention shifted from corona to cops shooting innocent black people.

Trenton's district attorney quickly filed charges against the two cops. "On review of the bodycam footage, I believe that the officer reasonably thought his life was being threatened, and so, in the heat of the moment, he took the life of Cyril Shaw. Nevertheless, I have filed third-degree murder charges against him, and the other deputy involved in the incident has been charged with aiding and abetting."

Investigation into Officer Symes's background showed that he was a veteran of the Trenton PD but had a checkered career involving multiple complaints about his use of unnecessary force against the public; he was a poster boy for bad cops. In theory, the incident could have been a rare occurrence when the two tribes could show a united front. All sides agreed that the shooting was unjustified and that the cop was a bad one, but partisan momentum was building, goaded on by the media's shouting that here was yet another example of systematic racism in Suit's America.

For Ludwig and Kunis, it was a perfect opportunity for collaboration. The PFA mobilized its operatives around the nation to stir up emotions, organizing protest marches in most major cities. Meanwhile, Kunis-funded agitators began to hijack the legitimate protests, turning them into anger-filled senseless riots. Entire neighborhoods throughout the US were burned to the ground during the chaos, and looting became another burden on the already struggling retail sector that had finally been seeing some hope of opening back up.

In truth, the anarchists, Antifa, and Black Lives Matter groups didn't really need too much encouragement to explode into destructive action; they too had been penned up for months and were just spoiling for a fight. Career criminals and gang members soon jumped on the riotous bandwagon, enthusiastically launching attacks against the police or anyone who tried to keep the protests peacefully focused on the issue at hand, namely police brutality against minorities.

News footage looked like some surreal version of *The Walking*

Dead; masses of protestors assembled each afternoon across the nation and marched, usually without incident, only to be replaced by rioters and thugs when the sun went down. The chaos was exacerbated in several cities by liberal mayors who instructed their police forces not to intervene in the rioting and to simply walk away—they did not want to be tarred with any hint that they'd engaged the long arm of the law against the protestors. Even when wrongdoers were taken in, the courts simply released them without charges, allowing a non-virtuous cycle to perpetuate. Thus, the country descended into weeks of anarchy. Nightly news about the pandemic was instantly replaced with nightly news about the riots and Suit's lack of response.

These weeks of violence and protest were, unsurprisingly, covered in two markedly different ways. For the mass media, it was simply the people peacefully stating their case that systematic racism in their country had gotten out of hand; if you are black, you will never get a fair deal with the cops. To this tribe, there were no such things as rioters; they were all simply disenfranchised citizens exercising their right to protest. It was as if entire city blocks that had been razed did not exist; the countless storekeepers who'd tried to defend their property and were beaten for it were ignored.

Interestingly, those same left-wing media outlets who'd supported policies of continued lockdown to "prevent the spread" now were silent as thousands of marchers and rioters thronged shoulder to shoulder in the streets. Some commentators even went on record to state that the right of protest trumps the need to be socially distant. They noted with pride that many of these young people were being responsible by wearing face masks, ignoring the fact that the masks were a great way to evade identification when police subsequently reviewed video footage for the perpetrators of crimes. Meanwhile, on the right, it was all about the rioters and lawlessness on the streets—and about police forces having their hands tied because of liberal city policies.

Ron was caught flat-footed by the rioting. For several days, his mantra was simply that law and order must be restored, and as with handling the pandemic, he looked to local governors to handle the crisis on a state-by-state basis. This was not the time for leading from behind, however; the nation had an expectation that in times such as these, the president should be "comforter in chief." His middling approval ratings sank to a new low.

"The bastards are saying I'm a racist," he complained to Megan one evening as they looked out of their quarters onto the distant silhouettes of burning police cars and hordes of punks scurrying around the White House perimeter like roaches around a pile of trash. "Your father is black for Christ's sake. Where do they talk about that? How can I be racist?"

"You know they look for any way to knock you down, Ron," she replied. "The problem is the Democrats have got the jump on you; they're already putting together a bill in the House to make big changes to policing policy. Meanwhile, what are the Republicans doing? Sitting on their thumbs and staring at each other. You've got to get ahead of this, darling."

"No matter what we say or do, it won't be enough for this mob. This isn't about race anyway. It's about *me*—it's about the election."

Ron continued to look out on the chaos and listen to the sounds of the night; police sirens, tear gas cannisters clanking, rubber bullet guns popping, and chants from the crowds: "Black lives matter," "Silence is violence," "Hands up, don't shoot." What a time to be alive. He was going to have to get used to it; the protests were far from over.

As time wore on, the tone and theme of the demonstrations morphed. No longer was this a "racist cops" issue; it was now was an "all cops bad" issue. Calls for justice for Cyril were superseded by calls to eliminate police forces across the country. The progressive wing of the Democratic Party was ecstatic; this was the kind of change needed in America, a change where the boot heel on the throat of the people could be removed. George Burton and his team opted to support this view; they needed the left's votes. His daily webcast shifted its theme from one of Suit's ineffectiveness against the pandemic to one of Suit's party and its inherent racism.

"You know that the Democrats have always had your back." He was discussing his love of black people. "We have always looked out for you. In my presidency, we will take care of everyone, you poor folk, the whites, everyone." The condescension peaked at his closing remark. "And remember, if you don't vote for me, you ain't black!"

"George, you've got to stop ad-libbing and stick to the script," Ludwig said. "The one group of voters we cannot afford to piss off are the African Americans. Without them, we're fucked."

"Peter, you know my track record with the blacks," George was now full of righteous indignation. "They love me. Look at North Carolina—I wouldn't have won that primary without their support. You worry too much, do you know that, Paul?"

The Burton campaign bumped onward toward the delayed primaries. It was merely a formality by now that he would no longer called the "presumptive Democratic candidate" and would become the actual one. All memory of the primary races and its candidates had been erased by pandemic and rioting overload.

Meanwhile, back on Capitol Hill, the Democratic House unveiled their "We Hear You" motion to show solidarity with their African American brothers and sisters. In an Olympic-gold-medal-quality piece of pandering, the Democrats' high muckety-mucks walked solemnly into the rotunda wearing matching scarves and hats of African Asante Kente cloth to show empathy for their African American comrades. They were totally oblivious to the fact that the Asante were massive slave traders in their time. No matter, en masse, the group kneeled to once again demonstrate solidarity with the cause: Black Lives Do Matter. It was tacky and tasteless, yet fanfared by the mass media.

Ron also tried to respond to the horrible situation as best he could: He developed an executive order to change certain aspects of Police behavior: a "three strikes you're out" policy to weed out bad blood such as Symes; use of supplemental social services to step in and deescalate situations where necessary; increased training for police; enlistment testing that would now include EQ tests to see if potential officers were emotionally cut out to compassionately interact with the public; and many more changes. The order's content overlapped extensively with the Democratic proposal, but of course, their response was that his executive action was weak and ineffective, simply providing proof of Suit's incompetence and indifference to the plight of black folk in the United States.

With the help of Ludwig and Kunis, the media remained laser-focused on stirring things up. Throughout the pandemic, the instruction to journalists had been simple: "If it isn't about coronavirus, don't bother. Now, it had changed: "If it isn't about race, don't bother."

The fires had to be stoked, the nation had to be kept off balance, and Suit had to be damaged. Every reported killing across America was now viewed through racial eyes, particularly those with officer-involved shootings. Incidents from years ago were dredged up so that new outrage could be displayed. Every opportunity was taken to display more anger and thus encourage more protesting and rioting. Coverage reached a new level of ridiculousness when, in an attempt to keep on message about racial biases, a financial news program spent an entire episode ignoring the recovering economy—or any other financial news for that matter—and discussed the lurid details of how Thomas Jefferson kept his financial accounts relative to his slaves. Young slaves were worth more, children born added to the asset base, old or injured slaves were written down, etc. It was a pathetically blatant way to keep poking the hornets' nest, to keep stirring the shit, but it was working.

The woke culture continued to strengthen. Companies were sending millions to Black Lives Matter, not knowing or caring who BLM really was, or what would happen to the money. It was simply a way of assuaging corporate guilt and signaling their virtue. Sports franchises, already teetering on the edge of ruin due to the pandemic-enforced shutdown, issued statements in support of BLM and its cause, not realizing or not caring that one stated aim of BLM was the defunding of police. Mobs began to topple statues across the country. Any hint of a racial connection gave justification for them smashing these symbols of oppression. Saner minds remarked, "Those who do not remember their history are doomed to repeat it," but the swollen masses of agitators didn't care. They just wanted change—or anarchy.

The craziness reached new levels of absurdity when products such as Aunt Jemima syrup were pulled from shelves. The originator of this product with her black face on its label was actually a true pioneer of black rights, a real entrepreneur, and the first African American millionaire, making her fortune from developing and selling her syrup. Who cares? She's just another symbol of white oppression. America was truly living in "interesting times."

Cyril Shaw's funeral was held with great pomp and pomposity. Pomp because the entire touching affair was orchestrated to perfection and covered by every news outlet in the country. Pomposity because the usual clan of hot-air generators showed up to tout the racial divisions that kept them in the money. A poor guy who'd been unjustly killed was becoming a dog whistle for radical thinking, his death merely an opportunity for radical change by those who wanted it.

๛෯๛

Back in Trenton, Stacey was quietly in discussions with the DA, having known him well during her time as governor.

"Look, third degree isn't enough, Cory" she said. "The people are going to demand more—and God help us if they don't get justice."

"Stacey, even a third-degree charge won't guarantee a surefire conviction. If we go for more, we truly risk losing the trial, and then what?" The DA was uneasy with this uninvited advice from a former governor who'd appeared out of nowhere to meet with him.

"Cory, you know I represent the party." Stacey was at maximum charm level now. "All our legal experts think at least second-degree is justified—or even first-degree. You know we'll support you in any way we can to secure the conviction."

Cory was ground down over the course of their meeting and finally agreed to upgrade to second-degree murder charges against Officer Symes.

On her way back to DC, Stacey called Kunis. "He'd only go with second degree, Milos."

"Well done, Stacey," he replied. "It's not a first-degree charge, but I think we can work with second."

They hung up—another missile ready for launch.

The media breathlessly reported on the upgrading of the charges. Some protestors took it as a sign that perhaps they were finally being listened to. The rioters didn't care.

As this latest stressful phase of life in America continued, increasingly wacky events took place. Throngs of people still protested or rioted, but an elite group of anarchists began a new tack. The Seattle area has long been known for its uber-liberal policies, and for some time, it had been a safe haven for all sorts of fringe groups and oddballs. Tent cities had long been a feature of downtown life there, complete with aggressive panhandlers and anarchists who attacked passer-by at will or blocked off streets so they could smash up any unsuspecting driver who strayed into their space. Their new initiative ensured coverage of the Seattle "lifestyle" with a vengeance.

During one of the usual nights of rioting and mayhem, a hard-core group of anarchists attempted to get into a district's police headquarters. The cops defended for a short time until being instructed to stand down and abandon the precinct building. It was an easy overthrow of the establishment. Within a few hours, in a well-orchestrated operation, fences were erected around a large part of the downtown area, and hordes of people began their occupation.

Antifa, anarchists, and thugs looked for more shops to loot; you name it, they moved in. Armed personnel within controlled entrances to the walled-in area, permitting only those woke enough to the cause to come in. Any unfortunate storekeeper or existing resident of the "free zone" was out of luck. By definition, they were considered hostile and had a simple choice: go along with things or leave their homes or shops.

As the occupation continued, people were expected to pay a "contribution" to the occupiers in order to avoid "bad things happening." Tribal coverage ensued with all the expected contrasts; just a mostly peaceful demonstration was one characterization, while the other view was that the rule of law had been crushed in Seattle.

When questioned, unbelievably, the mayor simply stated that, "It's kids enjoying themselves, nothing to worry about, it's just like Woodstock or the summer of love, leave them be."

The occupiers eventually issued demands to the outside world. "We need all student loans to be canceled; we need all police forces to be disbanded, we need black health care patients to be treated by only black doctors; and we need reparations; we need rents to be reduced and gentrification of neighborhoods to cease. Oh, and yes, we need water, vegan food, cigarettes, and booze."

America had finally entered bizarro world.

PREPARATIONS

Ron said, "So, Joyce—excuse me—Vice President Flowers, I'd like you to comment on the latest round of media hype that says we're in a second wave or surge of the virus."

"Thank you, Mr. President. We've heard from the media in recent days that we are in the throes of a dangerous second wave or surge. Projections of an additional five hundred thousand deaths are being touted by some experts, while the real data is being ignored. The facts are that well over half of our states have declining or stable numbers of cases. With just a few exceptions, every state or metropolitan area is seeing less than 10 percent positive test results. Of significance, the six states that are showing more than one thousand new cases per day are reporting that these increases are mostly due to increased testing that has concentrated on prisons, nursing homes, and meatpacking plants. As we know, all of these facilities are well-known hot spots, so increased positives are to be expected.

"We are testing around five hundred thousand citizens every day with less than 6 percent of them being positive. Sadly, the deaths continue, but the daily rate is now 750 and falling. That's a far cry from our peak of 2,500 per day, and of course, it's way lower than the five thousand plus per day that the experts predicted—those same experts who are now predicting gloom and doom in this so-called second wave. For those who continue to criticize our administration's response to the pandemic, I'd like to point them to a recently released report by a consortium of doctors and hospitals from around the world who have ranked each affected country based primarily on their responses to the outbreak and death rates. The United States was not the best, but is in the top third, and our response was rated as 'good.' America has performed far better than the majority of countries affected by this terrible outbreak.

"The media has tried to scare the American public every step of the way throughout this outbreak, and these grim predictions of a devastating second wave are no different. The truth is, no matter what you hear from certain news outlets, our approach has been successful; we aimed to flatten the curve, and we did. Our health care system was not overwhelmed, and we have adequate capacity to cover any spikes that occur. Of course, wherever spikes are identified, they'll be dealt with as quickly as possible. Remember, the restrictions imposed were never designed to prevent people from catching the virus; they were designed to slow its spread, and we have achieved that. Thank you, President Suit."

"Veep Flowers, folks, telling it like it is. I also want to remind you all of some more good news. Today's retail spending figures showed the largest monthly increase since records have been kept. Now, obviously we are a long way from pre-pandemic numbers, but this, coupled with the recent jobs data, shows that our nation is on the mend. We can get through this, America!"

More bad news for Peter, Milos, and the gang.

Ron was trying to keep a positive narrative going, being keenly aware of the countdown to Election Day. He decided it was time to get back on the road and restart his rallies. An announcement was made for a date and location in Texas. Response was overwhelming, whether it was due to genuine enthusiasm or simply a desperate wish to get out of the house, who knew, but no matter, almost one million ticket applications were received.

The media response was immediate; after an initial attack claiming that the president was grossly overstating ticket applications, the message became one of united condemnation of the president for putting so many citizens at risk of catching the virus from being all crammed together at the rally. These same pundits had praised the protestors/rioters for marching en masse, saying that civil rights were far more important than social distancing, but now Suit was effectively killing thousands by having them get together for his rally.

The PFA were keenly aware of the coming election too. Their multipronged attack on Suit had many public-facing actions. The corona outbreak and lockdown; the race riots; lawsuits over sex or funding or whatever; tell-all books; continued questioning of Suit's health or mental state; impeachment efforts; and more. However, quietly, behind the scenes, another two initiatives had been underway for some time. Ludwig and his team wanted to be sure that, no matter how the election played out, they'd have some aces up their sleeves. The first ploy had briefly seen the light of day during the early days of the pandemic when the Democrats' proposed aid bill included a total vote-by-mail option for the coming election, ostensibly to avoid voters being exposed to the virus, but really to make it easier to engage in the "old LBJ play" of stuffing ballot boxes and "losing" Republican votes. Five states use all-mail balloting, but the pandemic gave an excuse for an additional three Democratically held states to immediately jump on the mail-in bandwagon. In addition, every Democrat-held state was considering adopting similar measures too.

Now, converting to a mail ballot is a massive undertaking—printing, distribution, and counting all make for huge logistical challenges—but Ludwig wasn't seeking a total approach. He didn't need to either. In any presidential election, there are always swing states—places that are not solidly red or blue and who bounce back and forth between parties. About ten states could be considered swing states, so if mail-in voting for these was successfully implemented, voila!

The ease by which mail-in voting can be subverted is staggering: When voting by mail, a citizen typically receives his ballot, casts his vote, attests it, and returns the sealed envelope. Problem is, the envelope states the voter's affiliation on the outside! How easy would it be for a certain party's votes to magically disappear? Not only that, a citizen of a certain affiliation might receive multiple voting papers to complete, there have been multiple examples of this, where someone will receive eight or ten mail-in vote envelopes. Despite the media's long assertion that this doesn't happen, there are countless accounts of voter fraud. It's so bad that the White House keeps a website devoted solely to documenting proven cases. The ingenuity exhibited in these cons is impressive. Suffice it to say, mail-in voting in key swing states would be a big plus for someone wanting to skew the results, and Peter's PFA was acutely aware of this. Stealthily, this scheme was being implemented throughout key areas of the nation.

Initiative number two had also been in play for some time, flying under the radar and garnering little publicity. For many years, the cry of a presidential loser has been the same: "But I won the popular vote!" Stacey had used this very complaint following her loss to Ron. Since the beginning of the election process, whoever wins a state receives their electoral votes. This was the founding fathers' attempt to ensure that the wishes of smaller states were not overwhelmed by those of bigger ones, and that is why the United States is not a democracy but a federal republic. However, since Suit's convincing victory where he received almost 60 percent of the electoral college votes—despite being edged out by a few percent on the popular vote—Democrats had been quietly attempting to change the rules. Their proposal was to change things so that a state's electoral votes would automatically go to the candidate who received the highest number of national votes. So, you might win a state comfortably, but if your opponent edged you out nationally with the popular vote, too bad, you just lost those electoral votes. By the middle of election year, fifteen states had enacted such legislation with several more in the works.

A couple more initiatives were added to the mix. New ballot harvesting laws allowed people to go into neighborhoods and reap unused votes, and changes to the deadline for voting submissions allowed for more time to manipulate the count after Election Day. There were so many ways being developed to skew results. The Democrats had these edges—stuff the ballots or steal the electoral votes—and all this was accomplished without fanfare or anyone really noticing. It was brilliant. True to their modus operandi, one of the anti-Suit narratives began circulating that he was trying to cheat on the election. It was a classic blue tactic to accuse your opponent of the very thing you are doing yourself. Say that Suit is colluding—while you actually are! Say that Suit will rig the vote—while you actually do! The most effective lie is one close to the truth but in the opposite direction.

Amid a background of continued national rioting and occupation of liberal city centers, Suit's Texas rally was organized and held. Ron called it "the reboot of my election campaign." It passed off without incident: no riots, no confrontations, and no violence. There were a couple of interesting wrinkles, though; one cable news channel sent its six-person team to cover the event and, thanks to checks made by the organizers on all attendees, it was found that all six of the news crew were positive for coronavirus. Was this an attempt to generate a future bombshell story: "Suit rally spikes cases of deadly sickness"?

More worryingly, despite more than one million pre-rally ticket sales, far fewer people actually turned up; the arena was less than halfway full. It transpired that there'd been a massive effort by various left-wing groups to obtain tickets online with no intention of ever attending. Their aim was simply to deny access to those who really wanted to go. This was a clever and successful piece of sabotage. Of course, in the days following the rally, all mass media shouted about the disappointing attendance, a sure sign that Suit's rule was coming to an end.

Ron was not happy; after berating his campaign team for allowing such a wily trick to be played on them, he instructed everyone to work on ways to avoid any future such screw-ups. To make himself feel better, he sat down with AG Odom. "Ned, what's the word on the investigation? I need some good news"

"Mr. President, I believe that we're one month or so away from being able to publish our findings." Ned was, as always, being cautious in his assessment. "But I can tell you, sir, that the report will have clear recommendations for indictments, and a number of the Ludwig administration's people, together with certain career bureaucrats, should be feeling pretty uncomfortable right now."

Ron cheered up, but he still felt like he was carrying the weight of the world upon his shoulders. What would happen if he was reelected: famine, locusts, killing of firstborns? *This shit is biblical,* he thought dejectedly.

⋘⋙

Meanwhile, on the campaign trail, George was being carefully trotted out to the public, making limited low-key appearances, for example, one-on-ones with Democratic governors and small gatherings. All such events were grossly exaggerated by the news, making him look like a campaign warrior. Of course, all this was underlined by the nonstop polling that consistently showed Burton well ahead of Suit—and increasing his lead every day. It looked bad for Suit. In reality, the polling data was garbage, as it had been in the previous election, when Stacey was going to win by an overwhelming margin. Polls are so easy to skew; the latest being taken from a 75/25 Democrat/Republican mix of respondents, no big surprise therefore that the results favored the Democrat!

Members of the Group assisted in the dethroning of Suit in all ways they could, and one ingenious attempt was to silence his voice. In addition to his nightly briefing on TV, Ron and his team had been deftly using many forms of social media to get out their message. The owners of these outlets all coincidentally and simultaneously decided that they needed to modify their standards. Suddenly, much of the Team Suit outreach was deemed unsuitable, and was therefore censored or removed. The Group also helped Burton's campaign by donating a record amount of dollars to his war chest. Airwaves were flooded with the desired message: "Aren't you sick of the chaos? Don't you want a return to the good old days?" Time marched inexorably toward November.

Quiet conversations between the PFA and the democratically held House resulted in a reappearance of Tweedle Dum and Tweedle Dee, supported and abetted by Widow Twankey. Time for another inquiry and impeachment!

"We'll keep up the racial unrest and coronavirus fears, you get back to tying him in knots on the Hill," Peter said to the team. "We've got less than five months to close this out. Let's keep stirring the pot."

What sort of inquiry should it be? Why, let's challenge Suit's handling of the pandemic. But, perhaps now was also the time to start on Odom? Word on the street was that the AG's report would be naming names and be a pretty damning document. He needed to be discredited as much as possible and distract the public from his findings by questioning his integrity. They agreed to run two attacks in parallel and thus had their plan for the final phase of the campaign.

✑

NYC was being allowed to open back up, if only a little, but at least it was a start. For Sue and many others like her, it was a chance to get back out there, to return to work, even. Finally, they could feel a sense of worth again; the months of enforced isolation had been taking a toll on people's well-being, their sense of self, their ability for social discourse. Now hopefully things would finally improve, and they might be able to stop looking enviously at the other states they'd been seeing on TV that had released their citizens from lockdown so much earlier.

Following Sue's discovery of Joe's revelations, she had spent many hours fretting over next steps. Sure, the Manhattan Institute was an obvious place in which to confide, but how could she be sure? She'd dug up as much information on Dr. Casey as she could find, and he seemed like the real deal, but who knows? Consequently, Sue just kept reading through Joe's findings again and again, desperate to somehow get the word out, but scared of trusting the wrong people.

I mean, there's been people killed over this information—maybe even Maury, she thought. Even though there was a clear link between Tom Lincoln's, Joe's, and the detective's deaths, the only connection to Maury was a vague and probably coincidental link with Stacey Lincoln. *Except that there's no such thing as coincidence.*

Finally, she summoned up the courage and made the call.

"Miss Oakley, I've been waiting to hear from you. Your professor said I should expect a call some time ago."

"I'm so sorry, Professor Casey," Sue replied. "Things are difficult, what with the virus and lockdown. Anyway, my NYU professor thought you'd be the best person for me to talk to about some sensitive information I've obtained relating to Stacey Lincoln. I was hoping we could meet up and talk things through."

"Can't we just discuss it here and now?"

"It's, er, very sensitive, and I wouldn't be comfortable about discussing it on the phone." Sue's voice tensed at the mere thought of sharing her knowledge with anyone.

"Well, things are opening up, so I suppose we could get

together." Professor Casey could hear the worry in Sue's voice, and was intrigued. *What on earth could this girl have that was making her so worried?* "You know where we are, on Vanderbilt?"

"Yes, sir. I do." A time was set for the following morning.

They met. Sue did not bring anything with her; the USB stick was still buried in coffee back at her apartment.

"Professor Casey, do you know anyone in the administration? I have some, er, verified information about criminal activities carried out by Stacey Lincoln, and I feel like I need to get this to the administration so they can decide what to do about it." Sue was attempting to walk a tightrope—disclose enough to get help from Casey without saying anything of significance about the whole affair.

"Well, Sue, obviously our institute is in regular contact with various members of the president's team. As I'm sure you know, our work is to encourage free market ideas and domestic policies that will help the American people. Despite all of his, um, idiosyncrasies and unconventional approach to governing, we're behind President Suit and his goals. But, forgive me, I don't know anything about you—other than the glowing report from your professor—and I don't know anything about the information you say you have. Can you really expect me to help grant you access to senior administration officials?"

This was turning out pretty much as Sue had expected. *Now what?* "Professor … without seeming too dramatic and *CSI*-ish, people have died because of the information I have, so I hope you'll understand my reluctance in sharing it with anyone. You know, if some stranger came up to me and said things like I just did to you, I'd probably politely ask them to get the hell out, but I don't know what else to do. If certain people find out that I have this information, the next time you see me might be when I'm lying on a slab at the morgue, and no, I'm not being overdramatic. Look, if you can arrange for me to talk with someone senior enough in government about this matter, I'd be happy for you to come along and kick me out if you think I'm lying or faking." Her stomach was in knots, she was sitting on the edge of her seat, her feet were jiggling nonstop, and her hands were wringing together as she spoke.

"Well, Sue, please let me mull this over." Casey could sense the sincerity of this young woman, but should he put his credibility and reputation on the line for her?

They parted company, and Sue went back out into the almost-empty streets of the city and began to walk back home past familiar landmarks such as the library and the Empire State that all seemed alien now, not surrounded by the noise and hustle of the city, but by silence and stillness.

Professor Casey sat in his office, weighing options.

COUNTDOWN TO CHAOS

The news was not looking good; in one-third of the nation, infection rates were increasing. News outlets trumpeted about how some (Republican) states had been too quick to reopen, and now citizens were at risk. Meanwhile, Democrats insisted that lockdowns remain in place; some representatives even went so far as to say continued quarantine was vital, at least until after the election, if they were to defeat Suit. A recovering economy would not help their chances, so keep folk out of work, crash entire businesses, anything was better than four more years of him.

As usual, the real picture was more complex: Much of the data being presented was misleading. For example, the *WaPo* cited one state as having twelve thousand cases in June, while deliberately ignoring the fact that this was a cumulative number; the figure in May was ten thousand, thus making new cases in June two thousand, but that wouldn't be as sensational, so the headline was manipulated to suit the narrative.

Similarly, the WHO and others fretted about the rapidly rising worldwide number of infections, and this was indeed true. However, the increases all came from Latin American countries that had been "late to the corona party." Countries that had been hit early in the pandemic were now well on their way to recovery; many restrictions had been lifted, return-to-work orders had been enacted, and life had been slowly getting back to normal. This was particularly the case in Europe, and indeed, US hospitalizations and death rates were falling across the country, with the exception of some hot spots.

However, facts don't make for a good headline or lead story. Instead, "Infections Reach New Highs" was the preferred wording to keep folk scared. *Surge* became the buzzword of the day. China did its part too, declaring hot spots in various cities across its country. These were immediately locked down to great fanfare and publicity and then forgotten; the actual lockdowns lasted only as long as there was international media interest. It made for good optics though: the deadly virus continues to rear its ugly head, stay home!

The Democrat and Republican response to the pandemic could not have been more different in one crucial aspect. The GOP pressed on with its plans for a national convention, to be held in Ron's hometown of Houston, and the George Brown Convention Center had already been booked. Meanwhile, Democrats continued their narrative that large gatherings of people were unacceptably dangerous, and they were making arrangements for a "virtual" convention. Stacey's DNC team was leading the charge with these plans. Avoidance of an actual convention also reinforced their push for an all-mail vote at the election. It obviously was far too dangerous to allow people out to physically cast a vote; mailing it in would save thousands of lives. No matter that, across the country, grocery stores, hardware shops, and other such places were open and packed; you can buy food without risk, but showing up to vote will almost certainly kill you!

The rioting was morphing into an orchestrated ballet of mayhem. Anarchists masquerading as protestors roamed the cities, looting, beating and, in a new wrinkle, tearing down any statue they could attack. "We have to destroy our racist history" had been their justification, but now it didn't matter; all figures were fair game, whether anti-slavery heroes such as Grant or the Great Emancipator, Abraham Lincoln.

The Seattle free zone remained high on the media's priorities as a perfect demonstration of how young people were exercising their civil rights and enjoying a "summer of love" or a giant "block party." Even when thugs took over the zone and murder and mayhem began within it, it was still considered a fun social experiment—and the bad things were generally ignored. Even the delicious irony of the free zone inhabitants calling the police when gunfire broke out inside the compound was ignored by the left.

Mass media still exploited the race issue at every opportunity, continuing to couch all their articles and news pieces in racial tones, microscopically examining every single police action, always looking for evidence of racial bias. This approach occasionally backfired when they yelled racism at some incident only to discover that there was no actual racial motive. Such incidents were then subsequently ignored by the left, but immediately jumped on by all the right-wing news and AM talking blowhards, magnifying the two-tribes atmosphere of the country.

The scene was thus set for the tumultuous run-up to Election Day: a maelstrom of anger, frustration, and hatred, stirred up by all media, right and left.

George continued his "virtual" campaign, mostly from his condo, with the occasional highly covered outing to stand proudly in his mask and spout off about Suit's racism or incompetence, about how Suit had killed the US economy, and about how a Burton presidency would mean an end to the chaos and division of the past three-plus years. By now, even pro-Democrat pundits were making fun of George's low profile, remarking that the less folks saw of him, the more he went up in the polls.

The three met in George's condo to discuss post-virtual convention tactics: Ludwig, Burton, and Durelle sat on the balcony looking out across the city, observing the smoke rising, hearing the mobs yelling and police sirens wailing, sipping their glasses of wine.

Shawanda said, "Look, we've got to use the rest of the campaign to embrace progressive issues. Look around. The people are pissed; they've had enough of Suit's hatred and our own party's inaction. They want change, and a Burton-Durelle ticket has to guarantee that."

Ludwig said, "Shawanda, I know there's a vocal minority out there who have bought into your policies on police defunding, socialized medicine, student loan forgiveness, reparations, etcetera, but to win this election, we have to embrace moderate Democrats. Going too far left will cost us votes. George, where do you stand on this?"

"It's such a beautiful view, isn't it?" Burton said. "On what? Oh, you mean all the rioting and statue smashing? It's terrible, isn't it? I mean, some of my ancestors have statues. What happens when those punks pull them down?"

"So, you disagree with civil protest?" asked Shawanda, her voice rising.

"No, of course he doesn't," replied Peter. "Do you, George?"

Lights came on in Burton's eyes as he seemed to fully rejoin the discussion. "Under my administration, we'll make sure that we have a meaningful discussion with these, er, young people, to allow them to air their grievances. Then we will appoint a czar to focus on race and inequality." Burton seemed pleased with himself for remembering the script.

Shawanda seemed a little appeased, but she, like so many of her colleagues, couldn't help but notice that George wasn't always "all there." However, rather than seeing this as a threat, she considered it as a potential opportunity; should anything bad happen to him post-inauguration, she'd be president! Unfortunately, her concerns resurfaced the following day while she was watching coverage of one of Burton's sparsely attended town halls. He responded to a question about police brutality against minorities and managed to stun the moderators into silence when he pronounced that cops needed to abandon their shoot-to-kill policy: "I mean, look, if a, er, you know, um, if an unarmed man attacks a cop with a knife, their response should be to just shoot him in the leg, don't go for a kill shot, it isn't proper. And no choke holds, no, sir."

All the gaffes and lack of visibility for Burton made little difference; by now, delayed primaries were being held around the nation. Stacey had VoteNow! prepped and ready, but it wasn't needed. Democratic candidates had evaporated, leaving just George to cruise on as the presumptive candidate. With his biggest rival bribed into withdrawing, the road was open for an easy run up to the convention. With the media's attention focused on racial division and the corona surge, no one paid attention to the primaries anyway, except when the voting had gone wrong. When some polling stations had opened for voting, they practiced social distancing, masks, and limited access to the voting booths, all in the name of "stopping the spread." The inevitable consequence was long lines, long waits, and disgruntled voters—a perfect outcome for a party that continued to push the need for all-mail voting come November.

❦

Back in the White House, Ron was edgy and downhearted. "Damn it all, Megan. They just might beat us come November," he remarked over breakfast. "It's less than four months now to Election Day, and if I don't get the economy back on track by then, I'm toast. Remember what Blow Job Bill said? 'It's the economy, stupid.'"

"Ron, the pandemic isn't your fault, the poor economy isn't your fault, and the riots aren't your fault. Just carry on being yourself; it's all you can do. Hell, it worked for the first three years, didn't it?" As on other occasions of low morale, Megan was being the "booster-in-chief."

"Not my fault, maybe, but sure as hell my responsibility. You know, the only thing cheering me up these days is the prospect of debating that buffoon Burton. I'll chew him up and spit him out."

"Attaboy, Ron. Now finish your breakfast; you've a busy day ahead of you." Megan didn't mention that there were already rumors circulating that the Burton team would refuse to commit to any debates.

As per their threats, the House opened two simultaneous investigations: one into AG Odom's malfeasance through his politicization of the Justice Department and one into President Suit for his mishandling of the corona pandemic. The House leaders launched these inquiries mostly to add to the imbalance and chaos of the country at this time—but also to attempt to get ahead of the looming day when the AG's report into the failed impeachment attempt was to be published. They needed to grab the spotlight and dominate the news cycle in order to minimize the impact of what was likely to be a damning document.

Tweedle Dum and Tweedle Dee tag-teamed up for the hearings.

"The three branches of our great government have been blurred and comingled at the whim of our president. Under his direction, the Justice Department has carried out his orders without question or refusal. Attorney General Odom thus perverted the course of justice many times over. Most notably, he instructed the courts to overturn the guilty verdicts against a number of President Suit's election team, verdicts handed down by legitimate courts following the rule of law. We therefore demand his immediate resignation and expect him to appear before this panel to justify these outrageous actions."

"You don't have to go there, Ned," Ron said. "Executive privilege is legitimate here—tell them to go to hell."

"Well, Mr. President, I'm not sure that would be the best route to go." Odom was comfortable about appearing in front of the committee. "They're saying that dismissing those three convictions is a sure sign that I'm in your thrall—or as one of my predecessors said, 'I've got your back.' However, we can turn the narrative around. By testifying, I'll be allowed to disclose some hints of the bombshells that will be in the Impeachment Investigation Report. I anticipate its publication by the end of this month, and this hearing gives me an opportunity to offer a sneak peek, if you will."

Ron warmed to this idea, and a date was set for Odom's appearance.

Tweedle Dee said, "AG Odom, the purpose of these hearings is to establish whether you breached the boundaries of our branches of government by working under the direction of President Suit to pervert justice by your actions in forcing the dismissal of legitimately proven guilty verdicts against certain individuals. We will now hear your opening statement."

"Thank you, Mr. Chairman," replied Ned, "and thank you for the opportunity to come before this committee and explain my actions in the matters under review." Odom had been in this seat many times over his career, and it no longer held any fear for him. These politicians were only on their committees because of seniority, meaning that they were career swamp-dwellers, part of the self-serving community of DC "ins." After pausing to look around the socially distanced chamber, he continued his opening remarks. "As you all know, my department has been investigating the circumstances surrounding Congress's impeachment of President Suit over his alleged collusion with Russia and quid pro quo with Ukraine. We are finalizing this report, and I anticipate that it will be issued by the end of this month. I bring this up because the malfeasance you accuse me of has direct relevance to the criminal wrongdoings unearthed during these investigations."

The chamber perked up on hearing the word *criminal*.

"We have established beyond doubt that the guilty verdicts handed down to members of President Suit's campaign team were, in fact, obtained by subterfuge. We have established beyond doubt that certain members of the former administration sought to spy on the Suit campaign and transition teams using false information to justify their obtaining of surveillance warrants. I cannot name names at this time, but they will be published in the report—along with recommendations for prosecution. We have also established beyond doubt that the entire impeachment effort, an effort led by certain members before me now, was built on sand, sand made of lies piled up by individuals who crafted an elaborate and criminal scheme to remove the president from office. As we all know from our Bible teachings, a house built on sand cannot endure, and I'm confident that this entire house of cards will collapse following the release of my department's report. I must say, in my long career in Washington, I have never seen a more blatant and concerted effort to undermine the very foundation of our nation's democracy. In conclusion, therefore, I stand 100 percent behind my decision to instruct the dismissal of these wrongful verdicts, and I am now happy to answer any questions that you might have." He sat back and smiled at the row of politicians before him.

Oh dear! Some of the committee's panel knew full well that they had been complicit in the impeachment effort; would they be shortly under indictment? Could questioning Odom bring out damning details ahead of the report? Ned's opening statement certainly focused the minds of some in the chamber. The rest of the day was held in much the same way as all these partisan hearings go: grandstanding by politicians of both colors. The accusers strutted their righteous indignation about the travesties of justice carried out by Odom's DOJ, and previously primed Republicans tossed easy questions to Ned that gave him the opportunity to replay his opening statements. Unsurprisingly, at the end of the hearings, AG Odom declined to offer his resignation.

Also, unsurprisingly, the two media tribes reported very differently about the hearings. The left accused Odom of sidestepping the issue at hand, namely his instructions to dismiss charges against Suit's allies, while the right were elated that, finally, the terrible Ludwig administration would be held to account for its criminal actions.

AM pundits crowed from the rooftops, "I told you all along

that Ludwig was behind the whole impeachment fiasco! Time to put these crooks in jail!"

Various fringe social media sites either proved beyond doubt that Odom was being paid big-time to overturn the convictions or that Ludwig himself had personally planned the entire impeachment operation—with the help of the Russians.

At the conclusion of the Odom hearings, the House prepared papers of censure, and holding a majority, the vote was passed. To great fanfare and speechifying, AG Odom was formally censured.

Ned was pissed, now it was personal.

"Don't let it get you down, Ned. You're in good company," Ron said as they conducted a postmortem of the hearings. "I mean, Alexander Hamilton was censured too."

This was small comfort to Odom. He had spent his life trying to do good, to bring justice, yet now he'd been marked by a strong reprimand from Congress. These people would obviously stop at nothing to accomplish their goal of removing or discrediting the president.

"These people," namely Ludwig with his cohorts and Kunis with his Group, were meeting in the DC war room to review status. They were both pleased.

"Peter, on the party side, we have George set for the nomination, and our virtual campaign has been such a help regarding keeping him on message. I think it's unreasonable to expect another impeachment from the corona hearings, but I will make sure that there is a lot of high-visibility reporting of them, and every damning indictment will be heard loud and clear." Kunis intended to continue using the Group's media control to besmirch Suit in every way possible. "Oh, and congratulations for the Odom hearings, I did not expect to see a vote on censure, that was a nice move, and it will now bring into question every aspect of his report when published. He will have a black mark on his reputation for the rest of his life."

In a display of mutual backslapping, Peter said, "Your protestors have been very effective too, Milos, although I must say, they've been helped by some of our more liberal mayors and governors."

This was a neglected aspect of the unrest; every city that was enduring rioting and vandalism was a Democratic city. Every police force that had been instructed to stand down and simply watch rather than intervene had done so under the orders of Democratic mayors. Even the whole Black Lives Matter movement with its Marxist ideals and message that they will burn the whole thing down if necessary was liaising and coordinating with progressive parts of the DNC.

"Indeed, Peter, although once these people are set into motion, all I need do is provide funding; they are so rabid, so angry that all this chaos, all the riots, occupations, and statue destruction is self-initialized and self-directed. Young progressives are angry about everything. They just want change—even though they don't know what to change or why. A perfect example is this whole defund-the-police movement. I had nothing to do with that initiative; it simply came out of angry minds. I believe this is why Durelle was so successful in her primary campaign. She tapped into the frustrations and anger of young progressives. We can keep the unrest going for a long time, Peter. The surge in corona cases is a good example of media effectiveness and how the right reporting can set up a narrative that unbalances the public."

"It's amazing how everybody now thinks we must avoid contracting the virus rather than just flattening the curve, isn't it?" Peter was deeply impressed by the Group's control of the media and how it could shape opinion.

Their self-congratulatory talk over, strategies for the next phase were agreed. All this unrest, all this destruction, all this suffering was all in the name of removing Suit, but as always, the ends justifies the means.

The Republicans were not entirely sitting on their hands, although they were doing far less than they should, mostly tut-tutting and decrying the violence with no plan of action. However, they did at least try to address certain aspects of the country's current chaotic state. A Senate bill was prepared to address police reform. It continued much of the theme of the president's executive order, with a focus on training, de-escalation, improved social liaison, and other items—actually pretty much in line with the Democrats' talking points on this topic—but the bill was DOA. Without the sixty votes needed to let the proposal hit the floor for debate, the "Police Reform Act" died on its feet.

The House Democrats prepared a radically more severe bill of their own, one that would require all police departments to work with greatly reduced budgets, and it included requirements for disarming many of the frontline cops. As expected, this bill died on the Senate floor. While the country burned, the "Neros" in Congress fiddled. Ron did what he could, issuing executive orders that made monument destruction a federal crime, but it was pissing in the wind. If local police forces were instructed by their liberal mayors to just watch the rioting without stepping in, how would any new law have teeth?

The coronavirus hearings came up next, designed to throw mud and smear reputations ahead of the imminent AG report. As with all such hearings, it mostly provided a venue for politicians on both sides to stand up and make self-important speeches decrying their opponents while making themselves look good. Angry words and accusations are the language of Congress; if a new statue is ever erected before the entrance to that great building, it should depict a politician with arm held out, angrily pointing a finger into the distance. It would be called "It Was Your Fault," and then, of course, the anarchists could pull it down.

Experts were called in to testify on the origins, spread, and response to the virus. Depending on your affiliation, the administration was an abysmal failure or a knight in shining armor. President Suit had either ignored the danger or had been immediate in his response. Hundreds of thousands had died because of him—or millions had been saved. It is such an irony that, in an unprecedented situation such as the pandemic, individuals can claim to know exactly how things should be done, or more precisely, know how they should *not* be done. No matter what the administration actually did, the Democrats knew they would have done it better. In a rare display of agreement, if only on one single point, both parties declared Dr. Giovanni's handling of the response as excellent. He had been a key member of the Corona Strike Force, setting policy and generally talking sense during the daily updates. His conflicting statements and missteps were quietly put aside; a mask does no good, a mask is essential, etc. The takeaway was "Giovanni good, Suit bad."

Ron picked up on this topic during one of his nightly TV briefings. "You know, folks, the hearings going on right now are yet another display of how our friends across the aisle work. It's a show to discredit me and members of my administration. Now, you may think that what I've just said is a perfect example of my paranoia— they're all out to get me—but think on this, I established a Corona Strike Force, coordinated by Vice President Flowers and led by Dr. Giovanni. There's been universal praise for his response, and it has been generally well-placed praise. We did a fantastic job flattening the curve, saving lives, and creating private-public partnerships to produce safety gear. So, who appointed Doc G? I did! Who interfered with Doc G? Not me! Yet I should be hung, drawn, and quartered for my response to the pandemic, while Doc G should be given a Nobel Prize? Think about that, folks. Think about it. And another thing, the lefty state governors with the worst outbreaks claim that my administration didn't support them and that we gave bad advice. Well, America, I call BS on this! Without exception, every single request from the states was fulfilled. If you don't believe me, ask Dr. Giovanni. The so-called bad advice from the CDC is the governors' excuse for their appalling policy of dumping corona-positive cases into nursing homes, places that house our most vulnerable citizens. They claim that the CDC guidelines instructed them to do this.

Well, once again, I call BS! The guidelines clearly say that, as a last resort, patients who tested positive can be placed back into nursing homes—but only if suitable isolation precautions have been taken. Did the governors do this? No, they did not, and thousands died. I trust that the people of this wonderful country can see through this fog of lies, spin, and anarchy and reach their own conclusions. Let's get back on top, America. Let's get back to work. Let's be great again!"

Despite his sometimes legitimate protests, though, Ron was sinking in the polls. His defensive positions on all the racial and virus issues were not doing him any favors; he needed to take a more proactive position. However, drained by months of extreme pressure, he felt like he needed to get back out there among his people to draw strength from their support. He made a decision to hold an intense series of campaign rallies immediately—to the horror of the Democrats who once again claimed he was putting people's lives at risk. The rallies were a key element of Ron's campaign, and there was no way that he would not put them on. Less than four months before the election; it was time to get into high gear.

THREE MONTHS TO GO

The report dropped. Hundreds of journalists obediently lined up at the Capitol—masks and gloves on and socially distanced—to receive their hard copies of the hefty tome. Meanwhile, the document was simultaneously posted on the government website. Tens of thousands of people began poring over it, seeking out the headline items, disclosures that would make for a good sound bite. On the same day as its issue, talking heads across the nation, whether left or right, became instant experts in the whole impeachment investigation. A new cottage industry of paid pundits sprang up; anyone with the most tenuous connection to the affair was grabbed, a coveted asset for repeated exploitation by the media.

The president too had been studying the report, aided by VP Flowers. Ron was certain that any findings showing Ludwig's involvement would be buried by the media while the slightest hint of impropriety on the part of Suit's team would be sung from the rooftops. As he was poring over its findings, subpoenas were being prepared for several members of the Ludwig administration—and arrest warrants were even being drafted against a few individuals.

AG Odom wanted to perform a clean sweep through the scum involved in the whole sorry affair, but he knew that indictments for all the guilty parties would be a bridge too far; pragmatically, he elected to focus on the easiest to convict offenders and planned his actions accordingly. On the eve of publication, he met with the president to outline the upcoming events.

"It seems to me, Ned, that Ludwig was behind everything." Ron was basing his view on what he'd been told and what he'd read.

Ned replied, "Undoubtedly, Mr. President, but don't for one minute think that he will be indicted for anything. The office of the presidency is, in my view, sacred and privileged. Any president, including yourself, has certain protections from the law, and any attempt to prove a president is guilty of, or complicit in, crimes is a hiding to nothing. A president has so much leeway in everything he does that proving wrongdoing conclusively would be almost impossible. I will not waste my department's time on such a fool's errand; we must be satisfied with pursuing those parties who we know we can get convicted. You know, sir, there are many things you've done that I do not agree with. You've made many decisions that, in my view, have been wrong. But, as president of the United States you enjoy that discretion to govern the country as you see fit. The office is more important than the man, and that's why I took on this task to dig up the travesties perpetrated against this office and to pursue them to the best of my ability. The coming weeks will show how effective I've been in my efforts, but regardless of the final outcome, you know that I will always support you in the legal discharge of your duties, and I will always seek out those who attempt to usurp your legitimacy. Speech over, sir."

Thanks, Ned. I appreciate your candor." Ron reached out and shook Ned's hand. "As an outsider, there are precious few people in this godawful city who I can trust. Joyce is one, and I like to think that you are another. Do what you must, Ned, and I'll be behind you—whatever happens."

While the nation had been enrapt by the pandemic and race riots, Odom's squad had spent months empaneling grand juries and gathering evidence. On the day of the report's release, indictments and charges were handed out to a group of perpetrators who'd been deeply involved in developing the false narratives of Russian collusion and Ukrainian quid pro quo that had formed the basis of their impeachment efforts.

Ludwig's attorney general for most of his term had been Aaron Shell, and he was indicted on counts of obstruction of justice, falsifying of evidence, and other less felonious charges. Shell was in good company too; similar indictments were handed down to Joe Carney, the now-retired head of the FBI, and to one of Stacey's predecessors, Deborah Salem, an ex-chair of the DNC. Charges and arrests were sure to follow.

Meanwhile, following classic police procedural tactics, a number of lesser wrongdoers were arrested on a probable cause basis and hauled in. These individuals included Carney's assistant at the FBI and the FISA court judge who had repeatedly empowered and allowed the wiretapping and surveillance of members of Suit's teams, based on knowingly false information in the FISA warrants' applications. The paper trail for these two individuals' crimes was crystal clear. There was no need for a grand jury—just put 'em in cuffs.

Even better, with warrants issued and arrests made, these perps were facing many years of time, and they were now disposed to helping in the investigation of the big wheels behind the whole travesty of justice.

As Ned's exhaustive investigation had shown, DNC Chair Salem—almost certainly under Ludwig's direction—had worked with Russian operatives to develop a fictitious report that showed Suit's collusion with them. This report was then used by Carney and his FBI cohorts to initiate a comprehensive surveillance operation throughout the latter part of Suit's campaign, his transitional government, and his initial period of office. Either through luck or guile, most of the legwork relating to obtaining the necessary warrants for the wiretapping and other charges had been delegated to his second-in-command, and so the paper trail made arresting him a no-brainer.

Amazingly, secret records had also been kept between the FISA court judge and the assistant FBI director, and these clearly showed that the judge was in on the entire charade, resulting in slam-dunk charges against him too.

All this nastiness, all this underhandedness, just to get Suit, without any regard for the fact that he'd been elected by the will of the people? So much for democracy. Of course, there was other fallout from the AG's report. Several minor players were arrested and brought in, ready to save their skins by singing whatever song they thought would help mitigate their charges.

What of the media reaction to these revelations, this scandal the AG Odom characterized as the worst abuse of power in US history? It was exactly as you'd expect it to be. Fox News, AM radio, and right-wing newspapers devoted their coverage almost exclusively to the whole affair. Their years of suspicions now confirmed, this was vindication, the sweet taste of victory, of being right all along! The pandemic? Forgotten. Race riots and anarchy? Forgotten.

Meanwhile, CNN, the *Times*, the *Post,* and their blue brethren covered the report with a skeptical eye. Sure, the magnitude of Odom's findings was such that coverage had to be done, but the spin was unsurprising. "This is really just Suit's corrupt lapdog, Odom, getting payback against Ludwig. We all know Suit colluded, and we all know he did quid pro quo." Words such as "alleged," "claimed," and "reportedly" became frequent descriptors in any of their reporting, along with reminders that the report was the work of a compromised AG who had been censured for his shady dealings.

It was a tricky balancing act for all the left-wing media outlets. Under Kunis's quiet direction, they were told to keep hammering the narrative of the administration's incompetent response to the pandemic, coupled with continually stirring up racial unrest, but now they could add in a little corrupt and partisan AG report coverage.

The Democratic House began making noises about holding hearings to address "the veracity of these outrageous claims." This was to be expected, but it was a potentially high-risk move on their part. Scouring through the hefty report, even with its name redactions, it didn't take a genius to identify certain members of Congress who had clearly been complicit in some of the nefarious deeds perpetrated during the scandal. That some of these individuals were also senior members of the Judiciary Committee added a delicious irony.

Across the Capitol, the GOP-held Senate looked placidly on at the House shenanigans, with a collective "told-ya-so" look on their faces, and declared their intention to hold Senate hearings on the whole scandal. Meanwhile, the House adopted the old "look, a squirrel" tactic of distraction. They lost interest in AG Odom's sensational findings, brushing them off as a bunch of lies perpetrated by a compromised AG, and instead kicked off yet another Russian story line. This time it was all about Suit's cozy relationship with the Russians, to the extent that he was in cahoots with their leader to profit from the eternally running conflict in Afghanistan.

Per the usual uncorroborated sources leaking to the *New York Times*, Suit and Putin were accused of making billions personally via corrupt military contracts and arms supplies. This tissue-thin story nonetheless had legs thanks to mass coverage by the left and statements made by the Democratic House leader who was 100 percent sure that Suit was being blackmailed by the Russians over something (what exactly it was, she never disclosed). As might be expected, this latest Russian outrage eventually fell out of the news cycle when even the most anti-Suit haters could see that it was all BS. *No matter,* the media thought. *We can always fabricate another salacious Russian story and keep the whole Russia thing alive.*

What a year! Beginning with the best economy and employment in history, then pandemic, then rioting and chaos, and now, the worst economy and employment in decades, and all in the space of just a few months. If there was ever a time for President Suit to get in front of the people and offer comfort, hope, and solutions, it was now, and for Ron, that made it even more important to get his rallies back up and running ASAP.

"Good evening, America! How are we tonight?" Ron was in a large outdoor arena in the key battleground state of Florida. His crowd was mostly, although not exclusively, wearing masks, and people were spaced out per CDC guidelines. While this had obvious repercussions on the size of the crowd, some six thousand plus were in the stadium, all fired up and ready for a fun evening.

After running through a few set-piece remarks about his campaign platform, Ron began his stream-of-consciousness chat with the audience. "Where's George, huh? Considering he is my opponent for the most powerful job on earth, you'd think he might have a little more enthusiasm, wouldn't you? But no, there he is in his ivory tower back in DC, making his orchestrated webcasts and occasionally sneaking out for a photo op."

The crowd was doing the usual thing of booing at the mention of Burton's name and cheering at each slur that Ron leveled on him.

"If you believe the polls, this is a winning strategy for George. We'll ignore the fact that 95 percent of the special elections we've seen this year went to Republicans, including snatching districts away from longtime Democratic strongholds. We'll ignore the fact that, before the pandemic, our nation was enjoying its best economy in history, and we'll ignore the fact that, despite the horrible negative impact of our lockdown, our economy is racing back. Oh, and let's look at the rioting, shall we? Every single city that's been hit hard by these riots is a Democratic city in a Democratic state. Coincidence? I think not. Vote Democrat—and you're voting for chaos.

"But, folks, before the looters and criminals took over, the true roots of the protests were justified. African Americans do have legitimate grievances; they have been unfairly treated. However,

I like to think that they want law and order, I like to think that they want jobs, and I like to think they want a better life for their children. So, where do I stand of this? You'll see from my executive orders and other actions that I'm all about law and order. Look at the employment stats, and you'll see that minority employment has never been higher. Education? Well, our school system has for too long being in the thrall of unions. Teachers may have ideals, but under the direction of their unions, we've descended to a lowest common denominator approach, so it's time to get our kids taught properly again. Our education secretary will shortly be announcing new initiatives to increase the number of charter schools in our nation and to implement a school voucher system more widely. Why should you be forced to give your property tax money to a lousy school? Vouchers mean that you, the parent, can decide where your child goes for their education. All these initiatives will be especially helpful to our minorities."

Ron talked on, riffing on a range of topics, but education was one of the new arrows in his quiver; it was well-known that African Americans like charter schools and vouchers because it gives them a chance to get away from the usually poor schools of their neighborhoods. The inexplicable devotion of minorities to the Democratic Party had been shaken in the previous election—when Ron won significantly increased support from them—and hopefully this education plan would help cement that support.

The rallies continued, always with massive criticism from the press for Suit's flagrant disregard for public safety, and George continued his carefully scripted non-campaign. Mysteriously, news stories all began to simultaneously focus on the "massive surge" in corona cases, despite the simple fact that across the nation, the death rate had slowed to a trickle, and hospitalizations had peaked and were going down. No matter, more testing equals more positives equals more panic.

Often overlooked in the reporting was the small point that

many of the tests were actually looking for corona antibodies, not the actual virus, which swelled the positive results significantly. In addition, members of the CDC quietly noted that perhaps 50 percent of the tests were giving wrong results. No matter, with a strengthening economy and a populace trying to get back to normal, the media's message was to "get back into lockdown, shut businesses down, and wait until we tell you it's safe." Democratic governors and even some weak Republican ones obliged with the reintroduction of quarantine and other punitive measures.

In the middle of this latest round of lunacy, convention season arrived. Despite much hand-wringing and calls for cancellation, Republicans pressed on with their plans for an actual convention to be held in Ron's hometown of Houston. After the whole event had been finalized, the city's Democratic mayor threw a curveball just weeks before it was scheduled to open. Citing the current surge in corona cases in Houston, he instructed the convention center's management to cancel the event.

Things looked grim for the GOP until the secretary of the Treasury had a quiet, off-the-record conversation with the mayor. He pointed out that the massive amount of funding all urban centers would inevitably need to offset their tax revenue declines would be coming from the Fed's pockets—and it would be largely discretionary. You scratch my back, and I'll scratch yours, Mayor Turner. Billions of dollars were at risk, so against his better judgment and instructions from his party leaders, the mayor relented and allowed the event to proceed. Some face-saving was made by his instruction that the GOP must strictly follow all social distancing guidelines and other CDC recommendations.

The GOP convention was much like any previous one. Delegates arrived and partied, speeches were made, votes were cast, and a good time was had by all. It felt so good to be almost normal—if only for a few days—but the normality was not complete. Temperatures were taken, and face masks were the order of the day, usually decorated with the Stars and Stripes, or slogans ("Suits Me," "Suit Up for America," or "Let's Beat Burton!").

Social distancing was maintained in the layout and format of the convention, but luckily the George Brown Convention Center in Houston is huge and even with six-foot spacing requirements, it could easily accommodate all who came. Perhaps the biggest departure from a typical convention was the intensity of the protests. Antifa, BLM, Occupy, and the usual other crowds descended on Houston with a vengeance, naturally ignoring masks and social distancing measures.

The pattern was per all similar previous protests. Daylight saw generally peaceful marches and protests, with a modicum of scuffles with police and much speechifying. Convention attendees were expected to run the gauntlet of placards, obscenities, and threats as they entered the center each day. Night brought out the vermin; gangs of rioters roamed downtown, smashing, spraying, fighting, and having a good old time.

The city's mayor and his Democratic police chief played by their party-suggested rules, and they mostly let the chaos happen, passively watching the hordes of incomers creating mayhem while Houston's inhabitants looked on in horror.

"Why isn't anyone doing something?" Houstonians asked as gangs roamed the streets unmolested. Tranquility Park near the convention center was turned into anarchist HQ for the duration of the GOP convention—with tents, food, supplies, protest signs, weapons, and everything else a rioter needs being provided by persons unknown (read Kunis and the PFA).

As the convention wrapped up with its expected Suit-Flowers endorsement, the Tranquility tent city morphed into the "Houston Free Zone" as the anarchists realized they'd had such an easy time of it in the Bayou City. Alas, it was not to be; having seen the absolute disaster unfolding in cities such as Seattle, Minneapolis, and Portland, even leftie Mayor Turner finally decided that an occupied zone in his city would not be good for his image. The police moved in to dismantle the park and return it to the people, but would he have done this without some "persuasion" from angry Texans?

The media and the left gleefully assumed that the zone was to be there until the day after the convention closed, when a large group of citizens surrounded the park, allowing anyone in, but no one out. This clan of hundreds were orderly, organized, and disciplined— many of them with open carry. They were categorized by the media as an "army of threatening armed vigilantes," despite being orderly but firm. Who created this volunteer force was unknown, although rumors indicated it was a coalition of Suit's donors. Regardless of its origins, the tactic was successful. Within twenty-four hours, Mayor Turner realized that pressure in and around the park was building to a head, and he had to act or face an ugly escalation. So, bye-bye, Houston Free Zone.

The following week, the nation was treated to the weird spectacle of the Democratic Virtual National Convention. Stacey and her team had been working hard putting it together. The format was that of a giant webinar. In the DNC's headquarters, a meeting room had been set up—socially distanced, of course—that would hold the chair, the main committee representatives, and the Democrat lions like Ludwig and Burton. Elsewhere, throughout the nation, in every state capital, similar groups gathered in meeting rooms to participate via video link. Once bitten, twice shy was Stacey's motto for this event, and she was sure to not rely on Fatima Ludwig's cronies to set up the necessary tech for the convention, instead bringing in a top-class and expensive IT company. Extensive pre-convention testing had shown the setup to be robust and reliable.

Stacey was feeling pretty good about things going into the convention. After declaring the event open, she said, "Welcome to our Democratic National Convention. Extraordinary times call for extraordinary measures, and this virtual format is our party's mature and cautious response to the terrible global pandemic under which we are all living. As we all know, close contact with others at this time will lead to an escalation of the virus, and inevitably, more deaths. The responsible thing, therefore, is to prevent contagion by holding our convention virtually—just as we continue to press for an election format based on mail-in voting, which is the only safe way to vote under these circumstances. It's the right thing to do.

"Before we begin the business of the convention, I have a list of house rules that I need you all to observe. Firstly, when one party is speaking, all other feeds are automatically muted. This is to avoid garbling from multiple parties speaking at once. Participants may enter comments or questions in the comments section at the bottom of your screens. All comments will all be addressed once the party in question has finished speaking. If you have any urgent topic or an important point of order, you may hit the 'raise arm' icon on your screens, and that will immediately notify us of your urgent concern. These will be initially addressed offline by the committee and brought before all attendees if considered necessary."

Stacey went on to explain time limits for speeches and other procedural points, and she then moved on to the first item on the agenda.

"Now, because of the extraordinary times in which we are living, there have been a number of unusual circumstances surrounding this election. Obviously, Mr. Burton's campaign has been severely constrained by the national quarantine, and he has had to work under duress with many limitations. Another, perhaps more significant, aspect of this year's unique election season is the nomination of his running mate. Normally, the candidate's choice would be announced shortly ahead of the convention, but time constraints this year have meant that this decision was delayed. I will now hand you all over to George Burton who will make his announcement regarding his vice president."

George's aged head popped up on screens across the country.

As he looked down at his notes, a voice in his ear said, "Now, go carefully, George. Don't fuck this up. Just read from the page—and whatever you do, no off-script moments!"

George's eyes bounced up and down as he alternatively glanced at his notes and the camera. "My fellow Americans, before we begin, I'd like to thank you all for your confidence in me as your presumptive Democratic presidential candidate. I'm, er, touched by your faith in this old warhorse, and hopefully you won't change your minds when it comes to the official endorsement later in the convention."

"Stick to the script, George!" hissed the earpiece.

"A vice president is an important role, hell, I should know. That person rounds out a party's ethos, its beliefs, and its hopes for the future. When in power, a president and his vice work as a team, shaping the nation. It's a key job, and my team has spent many hours to reach its decision. So, without further ado, I'd like to announce my choice for vice president. She's a woman of immense capability and experience. You've all seen her a lot recently, in fact, just a few minutes ago. Please welcome vice presidential candidate, Stacey Lincoln!"

George leaned back in his seat, relieved that his moment was past. The second her name fell from George's lips, a raise arm" icon sprang up on the central console at DNC HQ.

"I've got this," said Ludwig as he patched in Shawanda Durelle to his headset.

Stacey's face was filling all screens as she took in the virtual applause and began her acceptance speech.

"Motherfucker," came an angry shrill voice through Peter's headset. "What have you just done? We had a deal. I demand that you retract the bullshit George just spouted and do what you promised. I'm supposed to be the vice president!"

"Shawanda, I can appreciate your anger," Peter said to soothe the woman, fully aware that this would be impossible. "We had to make, er, adjustments to the campaign, and that led us to Stacey Lincoln. I know, it's unfortunate for you, but a more moderate candidate is considered to be our only way forward.

"I'm gonna bury you, you bunch of welshing motherfuckers. Open my mic right now!"

Shawanda's outrage was not unexpected. A creaky voice with indeterminate mid-European accent came onto the line, although the screen face remained that of Peter Ludwig.

"Miss Durelle, I too can appreciate that you are upset by this development, but perhaps you should take a breath. Imagine a scenario where you publicize anything about our previous arrangements. That might very well give you a sense of satisfaction, of revenge. But, consider this, should you say the slightest thing about our previous agreement, then we of course would be duty bound to release all the details of your recent financial windfalls. I think that the public would be fascinated to learn how you managed to buy a luxury condominium in the most exclusive part of Washington, the very place in which you are now sitting. I could go on and describe other transactions recently completed, and of course, one mustn't forget that those rumors about your campaign funding improprieties could quickly resurface. How will your supporters feel when they discover that you can be bought? What will that do to your credibility and future career? Now, I'm certain that there is an important and lucrative cabinet position in your future, so my advice to you, Miss Durelle, is to, how do you say it, suck it up."

"She's hung up, Milos," Peter said through the headset.

⌒⊶⊰⌒

Following the truncated virtual convention, as the nation's media fed on news about Stacey's veep nomination, she sat with Kunis in a hotel room, away from prying eyes.

"Did I not promise that there was a reason for you to get back into political life, to take on your DNC role?" Kunis said. "I have fulfilled my pledge to you—and now you must continue to trust me, Stacey. We are in the home stretch."

"I was wrong to doubt you, Milos," Stacey answered, "but the whole Durelle deal had me worried for a while. I thought you might not follow through."

They clinked glasses to toast a successful convention.

DEBATES

"**W**orrying news from China, where reports are emerging about yet another new strain of virus with pandemic potential." Such were the almost-gleeful articles coming out in the *Times* and *Post*, who both seemed agog with excitement at the prospect of yet another calamitous pandemic. They tag-teamed this story with that of the impending "second wave." The current surge was apparently getting old in the eyes of the public; new threats had to be circulated to keep folk off balance. Helping in this important media task was the continued coverage of riots and protests throughout every large Democrat-held urban center across the nation.

By now, people both left and right were in danger of growing immune to the ongoing outrage of nightly chaos, with its burnings, beatings, and statue topplings, and they needed to be fed some new scary stuff. A potential ray of light shone down from Seattle when its mayor finally ordered her police force to move in and dismantle the tent city/free zone. This job was accomplished with relative efficiency, and little violence, which surprised many after seeing murders and mayhem unfolding within the zone's hastily erected walls in the past weeks. The free zone's displaced inhabitants simply dispersed to the shadows, no doubt waiting for another opportunity to create more havoc when conditions permitted. Seattle's large homeless population had loved the free zone, but now they too had to leave and go back into the shadows.

Thank goodness that the mayor had seen reason and had done the right thing for her citizens. No, wait—she hadn't. It was only after the mob stood in front of her mansion and began their noisy and violent protests in front of her that the mayor had a sudden epiphany: "People deserve protection and shouldn't feel threatened in their own homes." Wow, callous disregard mutates into common sense only when the mayor experiences what her hapless citizens have endured for ages.

In Congress, the group of Democratic progressives known as the Mob voiced their open support of all the fringe groups at the core of national unrest: They jumped on the "defund the police" bandwagon and embraced other radical agenda items such as rewriting history via the elimination of "offensive" national monuments. This House charge was led by Shawanda Durelle who, freshly embittered from her national convention experience, had opted to do what she does best: mobilize the left and turn the heat up on the establishment.

Shawanda couldn't be vocal about the unfulfilled promises made to her, but she sure as hell could make life difficult for the bastards who'd cheated her. Across the country, more liberal mayors and governors jumped on the bandwagon too, slashing their police departments' budgets and reducing force size. The obvious consequence? Crime rates skyrocketed in the affected cities. Murder rates doubled, theft shot up, and every criminal datapoint spiked.

While the nation as a whole—at least those who were Fox viewers—looked on with horror and despair at the daily stream of sobering statistics and video feeds showing old ladies being beaten senseless for a few dollars, or for being white, the people in power making such decisions continued to characterize the whole thing as an exercise in utopia or some sort of grand social experiment.

CNN viewers saw no riots, just "mostly peaceful protests."

The standard response to any criticism was to say that it was every American's right to protest and that they could not be seen to stifle freedom of speech. These lofty ideals of course conveniently omitted that the perpetrators of all the mayhem were not political activists or protestors: They were not "engaging in lawful protest." They were just gangs of rudderless punks who simply enjoyed causing chaos. It was so much better than living in Mom's basement.

At a higher level, but in a more formalized way, the Democrats and Republicans were preparing for their own battles. With both sets of candidates now official as a result of their conventions, the next step on the road to the presidency was the debates.

In the weeks leading up to these traditional three verbal wrestling matches, both candidates got out in front of the nation. Ron began to supplement his rallies with regular TV interviews with a normally hostile talking head. He felt obligated to do so partially because of the various social media platforms' success in stifling his preferred method of talking to the public. It just wasn't so easy these days for him to post something when he needed to get the message out; if deemed "unchecked" or "divisive," the Facebook and Twitter Nazis simply blocked or stifled his posts. Surprise, surprise, many of Ron's posts were considered unsuitable, thus necessitating engagement with a more traditional means of communication: network TV.

George had been brought down from his condo and was making more public appearances than he had done for months. Following the results of his medical examination, his team seemed to be finally getting the right balance of antidepressants, anxiolytics, and antipsychotics, and his behavior, while still often erratic and unpredictable, was at least a little more controllable. Pump him full of the right cocktail of drugs, cross your fingers, and perhaps he'd make it through an interview without crashing and burning. They weren't taking any chances, however, and his public appearances were carefully choreographed under strict rules of engagement. Early on in his reemergence, an interview in front of a group of journalists offered a good example of how the rest of his campaign was going to be run. Every question asked was pre-vetted and predetermined, and every answer given was read by George from a teleprompter—with earpiece backup as necessary. It was a stilted affair all round, but at least—for his team—it offered none of the drama and fear of an unscripted interview. To make the entire interview charade even more cheesy, every question was a softball. Instead of his opinions on the riots, George was queried about topics such as whether he was worried that he'd get complacent as his lead in all the polls grew.

It was quite a contrast to Ron's treatment at the hands of the mass media.

"Mr. President, given your recent statements and executive actions regarding the current protests and removal of statues, do you wish the South would rise again?"

"Well, Chuck, I'm disgusted by your question and its implications. I love all of America, always have, and I believe that people like you and your friends in the media are stoking the fires of racial prejudice by asking questions such as that. You ought to be ashamed of yourself."

This was the tone of pretty much all of Ron's combative appearances in the time running up to the first debate. At least he still had his nightly briefing to help get his message out.

"Yet another record set of employment and economic figures, folks," he declared one evening. "I know you won't see much news about this, but we are going back to work! Consumer spending up, employment claims down. I tell y'all, we just may be back to normal by the end of the year. But only if you elect me, of course! If good old George wins, then expect a sudden lurch to the left. He may claim to be the moderate candidate, the safe hands who will walk you back to those halcyon days of yore, but see for yourself, the man is over the hill. He'll be the figurehead, sure, but under a Burton presidency, America will be run by his handlers, the far-left people who are orchestrating all of this chaos."

How right he was!

As the debates neared, the Burton and Suit teams engaged in the usual sparring over what channels, what format, and even how many debates. Given the unique circumstances, it was a more difficult discussion than usual: no more the normal format of moderators amid a large audience and no more candidates next to each other on stage. There were arguments about whether the two men should be somehow encased in plexiglass bubbles—or if they could even run the debates from their homes.

Ron was keen to increase the number of debates because he was certain he'd kick Burton's ass on any topic. "Let's have as many as possible."

On the opposite side, Burton's team naturally enough wanted fewer debates and preferably a wholly remote and distanced format.

The entire process, as per usual, was overseen by the CPD, or Commission on Presidential Debates, who had the ultimate say. A supposedly nonpartisan body, many on the right were nonetheless surprised when the final details of the debates were published. Three debates were scheduled for mid-to-late September, each one to be held on a different university's campus. So far, so normal, but then it got interesting. There was to be no audience. Moderators were to be (naturally) socially distanced from each other and the candidates. Masks, while not mandatory, were encouraged. To discourage the two men from roaming around the stage and possibly getting too close to each other, they were to be seated behind desks. The biggest surprise was that all debate questions were to be supplied to the candidates in advance. The CPD's logic for this was to discourage the two men from yelling at each other or from running over in time. Justification for this extraordinary change was that "excessive shouting and talking spreads the virus and therefore should be discouraged." CNN et al hailed this wrinkle as a sensible measure, and Fox panned it as an obvious sop to Burton. Burton's team breathed a collective sigh of relief, and Suit's team groaned in frustration.

Meanwhile, out in the nation, the hospitalization and death rates continued to fall, but that wasn't how the pandemic was being reported. Instead, the media focused exclusively on the number of cases while simultaneously pushing for more testing, Well, duh! More testing equals more positives equals more headlines about record numbers of cases. Other little wrinkles were discretely emerging too; under the terms of Congress's emergency economic bailout package, hospitals had an actual financial incentive for treating corona patients because they received additional emergency funding based upon their corona treatments. So, voila, anyone admitted invariably was classed as "positive," cha-ching, cash into the coffers. In addition, data on corona case hospitalizations and deaths was being quietly massaged by individuals in the CDC. Any hospitalization or death from influenza or pneumonia or congestive heart failure was now included in the corona statistics, thus inflating them. Was the "surge" real or fabricated? No one knew. The only sure thing was that the numbers were not accurate, and the experts—as with all their prior projections—were invariably wrong.

And what of the AG's blockbuster report? Sure, it still got sporadic column inches and airtime, but it was usually buried by other stories: the riots, defunding police, toppling statues, the pandemic, and the latest Russian hoax. Individuals continued to be arrested or indicted, and more salacious details of wrongdoing on a federal level continued to come out. That was dry stuff; in today's instant gratification society, people want easily digested sound bites and not complex, labyrinthine plots.

In the week before the night of the first debate, one of the many companies that were frantically working on a vaccine against the virus announced that their first human trial had been successful and that perhaps a vaccine would be sent out to the public before year-end.

Of course, there already was a vaccine, held by Kunis's Chinese company, the same one that had developed the virus, but Milos was not about to release that however until his grand plan had played out. His surrogates had a quiet word with Giovanni, and in a Corona Strike Force briefing, the doctor responded to a journalist who'd asked about the vaccine.

"As many know, it typically takes two or three years to develop a vaccine, and some diseases are impossible to guard against. Now, we've all read the recent announcement that a vaccine may be available by year-end. That would make it only eight months from conception to release. As a doctor, I find that hard to believe, but even if it proves to be the case, I would strongly advise against any widespread use of such an incompletely tested drug until more is known of its efficacy; the possible side effects might far outweigh the benefits. As with all things related to this terrible pandemic, caution must be our watchword."

Good job, Dr. Buzzkill.

The first debate set the tone of those to follow.

"Good evening, and welcome to the first of three presidential debates. I'm Anderson Cooper, and joining me tonight as moderators are Donna Brazile and Jake Tapper. As you can see from this empty hall on the campus of the University of Notre Dame, here in Indiana, the coronavirus pandemic has meant that changes have been made to the more traditional format in order to ensure the safety of our candidates and ourselves." He went on to explain the rules of engagement, time limits for reply and rebuttal, and finally disclosed that all questions had been provided to the candidates ahead of time.

"The first question is for President Suit. In recent speeches and campaign appearances, you have emphasized law and order, clearly stating that police forces would not be defunded under your watch. Meanwhile, several cities across the nation have already voted to do just that. How will you address those mayors and governors who go against your wishes?"

Of course, Ron was prepared for this since both candidates

had been given the questions ahead of time. "Well, Anderson, what you're seeing in those cities that have not supported their police is a massive increase in crime. As you know, we live in a federalist system, so unless national security is in jeopardy it is not the job of the federal government to impose its will on states, but to support them. My administration stands ready to intervene should the governors request help. However, what you are already seeing is a massive backlash against their liberal policies; companies are pulling out of the places where chaos rules, and citizens are either leaving the cities or demonstrating strong support for their police. Our society is only civil because it has law and order. Remove this and you descend to the gutter, where every thug sees opportunity and every criminal is emboldened by liberal leaders' passive nonresponses to outrageous acts of violence and destruction. So, people, if you are enduring life in New York, or Seattle, or any number of cities that burn each night, speak up, force your elected representatives to act, and we will support you and assist in restoring order."

"Thank you, President Suit. Vice President Burton, you have two minutes for rebuttal."

George began his reply, his voice muffled somewhat by the mask he was wearing (unlike naked-faced Ron). He'd rehearsed his answers over and over, and he was being guided as usual by voices in his ear.

"Thank you, Cooper. When I hear the people call for the elimination of police, I listen. Look, there have been so many abuses by the police, particularly their systemic racism, and that has brought on this current round of mostly peaceful protests. I fully support the protesters, and when I'm president, I will enact new laws that restrict abuse by the police. We will work with city mayors and state governors to reallocate funding away from policing into social programs. The police should not be the answer to every situation, we need to have rapid-response social workers who'll come into a situation and defuse it using nonviolent means. Thank you."

"Good job, George," came the voice in his ear. The debate was underway and with one question down, eleven more to go, Burton had not screwed up! His handlers began to relax, if only a little.

"The next question is for you, Vice President Burton. During this current global pandemic, America has lost almost one hundred and fifty thousand lives, and with the current surge of cases, we are global pariahs, unable to travel to many countries around the globe. How would you have handled this crisis?"

"Well, Anderson, I would have handled it better. It's unconscionable that President Suit here has presided over the death of a hundred and fifty million citizens. He should have enforced the lockdown sooner, he should have been better prepared with safety equipment, and he should not have allowed positive cases into retirement homes. There are so many things he did wrong that I could sit here all night and not finish listing them off!"

Ron's rebuttal was brief. "Well, it's interesting to hear from George that 50 percent of our population has died of the virus, but I'm sure your fact-checkers will look into that and see no problem with it. Anyway, when I imposed the China and European travel bans at the beginning of this pandemic, I was hammered by nearly everyone who told me it was an overreaction. George here said it. You, Anderson, said it—as did the two people sitting on either side of you tonight. But now it seems I didn't do it early enough. I've read the Burton plan for handing this crisis; it's on his campaign website. I could go through it point by point and note that every single thing he lists, we've actually already done, but that would be a waste of time. It's window dressing, Anderson, and nothing more. Our response to this medical crisis has been rated by numerous independent global agencies as 'good,' in the top one-third of all countries affected. We're not perfect, but we've handled things better than most, and I'm proud of our efforts."

The evening thus continued generally as it had begun. Question topics covered statue toppling, immigration, the environment, and the usual things that debates are expected to cover. The economy came up in a question to George.

"Thanks for that question, Anderson. You know, this man across from me has run our economy into the ground. We have the highest unemployment in decades, we're spending trillions of dollars bailing out big businesses, and we are in a historic recession. I can't think of a worst performance by any president in history. My, er, leadership will turn things around. We'll have social programs to protect our citizens, and they won't need to work if they don't want to, no, er, I mean if they're, they're unable to. Government's job is to protect its people, and we'll do that."

Ron's reply was immediate; he didn't wait to be invited by the moderators. "George, I suspect your handlers are pretty pissed right now. You've just let the cat out of the bag! Your Freudian slip about folks not having to work if they didn't want to sums up exactly what's wrong with Democratic policies and governance. It makes people rely on the government. If Mr. Burton is elected, he will create an underclass of people who have never worked a day in their lives and who have no appetite for, or desire to ever work. They'll be leeches on society, sucking out money that's been earned by a diminishing labor pool who'll be taxed increasingly heavily. It's a downward spiral to oblivion, while president Burton and the people controlling him will look down in luxury from their ivory towers. What my administration did is get government out of the way so that folks could excel and succeed, and look at how successful that was: the best economy in history. George blames me for a recession and all the other negative numbers, but I don't own them; the pandemic does. Look at our latest jobs report or consumer spending data. We're already climbing out of the corona-caused pit. We built the best economy in our nation's history once, and we'll do it again!"

Ron had been correct about George's handlers; the second he'd said you don't have to work if you don't want to, George's earpiece had lit up with instructions to walk it back, to stick to the script, to focus. Perhaps his meds were wearing off—or perhaps he was just tired from having to pay attention so much—but as the closing remarks came up, George started winging it.

"Thanks for allowing me here tonight, Donald, Alderton, and, er, you, the other guy. You know, back in the day, I could whip this punk here." He stood and pointed across at Ron. "This guy here, I could whip his ass. When I was younger, I was pretty buff, check me out on Netscape, or whatever it is these days. I looked good: blond hair, muscles, chiseled jaw, an Aryan god. Okay, so now I'm a little older, but if he accuses me of living in some sort of ivory tower again, I swear I'll punch him! I'm a man of the people and a man for the people, all of you, you poor uneducated ones, the whites, the gays, you name it, I'm for it. Remember, vote for George Burton if you want us to take care of you!" As he was giving this final speech, George had ripped off his face mask and, in doing so, had pulled out his earpiece, which could now be seen dangling down, tangled up in the mask's straps. He was oblivious to the frantic yelling coming out of it as his handlers went ballistic at this latest off-script tirade.

"Okay, um, thank you, Vice President Burton," said a clearly baffled Anderson Cooper who'd just witnessed George's meltdown on live television. "President Suit, you also have five minutes for closing comments."

Ron had sat quietly through George's tirade, eyes wide in bewildered amazement, a slight grin of disbelief on his face.

"No thanks, Anderson. No, I'm good."

One down, two to go. Following the closing remarks debacle of debate number one, the commission opted to modify the debate format once more; they imposed a ten-minute delay in its transmission, so that any "unseemly" behavior could be edited out before the nation got to see it. Their rationale of course was that this was of potential benefit to both candidates, but the reality was entirely different.

During the second debate, George began conversing with his handlers. "Okay, guys, help me out here. They're talking about the

Paris accords, but I don't remember any goddam question about France … tell me what to say."

Everyone else in the hall looked at each other in puzzlement, but this obvious proof of Burton's cheating earpiece made no difference. Those words didn't make it to the public. Similarly, in the final debate, Burton simply froze up, going silent for perhaps thirty seconds, with a faraway look on his face. The moderators brought him back to reality only after repeatedly prompting him. With the rapid editing techniques used by the broadcast team, however, George's reply was seamless. Ah, the power of media.

⚜

Sue was back at work, socially distanced of course, with 50 percent occupancy. Like so many others, these restrictions didn't really matter because at least she was back earning a living and not cooped up! Her phone rang.

"Hello, Miss Oakley? It's Professor Casey from the Manhattan Institute. Listen, I recently met with one of Attorney General Odom's team to discuss some policy issues, and I actually did mention your request to talk to someone from the administration. He is open to hearing what you have to say, but as you might imagine, things are a little hectic at this time, what with the ongoing Russian inquiries and the election. He suggested that we revisit the topic after Election Day, say in December. I'm sorry if this doesn't work for you, but it was the best he could offer."

"Not at all, Professor Casey." Sue was slightly amazed that someone was willing to listen to her at all. "It's no problem to wait. I can work with any date that's good for you. Thank you so much. I can't believe you thought of me. Thanks again."

They hung up, and Sue got back to sanitizing a recently vacated table. *Wow, someone is actually willing to listen to me? What will happen when I tell them about the whole Lincoln conspiracy?*

THE HOME STRETCH

S treet battles continued across the nation as the ritual of nightly rioting unfolded on television screens and in cities everywhere. Empty-headed and ineffective politicians on both sides of the aisle argued the pros and cons of civil disobedience. The red tribe accused the blues of enabling lawlessness through their passive mayors and governors, and the blue tribe showed righteous outrage at the reds' desire to stifle legitimate protest.

No matter who was right and who was wrong, both sides were demonstrating exactly how useless politicians of any color truly are: speechifying and pontificating as the country burned. In all of this, the original and legitimate reason for the protests—that of the murder of a black man by a bad cop—had mutated into a broader movement to fundamentally change the fabric of America. Undo history, dismantle police forces, and remake America into a socialist utopia. It was classic bait-and-switch politics: capitalize on a crisis, any crisis, to get changes that you want.

Black Lives Matter was getting massive money injections from all over the place: Hollywood types assuaging their guilt; corporate entities hoping that a woke financial gesture would protect them from future accusations of racism; liberal activists who just wanted to continue fanning the flames of racism; and people who genuinely thought that BLM was a noble cause. Any reading of its manifesto would put that ideal to rest however; BLM was all about radical change, a sort of giant super PAC for progressives.

While actual fights took place on the streets, virtual fights were happening in courts across the country as the Democrats pressed their case for all-mail voting. The rationale was simple; it was far too dangerous to have voters expose themselves to the virus by being forced to physically go out. An individual could visit a hardware store—but not a polling station. Much better and safer to do it all by post.

To support this proposition, Kunis's Group had implemented a news initiative of "the second wave." As with the original pandemic, and the surge, after a certain time, the public tires of hearing the same bad news over and over. They begin to ignore the dire warnings and projections of doom and simply start doing what they feel is right. So, warnings of a second wave allowed a fresh dose of fear and terror to be injected into the public psyche.

The mail-in initiative was enjoying some success too. State courts were by no means granting blanket approval of all-mail voting, but enough states were broadening the rules or modifying mail-in criteria to allow vastly bigger numbers of mail-in votes or post-Election Day votes. It was becoming clear that the Democratic push in this area was doing well.

Ron had a small glimmer of hope when the Supreme Court, in an obtuse and confusing decision, ruled that the Dems' other strategy, that of influencing electoral college vote allocations, was against the Constitution. Surprisingly the vote was unanimous, and states had to allocate electoral votes to the winner of the popular vote in their state per existing law—and not to the national popular vote winner.

As Election Day drew nigh, it was becoming obvious that the contest was going to be tight. President Suit had a good track record, and incumbents usually win reelection. But, against these pluses,

America's massive left-leaning media machine had spun a narrative of Suit's incompetence, his divisive politics, and an administration that had led the nation into massive decline and discord. Anyone who truly thought for themselves could form their own opinions, but for the ardent tribal members who dogmatically accepted what they were being told by their preferred media outlets, the only question of importance was this: "Is our tribe bigger than theirs?'

Another hot-button legal issue was looming. Officer Symes's second-degree murder charge for killing Cyril Shaw was about to go to trial. In an impressive display of expediency, he was to be tried scant months after committing the offense, a true Democratic response to "his right to a speedy trial." However, cynics noted that the timing of this super-sensitive and controversial case just before the election was just another Democratic ploy, manipulating the narrative for maximum publicity.

Given that this was happening in her home state, Stacey had been active throughout the lead-up, pushing the timing forward and trying to get "her" people inserted into the proceedings. Officer Symes was enjoying a top-flight defense team, courtesy of an anonymous donor who had covered all his legal expenses.

Meanwhile, the prosecution team was the DA plus associates. Stacey herself had previously confided to Ludwig and Kunis that these guys were not the brightest bulbs in the chandelier, yet there they were.

The key element in any police shooting is the well-established precedent of whether the officer involved was in "reasonable fear" for his life. In the Shaw-Symes case, there had indeed been a scuffle between the perp and the cop prior to the shooting. Was it enough for "reasonable" fear? Cyril had been shot in the back. This was to be the crucial core of the trial, and both sides were trying to prove or disprove this key fact.

The first day of court had an almost-festival atmosphere. Outside, and kept apart by lines of heavily armed police, were two groups, subsets of the tribes. On one side, BLM and its associates were marching in circles around the courthouse with "Defund the Cops," "Black Lives Matter," and "Kill All Pigs" placards held high.

For the opposition, a crowd of Second Amendment folk were standing together, displaying "Blue Lives Matter," "Keep the Second Amendment," and "Support Your Police" signs. These demonstrations were to continue throughout the duration of the trial, mostly peaceful during day, but following the all-too familiar pattern of descending into chaos as night fell, with riots, looting, and violence.

Extensive voir dire was conducted, following an initial motion from the defense team to move the trial elsewhere, claiming that a fair trial would be impossible in Trenton because of ingrained bias against the cops. This motion was denied, and finally, after three days of back-and-forth, a jury was finally empaneled, equally split white to black and with a male predominance.

The opening arguments displayed the clear superiority of the defense team; they were all experienced trial lawyers who'd enjoyed many high-visibility successes over their careers. Meanwhile, the state's representatives lumbered and um-erred, sometimes seeming to lose the thread of their narrative. Background witnesses were called, experts testified, and the whole American judicial process lumbered on toward the key issue: reasonable fear.

Body cam footage showed undeniably that Shaw had fought with Symes before breaking free of custody and running away. But why would the officer shoot a fleeing man in the back when the perp obviously was not a threat at the time Symes discharged his weapon? Jurors were treated to endless reruns of the body cam images in super slow motion.

Prosecutors pointed out the obvious. If Shaw was running away from the police officer when he was shot, how could he pose a threat? The shooting was totally unjustified, simply a bad cop believing he was God. The defense team, however, called attention to Mr. Shaw in the final seconds before that fateful bullet ended his life.

"Look closely, ladies and gentlemen. Here, in the moment before Officer Symes fires, you can see Mr. Shaw turning to look back at the officer. Look even more closely. See that close-up of Shaw's right hand? What is he holding? It's not sure, but it looks a little like a gun, doesn't it? We maintain that Officer Symes had reasonable fear that Shaw was armed and was about to shoot at him. He had no choice other than to follow his training and shoot to kill, which sadly, he did."

So, on to closing arguments.

The prosecution's position was that Officer Symes was a bad cop, one who'd had multiple complaints filed against him over many years, yet one who inexplicably remained on active duty. Poor Cyril Shaw was clearly yet another victim of systematic racism by the police.

The prosecution closed:

"And so, ladies and gentlemen of the jury, this case is a textbook example of second-degree murder. Sure, Officer Symes didn't go to work that day thinking, *I'm going to kill me a black man,* but even without that premeditation, he intended to cause Mr. Shaw harm—and his actions showed a clear indifference to human life. That is the exact definition of second-degree murder. Please, do not be fooled by the defense claim that Officer Symes thought Cyril Shaw was armed; we have proven that he was not. Thank you for your time, and I know that you will arrive at the correct verdict."

The prosecution rested.

Defense closing remarks followed as the perfectly suited silver-haired attorney rose to address the court.

"So, do blue lives matter? Look outside at our world right now; we see anarchy, violence, and chaos. Crime rates are skyrocketing in every city that has not responded forcefully to this surge of criminal unrest. The only barrier we have between civility and anarchy is law and order, and our police officers provide that protection—a thin blue line of heroes who put their lives on the line every single day to protect the public. Certainly, at first glance, one might think that the defendant shot an unarmed man in the back, but as we have shown over these past several days, first impressions can be wrong. Officer Symes was there; he had the true view of events; he saw a man who had just fought with him turn around with what appeared to be a weapon in his hand, and in a split-second decision, he defended himself—exactly as he had been trained to do. If any of you twelve upright citizens have the slightest doubt before you retire to consider the verdict, put yourselves in officer Symes's shoes. Would you wait to see if you were being shot at—or would you take action, action that has been drilled into you from day one of your career? Officer Symes was in reasonable fear of his life, and I'm confident that you will side with law and order and find our client innocent."

The jury retired.

That was the signal for the media hype to be turned up to eleven. Frantic reporting that had blanketed America throughout the trial now went ballistic with speculation, all designed to stir up emotions and anger. No straight reporting here—just opinionated rhetoric intended to make waves and stir the shit. White cop, black victim, systematic racism, law and order: these trigger phrases were spewed out to the nation's airwaves. You name them, all the talking heads were now in front of the courthouse awaiting a verdict: Nancy Grace, Judge Jeanine, Dan Abrams, Judge Napolitano, speaking into television cameras, parsing every word spoken, and offering widely varying expert opinions as to the outcome.

Finally, after two days of endless commentary, protests, and riots, word came out. The jury is coming back in! Following required protocols and statements, the big moment neared.

The judge said, "Ladies and gentlemen of the jury, have you reached a verdict?"

"We have, Your Honor." The foreman handed the written verdict to a court officer who took it across to the judge's bench.

"In the case of *State of New Jersey v. Sergeant Louis J. Symes*, we find the defendant not guilty of second-degree murder." The judge read out the verdict dryly in a monotone, but the moment that single-syllable word "not" came out of his mouth, the courtroom erupted with yelling, cussing, and scuffling. Court officers tried to calm the chaos to little avail.

Outside the courthouse, an explosion was detonated by that single word. Protestors transformed instantly into rioters, throwing their placards at their opposition and rushing the cordon of police. The Second Amendment crowd surged forward too in an attempt to block the protestors. In the melee that followed, there were many arrests and injuries, the police tried helplessly to maintain order, and the rest of the day—and the weeks that followed—became a seething mass of unrest and hatred. As this drama unfolded, jurors were secretly taken from the courthouse—as was Officer Symes.

The whole scenario did not bode well for the upcoming trial of Symes's partner on lesser charges.

❧

Stacey, Peter, and Milos watched events unfolding on a screen inside Ludwig's home.

"Well," Stacey said, "a good result—just what we wanted."

"Exactly," replied Peter. "It's perfect. I think you both deserve congratulations, team. Stacey's efforts with the DA, Milos's defense team, we all pulled it off. This should keep Suit hunkered down straight through until Election Day."

Glasses were filled, raised, and clinked—a toast to more chaos—as outside, the nation burned.

ELECTION DAY

It was shaping up to be an Election Day unlike any other in America's history. Set against a backdrop of pandemic, economic hard times, unrest, racial division, media lies, and extreme partisanship, its citizens would have to decide between an ex-talk show host who had, until corona, brought the USA unprecedented economic good times but in a cacophonous atmosphere or an old, mentally declining lifetime politician who'd achieved nothing over his career but who was promising a return to normal life. The greatest nation in history had come down to this unpalatable choice between two far-less-than-perfect men.

George continued his carefully monitored campaign, giving virtual stump speeches from his condo.

"You know me, and you know what I represent. I am your return to normalcy. We have had four years of crises, chaos, and corruption. It's time to bring back true American values to the White House. Myself and Vice President Lincoln will do just that. And I assure you that, once elected, and with peace restored, my administration will then begin its task of transforming America into an even better place. Number one on my to-do list will be the establishment of a new cabinet position; Shawanda Durelle will be brought in as secretary for equality. It will be her remit to investigate every claim of discrimination, to review and revise police department budgets, and to evaluate reparations for our nation's African Americans. She will redress historical wrongdoings. You know this is the right thing to do. You know that four more years of Suit and all the unrest he creates will not be good for you or your country. You must support the Burton-Lincoln ticket."

His handlers were pleased: no gaffes, no ad libs, a good broadcast. One way they had been able to improve George's performance was the system initiated during the debates; now, all of his appearances were subject to a proviso that the campaign team had "final cut" privileges prior to broadcast. Unsurprisingly, the mass media outlets were fine with this, and George's public persona was improving daily as these edited, purified remarks were broadcast.

For the PFA and the Group, the final days before the election were looking good. Every poll in the country showed Burton with a massive lead, and even the most conservative pollsters were giving him a twelve-to-fifteen-point edge. It was theirs to lose, although as Stacey repeatedly reminded them, they had been in the exact same place four years ago with her own campaign. By promising Durelle a high-level position in the administration, they had defused her continued sniping, brought her base on board, and gotten all the followers of the progressive wing of the party to at least consider a vote for Burton. The Durelle announcement alone had given them a five-point bump. Despite his initial misgivings, Peter had to admit that it looked like Burton had been a good pick, and in a short time, the Democrats would be back in the driver's seat where they belonged.

❧❧❧

Ron and his team were working hard too. Rallies continued to be held in key battleground states, usually in outdoor stadiums as a sop to the corona concerns. All had been attended by hordes of enthusiastic supporters. His evening television broadcast also continued to get high viewership figures.

From his last campaign, Ron knew better than to believe the biased and skewed public polls; his team's bespoke analytics were far more reliable, and they were showing that it would be a tight, but winnable, race—and not the Democratic romp being bandied around by the media.

His evening monologue gave a good overview of the message he continued sending out to voters.

"Look, folks, you can see that we're climbing out of this coronavirus pit. Oh, I know that the media is telling you we have record numbers of cases and more positives than anywhere else on earth, but look past the hype and phony numbers. There are just two real indicators for tracking this pandemic. Ignore the rest. Our death rate is among the lowest in the world, and hospitalization rates have been falling for weeks now. Case numbers are a distraction; we test more than any other country; therefore, we find more cases. It's a simple as that. But that's what the media wants you to focus on, and that's why they were calling for massive testing early on in the pandemic.

"The Strike Force's plan to restart the economy has been a huge success. You're seeing monthly data that shows us roaring back, businesses are opening up, and people are going back to work. I'm hopeful that we'll be back on top by year-end. Why can I be certain of this? Because, no matter what you may hear from the cynics and doomsdayers, we are so close to having a vaccine. Phase 3 testing is wrapping up as we speak, and that means the public could be getting shots within a couple of months. Oh, I know this is 'unprecedented' and 'impossible to achieve,' but you know what? When we unleash companies from ridiculous regulatory burdens, they can achieve miracles. We showed exactly that over the first three years of my presidency, and we're showing it now in our response to the pandemic.

"We are a great nation, America, and we can do anything! Now, you may not feel that when you see all the unrest and extremism currently out there in our liberal cities, so I want y'all to focus on one word: safety. Will you feel safe under a Burton presidency? Old George is finally sounding coherent, but listen for the little editing clicks all through his speeches, and you'll figure out why that is. I'm sure you've heard him talk about how he'll return you to the good old days when there was peace and love everywhere, but did you listen to his most recent speech? Immediately after electing him as a 'safe pair of hands,' he'll abdicate to the socialist wing of his party and they will 'transform' the country. Think about this. All the crap going on around our nation right now is far-left. Left wing mayors and governors do nothing to protect their citizens while the mob destroys cities. Do you think all that will all go away if George is elected? It might, but only if he bows to their demands. If the mob doesn't get what it wants, then expect more chaos and violence—or even worse. With Burton as president, you have two possible roads in the future: a lurch to the left or even more rioting and unrest. On the other hand, you know me. You know that I am on the side of law and order, that I support our police, and that I won't allow them to be defunded or eliminated. So, folks, *safety* is the key word. Will you feel safer with me as president or Burton? It's your call."

Ron's remarks about the imminent virus vaccine were spot-on. Early in the outbreak, his Corona Strike Force had initiated a contest between the three largest drug conglomerates in the world, feeding them billions to work all-out on a vaccine. In a smart move that maximized chances for success, each company was approaching the problem from a slightly different medical angle—some focused on a protein-based vaccine and some on a plasma-based solution—but all were working around the clock to be the first across the finish line. The successful company would be guaranteed billions upon billions of sales to a planet desperate to get this damned virus under control.

As might be expected, Milos Kunis had a pretty good idea of

which company would win: his own. He already had a vaccine sitting on the shelf and just waiting to be distributed. The biggest problem for Milos was timing, he had to be first, but he couldn't disclose his vaccine too soon; it had to be after the election and Burton's victory.

⚈⚈⚈

The nonstop onslaught from all sides of the media continued. For the blue tribe, it was all about President Suit's enabling of systematic racism and his incompetent handling of the pandemic response. "Two Hundred Thousand Dead Americans," "Suit has Blood on his Hands," and "President Suit's Confederate Dream" were typical headlines.

The left-wing media didn't even bother twisting their stories to meet their ends anymore; they were simply making stuff up without any regard for truth. Ron's campaign speeches were being rewritten by editors to fit their narratives. While he may have given a speech about a united America, they translated it into "a dark vision for the nation." Any independent fact-checker would throw the majority of these news stories into the trash, but in the final days before the first Tuesday in November, facts were of no interest. It was all about feelings: what did you believe or wish was true? If you read, saw, or heard something that didn't fit your beliefs, then it was clearly a lie.

Over in the red tribe, it was just as biased. Fox and its ilk continued to push the Russian hoax impeachment inquiry narrative, citing Ludwig's administration as the most corrupt ever. Even now, as AG Odom's investigation continued to yield more arrests and more revelations about wrongdoing at the federal level, there should have been some expectation of a nation outraged, some national reaction to the biggest political scandal in US history. Instead, with the country burning or sickening and dying, who cared about past events? It's what's happening now that's important. The election was being distilled into a single issue. Do you like or loathe Suit? Forget facts. Forget rational thought. It was going to be a simple for or against vote—a referendum on Ron.

Given the high percentage of mail-in voting this time around, with more than half the states opting for this, an election-night celebration would prove to be impractical. Perhaps learning from its aborted celebration four years before, the Democrats announced that they would be holding a simple virtual campaign-wrap celebration.

Meanwhile, Ron's team booked the same hotel space it had used four years ago and planned for an actual event, albeit with the new-normal procedures of masks, temperature checks, and social distancing. And what of the voting stations? They were arranged to ensure six feet of distance between booths and voters. Some states implemented entrance temperature checks; if you had a fever, then no entry. All this was designed to reduce the turnout, but at least in-person voting assured a little honesty as citizens signed in at the stations with their credentials and politely lined up to await their turn at democracy.

By Election Day, twenty-eight states had passed legislation to allow mail-in voting, and this act of civic duty had been underway for many days leading up to Tuesday. Significantly, and ominously, many of the so-called battleground states had opted for mail-in voting. One consequence of such a high proportion of mail-in votes was to be the media's reporting on the election itself. There would be fewer exit polls possible, and of course, no early prediction of winner and loser, no election-night declarations. In fact, in a close race, it was likely that the outcome wouldn't be known for days or even weeks after Election Day because mail-in voters are typically given extra time. You can send in your ballot the day of the election or, in certain states, up to a week after. This was going to be a messy one, and both campaign teams had expectations of a long and drawn-out process.

When the big day finally arrived, actual voter turnout was

relatively low, possibly due to fear of catching the virus. On the other hand, the mail-in vote was clearly very high. Every pundit and talking head had no real words of wisdom to spew; they were in the midst of an unprecedented event. Nevertheless, these pontificators blanketed the airwaves with their expert views throughout the day and into the night. Going mostly unreported by them was that, in several locations where people could vote in person, crowds of "protestors" had gathered outside the polling stations to intimidate voters into either voting for Burton or walking away. Some of these individuals were armed and did not mince words; if you were a Republican, you'd best leave if you valued your ass.

♦

Up in George's Washington condo, the Democrat elite assembled to watch the results. Stacey's DNC team had been doing sterling work over the past several weeks and days, duplicating ballot sheets and culling mailed-in votes on their way to be counted. It had been remarkably easy. Postal workers are often Democrats; a little cash in their hands and duplicate ballots could be added while envelopes indicating a Republican vote could be quietly shredded. Genius. Stacey was therefore relaxed and feeling good about the outcome.

The three of them sat off to one side in hushed conversation while the rest of the group huddled around TV screens, occasionally posting something on the party's media sites or giving commentary to the party faithful via the campaign celebration's web link.

George sat out on his balcony, nursing a drink with a faraway look in his eyes. He wasn't thinking of the presidency, or the campaign; he wasn't thinking at all, having what he liked to call a "senior moment." Inside was the hubbub of the party, and outside was the sound of police sirens, riots, and helicopters—but on that balcony, all you could hear was George's persistent dry cough, as if something had caught in his throat.

Peter said, "I've got to say, Milos, I was really skeptical about your plan to use Burton, but we've pulled it off, haven't we? Mind you, thank God for corona, eh? I mean, without this pandemic coming on at just the perfect time, the outcome would have been so different. Suit would have kept breaking records with his booming economy—and we'd have been toast. It was a lucky break."

"You are correct, Peter. We were lucky." Milos swirled his cognac and puffed on a cigar. *Sometimes one must make one's own luck*, he thought.

Evening turned into night and then daybreak, and both teams continued their assessment of what results they could get their hands on. By then, the majority of physical votes were in, and it looked like a close contest—with a clear edge for the incumbent.

Ron's team was quietly confident that, should their trend analysis continue to prove accurate, they'd win enough electoral votes to hang on to the presidency.

The news media was in a tizzy. They wanted to call a winner, but they knew that the outcome hung on the mail-in votes, and they wouldn't finish being counted for a long time. So began a ritual of "we interrupt this broadcast" announcements, complete with dramatic music, as each state finally released its results. Like a slow-motion train wreck, the presidential contest was resolved in dribs and drabs, one state at a time, over many days. This death by a thousand cuts existence became particularly painful for the Suit team. As each of the twenty-eight mail-in states got around to announcing their results, it became more and more apparent that Burton was pulling ahead.

∽⤳⤲∾

Ron had been back in the White House for some time now, and he summoned AG Odom. "Look Ned, it's pretty goddam obvious to me that some, if not all, of these mail-in states have been rigged. Okay, I can concede that some of them might be legit, but there's states that I won handily four years ago, and suddenly I'm getting my ass kicked? It's wrong, Ned, and you know it. I mean, look at Michigan; I kicked Lincoln's ass there four years ago, but now they've implemented mail-in voting, using the pandemic as their excuse, and I'm being handed my head on a platter up there."

"Well, Mr. President, we all know that mail-in voting is much more susceptible to fraud than the traditional method, so we had teams in place at potentially sensitive areas to keep watch and verify the election processes. The problem is, sir, that there's a million ways to cheat but oftentimes no way to prove it. Sir, we're doing all we can."

"Thanks, Ned. I appreciate it. The last thing our country needs right now is an election scandal on top of all the other shit, but if there's been cheating, then the people need to be told. Keep digging; this shit is plain wrong." Ron sat behind his desk and stared out into the Rose Garden, a depressingly long list of things to do in his head. *It is what it is*, he thought as he finally got back to work, forcing himself to tamp down the frustration in his gut.

◈◈◈

While the presidential outcome seemed to be shaping up as a Democrat victory, so too were the House and Senate elections. As the days slipped by, the blue tribe became increasingly confident and vocal. Their news outlets were now openly predicting a Democratic landslide, and they were full of rebuke for the washed-up TV host who had brought America to its knees over the past four years.

Headlines shouted "Blue Wave!" or "President-Elect Burton!" The wittier outlets led with "America Finally Changing its Dirty Suit," and abroad, British papers announced that Suit had "Gone for a Burton."

Inexplicably, and despite his team's usually accurate predictions, it seemed Ron Suit was going to be that rarity: a one-term president. Ron vacillated between anger and relief over this. Despite any concrete proof, he was sure that he'd been illegally denied reelection, his own team's analysis essentially proving this, but he would not have to endure four more years of relentless criticism and scrutiny.

The AG's investigations into election fraud yielded little—other than providing a field day for the media to cry sour grapes and pile on about Suit being a sore loser. Some evidence of irregularities was proven in two states, but even when switching electoral votes there from blue to red, it still would not give Ron a win; it merely narrowed the gap. Odom and Ron both used these two sets of crooked results to suggest that there had, in fact, been several other questionable outcomes, but without hard evidence, it wasn't enough.

Stacey and her team had done the rigging well; Odom could smell smoke, but he couldn't find fire.

By early December, around the time when electors were set to make it all official and formally cast their votes, it was over. George Burton was to be the next president. That is, if he could make it to Inauguration Day. By then, George was under round-the-clock care, another victim of the virus. Unfortunately for George, he fit the classic at-risk profile. He was old, had diabetes and high blood pressure, and even though he wasn't obese, these black marks were enough to make it difficult for him to shrug off the sickness.

The nation was thus subjected to endless speculation about his health, and the riots and other issues took a temporary back seat in the news cycle as talking heads wept crocodile tears over his sickness. In reality, they were loving it—yet another twist on the most bizarre year in memory. What a time to be a journalist!

A sudden fascination with the Twentieth Amendment spread through the media like a virus. Dating from back in the thirties, one section of this document stipulates that if a president-elect dies before taking office, the vice president-elect assumes the presidency.

It was not a well-known piece of legislation until then—although both Milos and Stacey could probably have recited it by heart.

⧉⧉⧉

Lame-duck Ron accepted his loss and began transitionary meetings with Stacey since George was too ill to attend. They were awkward affairs; old rivals reunited but with the shoe on the other foot. Stacey tried hard not to gloat, sometimes with success, and Ron tried hard not to go full-on sarcastic on her, often failing.

"No doubt you'll want to get all the information on the pandemic as a priority," he said in one meeting. "You'll be able to bask in the glory of a successful vaccine, Stacey. It's pretty much ready for release and distribution. Ironically, the winning outfit is a Sino-US conglomerate. It's funny how China gave us the virus—and now it looks like they'll take it away for us."

"I'd appreciate it if you call me Vice President-elect Lincoln, Mr. President."

And so it went in frosty, adversarial meetings where Stacey began to assume control as Ron ceded it. By then, he was totally resigned to leaving office, even looking forward to it in some ways. His future had many paths forward. Fox had offered him his old job running *NSFW* again, although he was in two minds about this. *Is it fitting for an ex-president to be a talk show host? Shouldn't I be like most of my predecessors and fade into the background, organizing charities and generally doing good work, slowly turning into a forgotten footnote of history?*

Sometimes he fantasized about "doing a Ludwig" to furtively spend his post-presidential time sabotaging the Burton presidency—just him and a group of dedicated Suit supporters, ninjas fighting an evil empire. That didn't really fit his character however—too mean and nasty—but it was fun to think of it every so often. Regardless, whatever the future had in store for him, Ron concluded that it had to be better than the four years of shit he'd endured. In darker moments, a bigger question occasionally loomed in his head. Would the media allow him to fade away—or would they hound him for the rest of his life with endless lawsuits and negative press?

I'll cross that bridge when I come to it, he thought. *Right now, just make it through George's inauguration and then spend time with Megan.*

❧

In the last dying days of the Suit administration, Ned Odom was attempting to clear up as many loose ends as he could. He was sad that, with a Democratic administration coming in, all the good work done by his team on the impeachment hoax would surely die. Damning evidence would simply be placed in boxes and set on dusty shelves forever—or at least until some curious future historian resurrected the whole sorry tale of a president harassed nonstop throughout his term by malicious enemies who stopped at nothing to defeat him. It was just plain wrong that so much badness had pervaded the Ludwig administration and that much of it would go unpunished. If nothing else, though, Ned was a pragmatist. He'd been around the block many times over the course of his career. This period of his life was just another one to be filed under "case closed."

He was already mentally switching off when he sat with one of his aides to discuss some outstanding loose ends that needed tying up before the inauguration.

"Well, sir, I think that about does it," the aide said as they prepared to go their separate ways. "There was one thing, though, Mr. Odom. I visited with Professor Casey at the MI last week, more of a courtesy call to say goodbye than anything else. Anyway, he introduced me to this young woman who told a story of claimed wrongdoing by Stacey Lincoln. It was real cloak-and-dagger stuff, tales of murder and mayhem and all that. She gave me a USB stick that she says backs up her claims. I've not looked at it, probably should just throw it in the trash?"

Ned seemed disinterested, but he said, "No, give it to me. I'll take a quick look. I wouldn't put anything past those bastards at Ludwig's PFA. It might be a little fun bedtime reading." He took the device and slipped it into his jacket pocket.

Late that night, Ned plugged the memory stick into his laptop, more out of idle curiosity than anything else, and the files streamed down his screen. He clicked on one to see what this mysterious package was all about. After reading the first, Ned was no longer ready for sleep. He spent the rest of the night systematically running through every single file, fascinated and horror-struck by their contents. He drafted a handwritten note to Ron.

HAIL TO THE CHIEF

"**P**oor old George almost had William Henry Harrison beat, didn't he?" Peter said to Stacey as they walked away from the burial site. "I mean, at least Harrison got to enjoy thirty-one days of being president before the typhoid took him. As for George, well, he had a couple of weeks, not that he was aware of anything, being on a ventilator all that time. However, history will record that he was a president—so that's something. And now, Madam President, history will record that Stacey Lincoln was America's first female president!"

It had been a strange end to a strange election. On Inauguration Day, there was nothing—no pomp, no circumstance, no ceremony—just the head of the Supreme Court standing in his robes outside of a hospital room, looking in through the glass as he swore in George Burton as president of the United States of America. A small posse of officials stood at the justice's side, but inside the isolation room, the only company George had was a nurse clad in full hazmat gear, checking his vitals, adjusting drips, and pressing a Bible into George's limp palm as the judge recited the Pledge of Office on the other side of the glass.

From that fateful night on Election Day when he first noticed his cough, George's condition had deteriorated steadily and rapidly.

Within a week, he'd been admitted into hospital, and for the last six weeks, he had been comatose, intubated, and wasting away.

Despite their best efforts, President-elect Burton was slipping into oblivion. Meanwhile, a certain vice president-elect was eagerly waiting for every update from his doctors, outwardly hoping and praying for a miraculous recovery, inwardly wishing the old fool would just get on with it and die.

For Stacey, those weeks were almost unbearable, each extra day of his life forcing her to play the continued role of concerned colleague, a woman who would comfort George's wife and family, a woman who had to appear on television with messages of hope for George. She'd look into the cameras with reddened eyes and say, "Yes, we've seen a little improvement today, and prayer is a powerful thing, so please keep President-elect Burton in your thoughts and prayers." God, she was sick of it! At times, Stacey wanted to burst into his room and rip the tubes from his body, end it now, get it over with!

Milos was far more stoic. "Stacey, patience is a virtue, and you must have it now." The limo drove them from hospital back to his Washington offices. "I must confess that I didn't think George would have been with us this long. Perhaps the dose should have been stronger, but our friend is not long for this world. I can assure you that your own journey too will end soon. The voyage on which we set sail together those many years ago will come into safe harbor, and you will have reached your destination and destiny, Madam President!"

Kunis was correct. As she walked with Peter from the lengthy and somber pomp-filled state funeral service for a fallen president, Stacey straightened her back and fussed with her outfit—she had always looked good in black—as they approached the waiting press corps.

"Finally, I'm president, for God's sake!" she kept repeating to herself, almost as if she couldn't believe it. Sure, when they'd gotten word the George had finally passed, she'd been sworn in by the Chief Justice in a small anteroom at the White House, but now, as the military band struck up "Hail to the Chief," somehow it was all only just beginning truly sink in now. She was the most powerful woman on the planet, and rightfully so; her preordained position on this earth achieved at last.

Weeks later, President Lincoln sat at her desk, looking out onto the Rose Garden. What a few weeks it had been too. The rioting had all but disappeared, but more importantly, the newly released vaccine was being rapidly dispatched to every corner of the country where vaccination centers had been set up to dispense the miracle to anxious citizens.

An air of hope, of optimism, was sweeping the nation, helped by nonstop upbeat reporting and news coverage. After so long under lockdown, people were now sure that the end of the nightmare was finally in sight. A cure had been found—and now we can get back to normal!

A huge weight was being lifted from the nation's collective shoulders, and it showed. The country was opening up and an almost-festive air prevailed. The Group's media machine, abetted by the PFA, was bombarding the airwaves with relentless good news. "A fresh breeze is blowing from Washington," they proclaimed, "cleaning out Suit's corruption and heralding an unprecedented era of Progressive Liberal government. What a future our nation has to look forward to! President Lincoln to the rescue."

Stacey was liberating her people from the oppression of corona and the despotism of Ron Suit. With both Houses now in her corner, she was upbeat about the radical agenda her team was planning, one of open borders, free tuition, more government aid, and of course, crushing taxes on the rich and elite—except her donors. A total transformation of America was commencing under her watch. Stacey would go down in history as the most progressive president since Roosevelt.

Her ten o'clock meeting arrived, and Stacey's aide ushered in Milos Kunis. For the first time she could remember, Stacey noticed something strange on her friend's face; it was the hint of a smile. They sat on facing couches as she poured him coffee.

"So good to see you in here at last, my dear," Milos said as he looked around the Oval Office. "You deserve this, and I'm so pleased that I could help with your journey."

"Milos, I don't know how I'll ever repay you for this. There were so many times when I didn't think your plans would work—or when I didn't think I had the stamina or guts to see things through, but look at us, here we are!" She opened her arms with a sweeping gesture as she looked around the room.

"Well, Madam President, there are many things that we will need to talk about, but most items can wait." Milos inched forward on the couch. "However, I think it should be priority number one of your administration to reset the balance with our Chinese friends. Mr. Suit's trade agreement was bad for them, and the situation needs redressing." Milos finished his coffee and added, "I have some thoughts here in this paper that I'd like you to look over."

Stacey took up the folder and said, "Of course, Milos. I'll get on it straightaway. There's going to be many things we'll need to fix over the next four years."

She saw it again—a smile on his face—and she smiled back.

EPILOGUE

"Hello, America, let's see if tonight's news suits you!" Ron sauntered easily across to the desk as the TV cameras followed. He felt comfortable in this old skin; it was the perfect antidote to four years of hell. He'd agreed to try one season back with Fox, but tonight's show was the real reason he wanted to get back in front of an audience.

"You know, folks, tonight, I'm going to give y'all a history lesson, a story about President Lincoln. No, not the tall guy with the weird beard, but our current CNC. Funnily enough, this story begins with a young barista in Lower Manhattan. I won't say her name, but she had some interesting friends, and those friends unearthed some interesting facts about our newly elected president. Sadly, they paid a high price for these investigations—and died. But they weren't the only ones to die, and that's where it gets interesting. Let me explain …"

God, this feels so good, Ron thought as he began to unfold his narrative, an eye-popping story first related to him by outgoing Attorney General Odom. *Let's see how you get out of this, Stacey.* A smile crossed his face too.